HEATHER A. CLARK

# CHAI TEA
# SUNDAY

ECW PRESS

Published by ECW Press
2120 Queen Street East, Suite 200, Toronto, Ontario, Canada M4E 1E2
416-694-3348 / info@ecwpress.com

This is a work of fiction. Names, characters, places, and incidents either are the product of the author's imagination or are used fictitiously, and any resemblance to actual persons, living or dead, business establishments, events, or locales is entirely coincidental.

LIBRARY AND ARCHIVES CANADA CATALOGUING IN PUBLICATION

Clark, Heather A., 1977-
Chai tea Sunday / Heather A. Clark.

ISBN 978-1-77041-082-4
ALSO ISSUED AS: 978-1-77090-185-8 (PDF); 978-1-77090-186-5 (EPUB)

I. Title.

PS8605.L36225C53 2012      C813'.6      C2011-906951-2

Editor for the press: Jennifer Hale
Cover and text design: David Gee
Cover photo: © David De Lossy / Getty Images
Typesetting & Production: Troy Cunningham
Printing: Webcom   1   2   3   4   5

The publication of *Chai Tea Sunday* has been generously supported by the Canada Council for the Arts which last year invested $20.1 million in writing and publishing throughout Canada, and by the Ontario Arts Council, an agency of the Government of Ontario. We also acknowledge the financial support of the Government of Canada through the Canada Book Fund for our publishing activities, and the contribution of the Government of Ontario through the Ontario Book Publishing Tax Credit. The marketing of this book was made possible with the support of the Ontario Media Development Corporation.

 Canada Council for the Arts  Conseil des Arts du Canada  Canadä 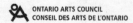 ONTARIO ARTS COUNCIL CONSEIL DES ARTS DE L'ONTARIO

PRINTED AND BOUND IN CANADA

 MIX
Paper from responsible sources
FSC   FSC® C004071
www.fsc.org

 ANCIENT FOREST ™ FRIENDLY

For Brian, Avary, Jacob and Emerson
— you inspire me more than words
could ever describe.

# PART ONE

1

The bright red kettle on our Viking stovetop whistled angrily, practically begging to be turned off. Yet, somehow, despite its obnoxious
shrill, I was oblivious to its cries. Lost in thought, I could hear only
what our doctors had told us earlier that afternoon.

"You okay, Nic?" My husband came up behind me, wrapping his
familiar arms around my waist and giving me a big squeeze. He turned
off the stove, silencing the room, and then sighed into my hair.

I turned to force a semi-smile at him, grateful to have such a con-
sistently supportive husband. After thirteen years of being together,

seven of them married, Eric and I were in full marital sync, many times anticipating the other's thoughts and words before they even happened.

"I'll be okay. Eventually, anyway. I just thought it would be different this time, you know?" I grabbed two mugs from our white cabinet and poured our tea — herbal for me, Earl Grey for him.

As I filled our mugs, boiling water sputtered out of the kettle, spilling on the counter and splashing my index finger. "Damn it!" I cried, instantly putting my finger in my mouth to try to stop the burn.

"Here, Nic. Put it under cold water." Eric guided me to the sink and turned on the tap. The lukewarm water streaming from the faucet soon turned icy, numbing the pain.

"Feel better?" Eric asked me when I could no longer take the cold. He took a clean tea towel from the drawer to wrap my hand. "Why don't you go and sit down on the couch? I'll bring you your tea. And then I'll order us a pizza for dinner. I know neither of us feels like cooking. Pepperoni and green olives sound good to you?"

"Mmm-hmm . . . my favourite. Thanks. I'm suddenly really exhausted." I rubbed my eyes, knowing I was smudging my mascara over my lids but too tired to care.

"And I'll pick up some mint chip ice cream on my way to get the pizza." Eric searched my mascara-smudged eyes. I knew he was trying to find some way — *any* way — to make me feel better.

"Sure. Whatever you'd like."

Eric picked up my hand to inspect the burn. "I'm no doctor, but I think you'll live." He gave my hand a little kiss and gently pushed me towards the couch.

I sank into the cushions, relieved to find comfort after so many hours sitting on the hard waiting room chairs. Eric joined me. He handed me my tea, and took my feet in his lap to try to massage away the anxiety he knew I was feeling.

I closed my eyes, inhaling deeply, and murmured the words I had said so many times throughout our marriage. "Seriously . . . what would I do without you?"

"I really don't know," Eric teased. "But you sure are lucky."

And lucky was right; I had married into pure stability. A gentle giant, Eric was as kind as he was strong. Anyone who knew him instantly recognized his patience and trustworthiness. And as my sister Maggie always pointed out, the icing on top of our perfectly made wedding cake was how madly in love he was with *me*. I knew how lucky I was to have the husband I did. Everyone who knew us knew it.

Eric and I had met during our summer break between second- and third-year university, when we were both hired to be lifeguards at a local water park. I was a rookie and he was one of the king veterans who constantly picked on newbie guards interviewing for the coveted position of waterslide babysitter. As my final interview pool drill, I had been required to rescue Eric, my unconscious, non-breathing victim from the dead centre of the pool. Although Eric was six-foot-two with 220 pounds of solid muscle as distracting as it was heavy, I somehow managed to get him to the side of the pool and properly rescued. He lived. And our relationship was born.

Six years later I became Mrs. Eric Sedgwick. Except that I was technically still Nicole Fowler, or Nicky Fowler, to those who knew me best. We were married on a cliff at Keoneloa Bay in Kauai, above the Grand Hyatt Resort in Poipu, overlooking the rugged Hawaiian coastline. Alongside a gawky island teenager plucking out emotionally stirring native songs on his tiny ukulele, and the Hawaiian minister wearing a maile leaf lei, we were surrounded by only our immediate family and best friends as we said our I Do's.

Our clifftop wedding far behind us, I blinked back tears and turned to bury my head in Eric's chest. Although slightly less defined than it had been years before when we first met in the middle of a pool, his chest was still as strong. And it felt like home.

"You sure you're okay?" Eric asked me.

"I will be. I'm just frustrated. And sad. I really thought they would have good news for us. It's our turn." I inhaled quickly and my breath caught in my throat.

After years of trying to get pregnant, our fertility doctor had confirmed that I wasn't. Again. It was my fifth negative pregnancy test at the clinic, only this time the devastating news came with an even bigger blow — Dr. Sansi, the fertility specialist who had gained our trust, respect and life savings throughout our need-a-baby expedition, felt that we should take a few months off. She thought the stress might be playing a critical factor in all of our monthly failures, and we only had one more shot at successfully becoming pregnant.

We first suspected something was wrong after I went off the pill and we threw caution to the wind. Although we weren't yet ready to officially "start trying," we were close enough that we'd be okay if something happened. Yet nothing did — and it surprised us, given how energetic and frequent our love life was.

After eight months, panic started to set in, and our spontaneous love life turned into morning temperature checks and routine sex every other day. Afterwards, I would lie in our bed, my bum propped on pillows and my legs raised straight in the air, until I could no longer hold the pose. Yet we still only got minus signs every time I peed on one of those damn sticks.

The months turned into one year of no baby. Then eight more months while we waited on the baby factory list. Finally, we got in to see Dr. Sansi.

We were instantly thrown into testing. I was poked, jabbed and prodded by a funny-looking instrument wearing a condom (medically known as a transvaginal ultrasound, which I was conditioned not to say given Eric's weirdness to the term) and had my cycle monitored by endless rounds of blood tests.

Eric's role in the whole investigative process was much simpler. And as I can only imagine, a bit more fun. Yet his results gave us the devastating answer we didn't want to hear: he had been diagnosed with the condition of azoospermia and, despite its cartoonlike name, there was nothing funny about it.

Eric had a zero sperm count. Zero. Zilch. Zip. Notta one sperm, healthy or even damaged, which meant there was nothing for me to get pregnant *with*.

If we wanted to have children, we needed to consider a sperm donor, which really wasn't an option for us given my belief that only half-looped men would actually donate their sperm to the masses — and who would want a guy like that to be the father of your child?

Without going with a sperm donor, adoption was our only other option.

Needless to say, we were both emotionally destroyed. I cried for three days straight, and it was the first time Eric had actually joined me in my constantly recurring sob sessions.

On the third day, we got a call from Dr. Sansi's office asking us to come in to speak with her. When we arrived, red-eyed and puffy-faced from so many days of crying, Dr. Sansi told us there was one last thing we could explore. "It comes with *risks*," she said. "But it could be an option for you."

Eric begged the doctor to continue. Dr. Sansi nodded and then explained that while it was probable Eric's sperm was being counted at zero because there just wasn't any there, there could be a micro-scopic chance of some being tucked far, far inside. If it was there, the numbers would be so teeny tiny, and the sperm so immature, that they couldn't be passed through Eric's passageway while making love to me.

The only way to know for sure was to do a microsurgical epididymal sperm aspiration, which, as the name suggests, basically meant cutting into my poor husband's family jewels to see if the doctor could find a microscopic pocket of sperm. Dr. Sansi again stressed there were surgery risks, but assured us that our findings didn't need to be big; after all, we only needed a few.

Immediately we told Dr. Sansi that, yes, of course we wanted to proceed. We were desperate. We would try anything. Do anything. Dr. Sansi put us on yet another waiting list, and we watched the clock tick by for four months until we got in to see one of the few male fertility surgeons in the country who could perform the testicular micro-biopsy procedure.

The first surgery turned up nothing. So, for the second surgery, we decided to take a bigger piece of the pot, with even larger hopes of striking gold. And it was then that we hit the sperm jackpot.

Dr. Sansi personally called us at home as soon as she found out the results from the specialist, and was talking a mile a minute as she delivered the good news. The sperm guru, as Eric and I had nicknamed him, had successfully located the teeniest, tiniest amount of sperm, but it was enough to successfully fertilize some of my eggs in vitro. And that was all we needed.

I could practically hear Dr. Sansi grinning through the phone. After indirectly experiencing all of the pain we had gone through, she felt nearly as invested in our family-building success as we did.

With no more time to burn, Eric was soon giving me the injections required to arouse my ovaries into producing multiple eggs, and I was once again turned into a human pincushion with blood tests every day. But the cramping, hormonal mood swings and wicked headaches were all worth it when we learned that the doctors had been able to successfully remove twenty-four of my eggs. And it was even better news to find out that eleven of the twenty-four eggs had not only been fertilized, but seven had made it into the wonderful world of blastocysts (otherwise known to the non-medical players as the embryo stage that has been proven to increase a woman's chance of getting knocked up).

We had seven chances at pregnancy.

Seven shots at creating a bambino all our own.

Needless to say, we were ecstatic — and so relieved to know our prayers had been answered.

At our fresh embryo transfer, Dr. Sansi felt that it would be best to insert the three strongest embryos. Although a typical transfer maxes out at two, knowing there wasn't an abundant reserve of sperm that we could keep digging into, we agreed that it was best to increase our odds.

The seven embryos were rated, and we learned that four of them were Grade 1 (translation: the best). We thanked our lucky stars for having the top embryos you could get — secretly thinking this must mean a rocket scientist child was in our future — and I spread my legs in the treatment room next to the embryology laboratory, wishing I could ease the discomfort by keeping them crossed just like I was doing with my fingers and toes.

And then the waiting game continued — until Dr. Sansi phoned us two weeks later with more bad news. None of the three rocket scientist embryos had implanted.

I wasn't pregnant.

With nothing else to do, we catapulted ourselves into the next round, a frozen embryo transfer. Two were thawed and thankfully both survived. Dr. Sansi transferred two embryos — a Grade 1 and a Grade 2. Once again I spread my legs and crossed every other body part that would oblige.

But our trip to the fertility centre earlier that afternoon proved our turn had, once again, passed us by. Which meant we only had one more shot. And our last kick at the can came with two embryos that had been graded like they were remedial school kids.

Yet those were our final — and only — hope.

2

Something hot and bright was hurting my eyes, and my somewhat pleasant dream was suddenly altered. My sister Maggie, looking like a version of her grown self with the exception of newly styled hair, was throwing fluorescent sand at me from an oversized pink beach bucket. Except we were in my bedroom, and I was confused about where she had found the sand. When I realized having an entire beach thrown in my eyes actually wasn't hurting, I tried to open them a bit wider, and recognized it was actually the sun streaming through our California shutters that was bright and burning.

"Morning, hon," Eric gently whispered into my ear, propelling my wakefulness into a higher gear. He handed me a venti non-fat latte, sans caffeine — I had been off the good stuff since we had stepped up our baby-making attempts. He sat beside me on our king-sized bed and pulled at my arm to help me sit up.

"What time is it?" I asked, rubbing my eyes. "I feel like I slept forever."

"Well, lazybones, since it's just after ten o'clock you pretty much did," Eric teased, sipping at his own latte before crawling in beside me and opening the Saturday morning paper on his side of the bed. Without asking, he handed me "Homes & Gardens," my favourite section to read on Saturday mornings.

"And, since you're now so rested, I've got a romantic, surprise night lined up," Eric continued, not glancing up from his paper. "All you need to know is that you have to be ready to go by seven o'clock. You don't have to be overly dressy but, if I know you, you'll probably want to wear something nice. Maybe the black dress you just got?"

"Hmm . . . intrigued . . . ," I responded, trying to muster up a sliver of positive energy for the secret plans that otherwise would have made me genuinely excited. I knew that neither of us could shake the devastating news we had learned the week prior, regardless of what we did that night, but if Eric was going to try to mask it, then, damn it, so was I. "Any hints? Clues? Come on, Eric, don't leave me in the dark all day. I'll go mad."

"I guess that's too bad. Just think . . . the payoff will be that much better after knowing nothing at all." Eric continued to read the sports section, not giving in to my attempts to draw out a confession.

"One clue! Just one." I climbed over the sheets until I was directly on top of him and he couldn't shake my stare.

"You drive a hard bargain, Ms. Fowler. No wonder your Grade 3 students don't have a chance at getting away with anything in your classroom!" Eric laughed, his blue eyes shining, but still lined with pain. "Okay, here's your clue. We're headed to one of the richest countries in Africa without really going there."

"Seriously? Seriously. That's my clue? You promised me a good one." I got off Eric's lap and picked up my section of the paper, pretending to ignore him.

"Okay, okay, I see how this is going to go. Fine, sucky pants, I'll give you one final clue. Tonight, we'll still be in the city but feel like we're in *Casablanca*."

*Casablanca*?

The clue didn't help me — and I wondered if he was bluffing.

But that night, true to his word, we both got dressed up for a night on the town and stepped into a tiny piece of Morocco — which, by no coincidence, had been one of my favourite places we had travelled to since we had been married.

Eric had made reservations at Babouch, a Moroccan restaurant that had recently opened to rave reviews. It was impossible to get in without reservations made weeks ahead of time, and I didn't ask any questions about what strings Eric had to pull to make it happen. As a partner at one of the city's top law firms, Eric often had celebrity-like access to the best restaurants and shows — a perk we had both enjoyed for many years.

Sitting in our own private dining room, made from walls of red and gold velvet draped from oversized beams, Eric requested that the maître d' draw back the doors so we could watch the belly dancer show. Munching on olives and b'stilla, Eric and I watched a group of dancers shake their way through the restaurant. Some of the dancers were veiled, creating a feeling of majestic secrecy for any onlooker. Others used Moroccan finger cymbals, which I remembered being called *zills* — one of the many pieces of slightly useless knowledge that I had picked up on our trip.

Halfway through the dance, three of the belly dancers encouraged diners to join them. Those who had enjoyed too much Moroccan wine seemed to be the first to eagerly step up, and I couldn't help but smile to watch them have so much fun.

"This was a lovely idea." I smiled at my husband who looked exceptionally hot in a dark blue Hugo Boss suit paired with a crisp, white shirt and no tie. It made his blue eyes seem even more intense and looking into them was making me feel warm all over. "Thank you for thinking of it." I picked up my own glass of wine and toasted my husband for being so thoughtful. It was the first glass I'd had in months; despite my great love for all things vino, I'd stopped drinking when we had started our treatments. As one who never shied away from a glass or two of wine, or even a bottle or two on some occasions, it took some effort on my part, but I had wanted to be fully committed to the process. That night was the exception; after all, we would be taking a few months off before trying again.

"I'm glad we came too, Nic. We need it. It's been such a rough couple of years for us and I know how badly it hurts." Eric reached over the table to take my hand. "Tonight we will have fun. And soon we'll start again. We can't give up now. As long as we've got a shot, we still have a chance at becoming parents. We have to remember that."

"I'll toast to that," I replied, clinking his wineglass once again.

"There's one other thing." Eric wiped his hands free from hummus on his thick linen napkin and reached into his pocket. "I want you to have this."

He removed a black velvet box from his pocket and handed it to me to open. Blushing in both anticipation and slight intoxication, I gently lifted the lid to find a small cross lined in flawless diamonds. It was attached to one of the prettiest, most delicate white gold necklaces I had ever seen.

"Eric, it's stunning. *Really* beautiful. Thank you." My eyes welled up with tears. I couldn't take my eyes off the necklace — or the diamonds twinkling in the candlelight.

"I thought you deserved a real treat, Nicky. I was having lunch in Yorkville last week and walked by a little jewellery store. I saw the cross in the window, and I instantly wanted you to have it." Eric looked down at the chicken Marrakesh he was eating and cleared his throat. "I thought you could wear it as our sign of hope. We *will* be parents, Nic. I know it. I feel it with every part of me, and I want you to believe it too."

Listening to his words, an array of emotions took over: gratitude and adoration for the husband who loved and understood me in a way I didn't even think was possible. Sorrow for the guilt I knew Eric had carried with him since he learned about the source of our problems. And absolute heartbreak for what we were going through as a couple.

We would be wonderful parents. We deserved the chance to prove it. To have a baby of our own. Yet, for a reason neither of us could imagine, we had been dealt the shittiest of hands in the game of fertility.

I scooted around the table to join him, handed him the box and lifted my hair. "Will you put it on me, please? It's *so* beautiful. I never want to take it off." I turned my back to Eric to make it easier for him to put it on me. Expertly, he worked the clasp. I turned back to face him, kissing him slowly and fervently in an effort to show my gratitude and hint at what was to come.

When we parted, the waiter approached, indicating it was time for dessert. "May I bring you something? A brulée royale perhaps?"

I shook my head no, but Eric had a different idea. "I've definitely got room for dessert. The molten oasis, please. Two spoons." Eric winked at the waiter, knowing my obsessive love of chocolate.

When it arrived, I forgot about being full and dove in. Once we had scraped up every bit of the silky chocolate, I took a sip of my tea and touched the cross necklace around my neck. For the first time in a very long while I felt happy. Well . . . almost happy. But it was as close as I was going to get.

⎯

Eric and I agreed to take the advice Dr. Sansi had given us; we would take a few months off before trying our last round of frozen embryos. We both needed a break, emotionally and physically, and my frame of mind needed to be in the right place for the in vitro to work.

Given my need for happy hormones, I extended my search for some serious serotonin. After reading too many articles online about how to become pregnant, I became obsessed with the softer side of fertility. And by softer, I mean downright loony. Sure, I did the typical stuff, such as Bikram yoga and a weekly massage, but I was also infatuated with alternative methods that some mothers swore helped them get pregnant.

I tracked down the top fertility hypnotherapist that I could find and drove an hour each way for my sessions. Billy the Fertility Guy, as he was called in the business, was about a hundred years old and vowed his sessions would help reduce my stress and increase a sense of control in my life. I met with him once a week for in-person sessions and meditated on a daily basis by listening to the CD he gave me.

When I wasn't working with Billy or listening to his CD, I strove to become "harmoniously balanced" through the help of reiki. In my first session, I met with my reiki master to become reawakened through an initiation process called attunement. Apparently — and I must admit that I never fully came out of my skepticism shell with all of the new-age gibberish — a reiki master would open up my path so that more life force energy could flow through my body. Before beginning, I read that I might have a mystical occurrence, and would experience visions, colours or body sensations. In truth, I really felt nothing at all except a very deep relaxation.

When I told this to Bib, my reiki master, he responded by saying that this was normal for some, and that the deep relaxation I felt had released blockages within my physical, mental and emotional bodies.

"Nicky-san, the releases I gave you have allowed the natural flow of energy through your body, releasing toxins and waste products," Bib said, shaking his head after picking up on my disbelief. "You may now receive, hold and store more energy in your body so that you can accelerate your positive vibrations. Have faith, my dear Nicky. Have faith."

Despite Bib's committed belief in reiki, I remained doubtful — yet optimistically hopeful. So I moved on to a reiki drum healing ceremony after Bib promised it would help.

"I will bring you a profoundly uplifting experience through the combination of reiki energy and the ancient, sacred energy of the drumbeat," Bib said, preparing the room as I looked on. "The combined vibrations of the energies will reach into every cell and layer of your body to create a harmonic resonance in which healing can occur on a deeper level."

During my drum healings with Bib, I lay fully clothed on a low treatment table. He used a shamanic drum to produce specific rhythms over my body, sometimes drumming close to me and other times farther away.

I did my best not to laugh, and Bib would fervently shush me, telling me to close my eyes and get lost in the beat of the drum. I have to admit, somewhere into each healing session, I fell into a deep trance. Then again, I could have been just sleeping.

And then, despite Maggie's constant chatter telling me I had officially entered into the world of crazy, something happened while I was venturing down my loony-tunes path that must have worked. Because on a bright and sunny morning a few months later, after our final round of in vitro, I found out I was pregnant.

3

The first twelve weeks of my pregnancy were pretty easy. I had some mild nausea, but nothing overtly crazy like some baby-bumpers complain about. One woman in my Mama2Be group confessed that she couldn't stop craving dirt — it was a condition called pica, her doctor told her. Another complained about getting up close and personal with her toilet every hour of the day; the only thing she could keep down was chocolate cake. But it had to be devil's food cake. With white icing.

Eric and I promised ourselves that we would hold off on telling our families the big news until I was thirteen weeks pregnant and we were officially out of the first trimester fear zone. We hadn't thought

we'd be able to keep it to ourselves, but Dr. Sansi had urged us to wait —
she knew Eric and I were both a frazzle of nerves, given what we'd been
through, and she was worried that well-intentioned yet unpredictably
overbearing family members would add to our strain.

The days ticked by until, finally, we were able to break our news.
It happened on the most scorching day in June, and we used my parents' pool as an excuse to visit. They were tipped off over mid-morning
freshly squeezed lemonade, and Eric and I soaked up their reactions
alongside the sunshine. My parents came through with the requisite
grandparent reaction, complete with squeals and weeping with joy. My
mother wiped away a tear, laughing at herself for getting so emotional,
then crying all over again. My parents had continually provided us with
support through our whole IVF ordeal, and knew almost every personal
and intricate detail about what Eric and I had been through — except
for the tiny fact that we had started our last round. We had decided to
keep that part to ourselves in an attempt to alleviate any additional
pressure. "We thought you were still doing hot yoga and meeting with
that crazy reiki guy. A baby, Nic? A baby! Amazing."

"No more hot yoga for me. And that crazy reiki guy must have
helped!"

My father slapped Eric on the back, beaming from ear to ear.
I couldn't tell whether the flush in his cheeks was from the warm
weather or sheer grandpa pride.

"We've got to call Maggie!" My mother said, jumping up after setting her lemonade down in the shade. In the typical way I had witnessed
so many times in my life, she doled out instructions to my father. "Paul,
go and get the phone! And can you track down Maggie's number?"

Maggie had spent the previous year backpacking through Asia,
and was currently in a small village called Ban Sida, somewhere in
Laos. Maggie and a backpacker named Pradheep, a Canadian-Indian

girl she had met at a Buddhist temple in Luang Prabang, had just tackled the steep uphill climb through the jungle into Ban Sida so they could help villagers plant rubber trees and rice. Although I applauded her philanthropy, it wasn't an ideal location for phone service.

My father emerged from the house five minutes later with both a number and the cordless phone in hand. Maggie's reaction was just as I predicted — animated and piercing, even over a crackling phone line with horrible reception. Her high-pitched tone took my mind to a long-ago time when Maggie and I were little girls. It was sad to hear her unchanged shriek overtop of the soft buzz of a bad telephone line. It reminded me of how far away she was, and just how much I missed her.

"Oh, sis, I was just about to book a fall ticket to Moscow, but it looks like I'll be landing at a different airport now! I can't wait to meet my little niece or nephew. I will definitely be there. I wouldn't miss it for the world! I'm just so happy Dad tracked me down. It's really quite shocking that we're speaking right now. You should see it here . . ." The phone cut out momentarily, before Maggie's stream of consciousness babble picked back up and she chattered on about Laos and all that she had seen.

After a few minutes, she veered the conversation back to our baby. "Do you have names picked out yet, Nic? Maggie, maybe? Sure has a nice ring to it, yes? I definitely think it should be considered."

She took a breath, and I laughed. I told Maggie that, yes, we had talked about a few names but, no, her name wasn't on our short list.

"Okay. Then how about Julia?" Maggie pushed, moving to her middle name.

"We'll see, Mags. You just focus on getting yourself home so that you can hold your baby niece or nephew," Eric's voice chimed in from the phone upstairs, where he was listening in. I knew he'd be nearly as excited as me to learn that Maggie was coming home when our baby was born. As one of four boys, Eric had never had a kid sister and Maggie had become like one to him.

We chatted for a few minutes longer and said a reluctant goodbye to Maggie. After hugging my parents one final time, Eric and I got in our car and drove the three hours north to his parents' cottage in Muskoka. Although Toronto was still officially home to Eric's parents, they traded in their smoggy summer days in the city for boating on Lake Rosseau — a venture that had become particularly easy since Eric's father had officially entered into retirement by selling his three pharmacies in Toronto.

We had spent a lot of time at the cottage in the down days of fertility treatments. It had become a place of mental escape for us, the healing powers of the water never ceasing to amaze me. Somewhere on our rough road, Eric's family cottage had come to feel like a home away from home for us and we loved going there as much as we could.

In complete contrast to the mezzanine bedrooms and exposed brick of the Candy Factory Lofts where Eric's parents spent their winters, their cottage was designed to mirror the coastal classic style inspired by Cape Cod. It brought the natural elements of lakeside life indoors, with antique hemlock floors and picture frames made of birch. The slip-covered toile sofas and handmade quilts created the feeling of true Muskoka living for anyone who visited — and also contributed to the cottage being featured in a double-page spread in *House & Home* the previous summer.

Eric's parents, Brian and Amelia, were surprised to see us join them on the dock, having just settled into their matching red Adirondack chairs with an open bottle of Barolo and two newly filled wineglasses sitting between them.

"My goodness! To what do we owe this surprise?" Eric's mother asked, jumping up to give us both a hug as our flip-flops hit the dock.

"We were going to call, but we thought it would be more fun to surprise you," Eric responded, giving his mother a big squeeze.

"We brought dinner," I added, wanting them to know we didn't expect them to feed us. "We picked up some steaks from the Cottage Butcher in Bala, and some vegetables and potatoes as well. We didn't know Gravenhurst had a farmers' market, but it worked out well. We drove through just as they were starting to close."

"Lovely—this will be wonderful," Brian said as he stood up. "We're so happy you're here. Let me just get a couple more wineglasses."

"Just make it one, Dad," Eric said, squeezing my waist from the side. "And a fruit juice or water for our future mama." Eric placed his other hand gently on my tummy as I looked up at him, grinning.

"What?!" Amelia screeched, holding her hands to the sides of her head. "Oh darlings! What amazingly wonderful news."

"We were going to tell you at dinner, but I guess Eric couldn't wait any longer," I said, laughing. "Yes, I am definitely pregnant. Thirteen weeks and one day, to be exact."

"Well, tell us everything!" Amelia pried, hugging Eric, and then me.

Brian joined the hug, his words muffled through the enclosed grip. "A brand new baby for you, and an eighth grandchild for us. How great! And what a reason to celebrate."

Amelia enthusiastically nodded her head, her diamond hoop earrings dancing in the sunlight.

"I'll get the third wineglass and a bottle of sparkling peach juice. Is that okay with you, Nic?" Brian asked, holding his hand to his eyes to shield them from the sinking sun.

"Perfect," I answered, returning his grin and getting comfortable on the chair Eric had brought me from the boathouse. Despite my not even showing yet, Eric felt an Adirondack chair wouldn't be comfortable enough, and wanted to get me something more upright. It was typical Eric: thoughtful and protective, but sometimes overly so.

When Brian returned from the cottage, he poured a glass of wine for Eric and raised his own glass in a toast. "To my youngest son and his lovely wife, Nicole. I cannot think of two people more deserving of parenthood or the joy it will soon bring you. You will be loving parents and our grandchild is lucky to be born into your family." Brian raised his glass to meet ours and the bubbly yellowy orange of my peach juice contrasted against the light red of the Barolo. I clinked their glasses and thought about how nice it was to hear such soft and loving words come from Eric's father, whom I had only known to be business-like and stern in all of the years I had known him.

As I lowered my glass, I could practically feel the quickly beating heart of our developing baby and my stomach flip-flopped as I realized that, next summer, our seven-month-old baby would be sitting with us on the cottage dock.

"Will you find out the baby's sex?" Amelia asked.

Eric shook his head no while swirling the wine in his glass; wide stripes slowly rolled down the sides of his glass before he continued. "We thought we'd wait. Keep the surprise for as long as possible, you know?"

I took a sip of my peach juice as I watched Eric inspect the wine's legs. While I had agreed to his request of not finding out if we were having a boy or a girl, I knew in my heart we were having a daughter. And the daily baby email I had received that morning told me she was about three inches long and could already be sucking her thumb.

"Makes sense. Well, what about names?"

"Nothing yet, Ma. We've thrown around a few, but have decided not to share until we narrow it down."

"Totally understand. Okay, well, I didn't want to tell you before now, but I've got a bunch of baby clothes tucked away at home," Amelia gushed. "I couldn't help myself. I would find these adorable little out-fits, and I knew I would one day be able to give them to you."

"That's very nice of you. Thanks, Ma. "

I nodded, smiling at Amelia. I sipped my peach juice, glowing at the thought of the tiny baby clothes that were waiting for us. "And what about a shower?" Amelia continued. "We simply have to throw one for you. Perhaps we could have it here? We'll invite all of Eric's aunts, and Jocelyn, Laurie and Emmy too, of course."

"Have you told them?" Brian asked, referring to Eric's brothers and their wives.

"Not yet, Dad. We wanted you to know first." Seemingly happy with the wine's legs and clarity, Eric took a long pull from his wine-glass. I could tell he was overjoyed to have told his parents, and the realization of becoming a father was beginning to sink in. But at the same time, I noticed a certain tightness forming in Eric's jaw, the way it often did around his parents. While he was close with both of them, he didn't like their — at times — overbearing nature.

"They are going to be as happy as we are that you're adding to the Sedgwick rug rat pile," Brian joked, referring to the nickname he had given to his growing fleet of grandchildren.

"Well, there's no point waiting any further," Amelia said, fin-ishing the last sip of her wine and collecting the empty bottle. "Let's go up to the cottage and spread the news!"

"You guys go ahead. I'll put Nicky's chair away and join you in a minute," Eric suggested, crossing the dock to hold my hand as I stood up from the chair.

I agreed with his suggestion, but deep down I knew he really just needed some time to himself. As thrilling as our news was, it was also a bit overwhelming for him. In our years together, Eric frequently needed "moments of pause" as I called them, when he could organize his thoughts and let the big things in life sink in. It wasn't overly surprising that he wanted a few minutes by himself before we let his whole family know.

"You sure, dear? We can just put the chairs away after dinner," Amelia coaxed him, pushing Eric towards the cottage so we could call his brothers.

"No, Ma, really. I'll be up in a minute. You guys go on ahead."

"But aren't you dying to tell your brothers?"

"Soon, Ma. Just give me a few minutes. You guys go ahead."

Despite the occasional friction Eric had with his parents, his repeated resistance took me slightly off guard. I had never really given his need for alone time much thought; I simply responded by letting him take the time he needed by finding someone else to carry on my never-ending conversation with. But with my developing baby now taking up all of my focus, I wondered how the impeding world of fatherhood would affect him and his need for frequent solitude.

Amelia finally gave up and turned to catch up with her husband who was already halfway to the cottage. With Eric's parents so far ahead of me, I took my own moment of pause on the Muskoka steps leading up to the cottage to turn and watch Eric. His gaze was permanently fixed on the lake as he shoved his hands in his pockets, letting his thoughts get lost in the overarching pink and orange sky.

## 4

As my pregnancy progressed, my belly bump grew. Despite Eric's constant doting and worrying, the OB/GYN who took the place of Dr. Sansi
once I had successfully completed the first trimester assured me that
my monthly checkups were normal. Our little peanut was growing
beautifully and, as the doctor always described, as happy as a clam.

At eighteen weeks, I went for the standard prenatal ultrasound. I
was told to drink plenty of water and not pee, which was about as easy
as not blinking when someone blows straight into your eyes. By that
point, I had six inches of baby sitting on a very full bladder.

The technician brought me into the dim room and squeezed

warmed jelly on my belly. She placed the transducer (I had become an ultrasound naming expert during my time with Dr. Sansi) on my abdomen and started to take the baby's measurements.

I lay on my back for forty-five minutes, dying to see what she was looking at, until, finally, she asked if I'd like for her to get Eric from the waiting room so that we could see the baby together.

"Yes! Please!" I replied, grateful that we could experience seeing the baby together. Eric walked in behind the technician, and then she showed us the baby's itty-bitty pulsing heart and let us listen to its magical beat.

Then the technician panned the baby to reveal two arms, two legs and an adorable face with two ears, two eyes, a nose and a mouth.

"Is that . . . ?" Eric's voice trailed off and he pointed to something resembling a small tube that had floated onto the screen.

"No," the technician laughed. "That's the umbilical cord. But I do know if it is a boy or a girl, if you'd like to know."

Eric had stayed firm on our decision to not know the baby's sex, but I could tell the pendulum was starting to sway to my side. He shifted his feet and cleared his throat, obviously a bit uncomfortable and not knowing which way we should go.

"It's up to you, Eric. You know I'm happy to find out or wait."

"Oh, okay, well, let's just do it. Let's find out. I thought it would be better to find out the day the baby is born. But it seems more real now that I know someone *else* knows the sex of our baby. I think I need to know too." Eric squeezed my hand. "Let's go for it!"

I nodded at the ultrasound technician, signalling that I agreed with Eric.

"Well, since you've decided to find out, why don't I just show you?" The technician punched in a few buttons on the ultrasound machine in order to bring up a new screen. "Here are the baby's legs, which we saw before. Here is the middle of the baby's legs, and you can clearly see that there is nothing there hanging around. If it were a boy, you would see a swollen lump directly in between the baby's legs. It's a pretty clear shot, so I would say with some serious certainty that you are having a little baby . . . *girl!*"

A girl! I knew it.

Some might call it maternal instinct, while others would point out that I had a fifty-fifty shot at guessing the baby's sex, but every fibre in me had screamed we were having a girl.

Eric wiped away the tear that had started to roll down my cheek. "Congratulations, Mama. Looks like we'll be bringing home a daughter in a few short months. We better go and buy some pink!"

My belly had continued to explode, acting as a cozy home for our baby girl and a warming blanket for me. Despite always being cold in my pre-pregnancy days, I was constantly hot, and chose to ignore Eric's grumbles when I insisted on sleeping with all of our windows open.

The autumn air became cooler, and a hint of winter was promised in every new morning frost. The bright red leaves on our backyard maple trees were a long-lost thought, and the chill in the air brought shivers to anyone who stepped outside.

Except me.

My belly had continued to explode, acting as a cozy home for our baby girl and a warming blanket for me. Despite always being cold in my pre-pregnancy days, I was constantly hot, and chose to ignore Eric's grumbles when I insisted on sleeping with all of our windows open.

As Christmas drew near, Eric and I went about our annual holiday duties. He put up the lights while I baked gingersnap cookies and made peanut butter balls for all of our nieces and nephews.

Three weeks before Santa was due to arrive, while we were sitting in front of the fire munching on warm shortbread cookies straight from the oven and drinking hot chocolate with marshmallows (extra for me given that I seemed to feel better after copious amounts of sugar), Eric brought up names for our baby.

"I think we should really pick our name, Nic. It's getting close," Eric pressed, wiping crumbs from my belly, which, somewhere along the way, seemed to have become a food trap for anything that didn't quite make it into my mouth.

"Uh-oh. Here we go again. We've been through the baby name book every day for the past three months. Nothing is jumping out!"

"Doesn't mean we don't need to pick a name. We can't raise a little girl named Baby Sedgwick," Eric teased.

"Okay, what new names are you thinking of?" I asked, taking a big bite. The maraschino cherry pressed into the centre of the cookie was gooey compared to the satiny crumble of the shortbread.

"Well, I was thinking lately that I really like *Emma*," Eric replied. "What do you think?"

"Hmm. Too popular," I answered.

"Okay, how about *Matilda*?"

"Too trendy. And too Hollywood."

We were having another repeat of our daily conversations and getting nowhere. For some reason, I just couldn't seem to commit to a name. Nothing seemed good enough. Nothing seemed right.

"I know — *Whitney*!"

"Uh . . . no. I'd feel like we were raising someone destined for MTV."

"Well, we can't have that." Eric scratched his head. "Maybe we should take a different approach and consider the names of our relatives. My grandmothers don't really help at all, given that they were Stelladora and Beatrice."

"Um, yeah, just a little old-fashioned." I looked into the fire and thought of our grandmothers, and any iteration that came from their names. And then it hit me. "But what about Ella?"

Eric stared at me in disbelief. "I can't believe you finally like a name! That's a version of my nana's name . . . I love it. Are you sure about it?"

"Yes. I definitely like it. A lot. And I love that it is special."

"Well, then, Ella it is." Eric smiled at me. "Now what about a middle name?"

"Don't push it, Eric. It's a wonder that we even found a first name."

"Just hear me out. I think I have a great suggestion. What about Ella Margaret? I think a plane ride back from Laos warrants being named after, yes?" Eric suggested, referring to my sister. "Not to mention that Margaret is your mom's middle name."

"And my grandmother's middle name, actually."

"So it's perfect!"

"Ella Margaret," I said out loud, realizing that I loved it. It had a charming ring to it that felt like home.

"Do we have a winner?"

"I think we do. It really feels like the right name," I confirmed, kissing Eric and sinking into him next to the warmth of the fire.

"Mmm-hmm. I love it too. And I love you, Nicky." Eric nuzzled into my neck, and my insides stirred.

I deepened the kiss. Reached out to my husband in a way that I had avoided since living through the hormone crazies of my second trimester. And Eric immediately reacted, drawing me closer with a response so intense it felt like obsession.

Within moments, heat as strong as the fire we were sitting beside snaked through our bodies. My breath caught on the fervor of its intensity, both of us desperate for the peak that was as selfish as it was giving.

On the Saturday morning after we chose Ella's name, Eric finished painting the nursery. He had been working on it for over two weeks, taking painstaking efforts to ensure every detail was perfect. He had painted the walls light green before adding giant lilac bubbles to one wall to match the decor I had selected. He had been fastidious about every inch and I knew the finished room was going to be perfect.

"Do you think we can move the furniture in now?" I asked Eric, taking in the newly painted room. "I can call the store manager to see if everything can be delivered today. I know it's short notice, but they said to just give them a ring when we were ready."

We had purchased all of Ella's furniture at a trendy baby boutique and they were holding everything in storage for us until we needed it. We had spent a large chunk of change at the store, purchasing everything from our overpriced baby stroller to organic baby bibs, and I had gone a bit overboard with the number of sleepers and outfits I had purchased. I just couldn't seem to contain my baby excitement and it showed through my shopping bills.

The store manager confirmed everything would arrive that afternoon, and within hours of Eric's last brush stroke, the doorbell rang and two burly men sporting late-afternoon stubble and sweat marks down their backs carried all of Ella's furniture into her room.

Eric and I spent the rest of the day taking our purchases out of boxes and putting everything away. I washed all of her clothes in Ivory Snow while Eric surrounded himself with tools and bolts in order to put together the glider.

I removed the delicious smelling baby clothes from the dryer and neatly folded her onesies and jammies before putting them into drawers. Ella's closet was a sea of pink, including the little dresses I had purchased on my own and the outfits that so many of our generous friends had given to us at our baby showers. Her change table held little white baskets lined in lilac and green bubble cloth, which we had filled with unopened baby creams and newborn diapers.

"It's exactly as I imagined it," I sighed, stepping back from Eric to admire Ella's sweet baby room. Every detail had been finished. I sat in the glider, holding the pillows that had been customized to match the decor of the room, and imagined myself rocking my baby girl to sleep at night.

"I love it too." Eric kneeled beside me, putting the pillow aside and taking my hand in his. I leaned towards my husband and somehow managed to kiss his forehead. My bulging baby bump had become a source of restraint for me, and even the smallest movements were proving difficult.

As my body tilted forward, the cross necklace that Eric had given me at Babouch leaned with me, and then gently hit my throat as I returned to a sitting position. I touched the delicate necklace with my fingers, happy to have it fastened securely around my throat. I hadn't taken it off since Eric had given it to me. It served as a constant reminder of the adversity we had faced and, with it, the marital strength that had ensued.

"And now we wait," Eric said, interrupting my thoughts. "I'm going for cookies. Want some?"

"Always."

"You stay comfortable and I'll go get some Christmas cookies and two glasses of milk so we can toast Ella's new room."

Eric jumped up and took a final look around before heading downstairs to get our well-deserved afternoon snack. As I sat back in the chair and watched him retreat downstairs, my heart filled with warmth at the thought of how lucky we both truly were.

And then I felt it.

5

A twinge of pain hit my lower abdomen, followed by a light gush when I shifted in the glider. Uncertain of what was going on, I waddled to the bathroom and quickly noticed a pale pink streak of blood lining my underwear. My breath quickened. I wiped myself with a tissue, and found more streaks of light red.

"*Eric!*" I cried, suddenly feeling nervous and sick to my stomach. "Can you come here? I need you."

Hearing the urgency in my voice, Eric appeared almost instantly. He held the plate of cookies in his hand.

"It's blood. I'm spotting and I don't know why." I held the tissue up to the light and panicked again when I saw it.

Eric took one look and set the cookies down. He left to get the phone. I could hear him talking to the nurse who was clearly telling him to bring me into the hospital.

"They want to check you out, hon," Eric said. He rubbed my back and wiped away my tears. "Just think. This could be it! Remember what they told us in our prenatal class. Early labour often starts this way."

He guided me to our closet and I threw on the first outfit I could find. Eric grabbed the packed hospital bag that was waiting patiently beside my dresser, packed two months earlier, and held my hand as we walked down the steps.

Eric called his parents to fill them in on what was going on as he ushered me towards the car. "Yes, yes . . . I think she is fine. We're just taking her in to check her out. Plus the nurse thinks it could be the onset of early labour. I'll call you as soon as we know anything more."

"Slow down!" I cried as Eric peeled out of our driveway and raced down the street. My knuckles turned white from holding onto the car door so tightly. "I know we need to get there, but we aren't going to make it if you crash this car!" Ignoring me, Eric blew through a red stoplight. I cranked my head to look behind us, hoping that I wouldn't find rotating cherries on top of a police car. I didn't, and Eric kept his foot securely pressed on the gas pedal.

About halfway to the hospital, my lower abdomen started to contract and I knew I was in labour. The on-call baby doctor, who introduced herself as Dr. Marlow when she walked into the room where Eric and I were waiting, checked dilation and quickly agreed with my self-diagnosis. Despite being a few weeks shy of full term, our baby definitely wanted out.

Putting her hand on my knee, Dr. Marlow explained that, typically, a woman in such an early stage of labour would be sent home. It could be days of labour before Ella actually made her grand entrance. But Dr. Marlow wanted to watch me for a few hours to check my progress.

It was at the precise moment that Dr. Marlow was explaining all of this that my water broke in a huge gush, making the linens I was lying on sopping wet. "Well, looks like you just bought yourself an admission. This is the real thing!" Dr. Marlow smiled. "Let's take a quick look on the ultrasound to assess final position and we'll go from there."

The nurse wheeled in the portable L&D ultrasound and squeezed the familiar jelly — this time *not* warmed — onto my aching abdomen. She narrowed her eyes at the black and white TV image before her. She frowned. Every muscle in my body matched the contractions that were going on in my gut.

"What is it, Dr. Marlow?" Eric asked, his hand squeezing mine a little too tightly.

"Looks like your baby is breech. Frank breech, to be exact," she responded, her eyes still squinty and focused. They never strayed from the ultrasound picture. When she appeared to feel confident with her image interpretations, she removed the transducer from my belly and wiped away the gel.

"What does that mean?" I asked. Sweat beads lined my forehead and I struggled to breathe through a heightened contraction.

"There's nothing to worry about at all, but your baby is upside down. She must have turned last week and now her bum is where her head should be. A vaginal delivery with a breech baby is risky so I'm going to book an OR and give you an urgent C-section. It is a very routine surgery and it will happen very quickly. My guess is that your baby will be here in the next hour or two, depending on when we can get a room. I'd call your folks or whoever else you might want to be here. This is really it."

Eric squeezed my hand again, but this time it felt lighter and more excited. "I'll go call our parents and tell them to come now. You okay if I leave you for a few minutes? I can't get reception in the hospital and need to step outside."

"Yes, yes . . . you go call them. I'm clearly not going anywhere." I smiled at him, wanting to take in every moment of the milestone. In front of Dr. Marlow Eric gave me a long kiss on the lips, which made me blush with embarrassment.

Fifteen minutes later, Eric returned along with the nurse who had been put on my charge. She introduced herself as Nurse Nancy, which I knew Eric would have found amusing in a different situation, and told us that she needed to take me — without Eric — so that I could be prepped and given my spinal. Eric would be able to join me once I was completely frozen from the waist down and the thin blue curtain that we had seen in almost every episode of *Grey's Anatomy* had been set up to separate us from the blood.

I waddled to the OR and was introduced to the on-call anesthesiologist, Dr. Tam. Nancy helped me on the operating table and told me to sit on the side and round my back so that Dr. Tam could stick the needle in my spine. She promised to stay in front of me so that I could prop my body up against her and hug her shoulders.

"The biggest thing is that I need for you to stay completely calm and remain still," Dr. Tam murmured from beneath her surgical mask, as though it should be easy breezy to stay perfectly still when curled over a protruding, pregnant belly and someone is about to stick a six-inch needle into your lower spine.

"Squeeze tighter," Nancy instructed. "It's okay, honey, it will be over soon."

And so it was. Within moments, almost the entire surgical team, who had entered the room while the needle had been in my back, were helping turn me over and get me into position. "We have to go quick," Nancy explained. "We only have a few moments before you will be unable to move."

When Dr. Marlow was satisfied that I was completely numb from the waist down, they called in Eric, who had changed from his street clothes into head-to-toe hospital scrubs, including something that looked like a big, blue shower cap on his head. He walked through the small operating room and took his position at my head. My arms had been spread out and strapped down on either side of me, my body making a big *T* position on the table, and Eric reached out to take my right hand in his.

Although I felt no pain, the intense tugging and pulling going on inside of me was severe enough to make me wonder if the ring of fire that accompanied natural births would have been better. I had no idea what they were doing, and didn't want to know, but it felt like someone the size of a Mack truck was doing a line dance on my stomach and lungs.

"Here she comes," Dr. Marlow called out over the blue curtain, only minutes after the surgery had started. I was shocked at how quickly things were moving. "Give me about one more minute and your daughter will be here."

"This is it, Nic. We're finally going to be parents," Eric whispered into my ear. "I love you, baby." I tried to take in the moment, but my brain would focus on nothing but the obese line dancer jumping all over my belly and preventing me from being able to breathe.

"Here she is!" Dr. Marlow held our beautiful baby over the blue curtain and we got our first glimpse of our angel. She was red and puffy with icky, white vernix all over her bald head. And she was perfect. "She is definitely a girl!"

The doctor handed Ella to the nurse who whisked her to a table about six feet from my head. I cranked my neck in an attempt to get a glimpse, but couldn't see anything more than the nurse's back. A few pink blankets were being thrown around, but I couldn't get a glimpse of Ella.

I strained my ears to hear her cry, but heard nothing. I waited some more, but only heard my own heart beating in my brain, its sound echoing into my eardrums.

"Eric? Why can't I hear her?" I tried to move off the table, but got nowhere. The pressure on my gut had ceased, but my body was still filled with lead and I couldn't move a millimetre, not to mention Dr. Marlow was still putting me back together and stitching me up.

"*Shhh . . . shhh*. It's okay. Ella is with the nurse, who knows what she's doing. I'll go have a look." Eric gave my hand a squeeze and went to stand beside the nurse, who was hovering over Ella. He whispered quietly with her, before returning to my bed to retake my hand. "Ella is breathing on her own, which is great, but she's having a bit of trouble, so the nurse is going to give her some oxygen. She said that babies often don't cry when they're born by C-section. Makes sense though. Right, Nic? Many times they are sleeping when the doctor reaches in and lifts them out, so they barely make a noise. Ella is in good hands, doll. She'll be okay."

Yet I could see the doubt registering on Eric's brow. He also felt the unspoken medical diagnoses that had been dancing around us since Ella's birth. Something wasn't right, but *what* we did not know. Without needing to say a word to each other, I knew both Eric and I were wondering whether or not the doctors were aware of the problem and not telling us the update — or if they were completely unsure themselves.

After about two minutes of the nurse working on Ella, a second one joined her. From what Eric told me, they were aggressively rubbing her all over, trying to get her blood moving and her breathing stabilized. Five more minutes passed and the nurses told Eric that they felt Ella should go to the nursery. "It's just a precaution," the nurse who had joined Nancy explained. "She'll be in a better place in the nursery where we have more available to us to get Baby's breathing under control."

It irked me that the nurse wasn't calling our baby by her name. From the minute she entered the world, we had given her the name Ella, and the nurse had heard us calling her by her *name*.

The nurse continued, "Dad can come with Baby, if you'd like, or he can stay here with you. Whatever you'd like."

"Our baby is Ella. Would you mind calling her by name, please? And Eric should go with her. I'll be okay." I grimaced, pain starting to hit my body, but not from the staples being punched in by Dr. Marlow. "Go, go, Eric . . . I'll be fine. Please, I want you to be with her."

Eric squeezed my hand and kissed my cheek before hurrying off in his head-to-toe hospital scrubs. He followed the nurses who were wheeling Ella in a baby cart — lined in a multitude of pink blankets — out of the room and down the hall to the nursery.

Caught up in my own rampant hurricane of thoughts, I didn't even notice that Dr. Marlow had finished the surgery. I was lifted by a medical team of four onto my hospital bed. They wheeled me into the recovery room, but said nothing. I was grateful for the silence. I couldn't speak and I didn't want to.

After an eternity of waiting, Eric joined me in recovery and told me Ella's breathing had improved slightly, but still wasn't where the doctors wanted it to be. They had intubated her, and she was in an incubator.

"Dr. Lorel, the pediatrician on call, has ordered blood work so we can better understand what is going on. They said they will come and get us once they have the results." Eric squeezed my hand again. "Your parents are in the waiting room, and mine are on their way. She'll be okay, Nic. She'll be okay."

"I'm scared," I squeaked out, interrupting him. The voice coming from my throat wasn't my own. "And I'm supposed to be holding her right now. She needs her mommy."

"I know, baby. She'll be with you soon. Right now she's in the best spot possible for her. Dr. Lorel isn't leaving her side. And we'll know more soon."

"Can I see my mom?" I asked, suddenly wanting no one but my own mother to hold my hand.

"I'm sure it would be okay, given the circumstances. I'll go to the nurses' station to make sure. You sit tight."

Eric returned with my mother in tow. She walked straight to my bedside and gingerly took me in her arms, kissing my head, careful not to strain my post-surgery body. "I know, sweetheart, I know. It's very scary. We're all scared. But Ella is with the best doctors and nurses, who are taking great care of her."

She let go of her hug, and took my right hand in her own. On the other side of my bed, Eric took my left hand and the three of us waited together, linked by hands, until the doctors came to give us more information.

The doctor who had been watching over our baby girl was a man about my mother's age. He had a thick neck and green eyes. He walked through the recovery room door and frankly handed us our fate, albeit gently.

"Your baby is struggling. We've intubated her, but she isn't responding in the way that we'd like. She's going through some cyanosis, which means she has some blue colouration in her skin and mucous membranes, caused from the higher counts of deoxygenated hemoglobin in her blood vessels." The doctor cleared his throat, and continued, "I ordered blood work, and we learned that the albumin levels in her blood serum are abnormally low, which is something called hypoalbuminemia. I say that word in case you hear other doctors speak about it. Your baby is also severely hypoglycemic, meaning that she has drastically lower than normal levels of blood glucose. And she has coagulopathy, meaning that something is going on in her body to prevent proper blood clotting. We're concerned given that the coagulopathy has increased her susceptibility to bleeding. We need to carefully monitor that."

Eric dropped my hand. My mother held on. The doctor continued, "To be honest, we don't know what is going on right now. We'd like to transfer her to Mount Sinai and admit her into the NICU for continuing intensive care and more tests. They are better equipped to handle her medical condition, and she'll be transferred by a specialized neonatal ambulance that is already en route from Mount Sinai to pick her up. You are more than welcome to go with her, or you may stay here to recover. If you go, you will need to be transferred by a second ambulance at a later time. But, please, know that wherever you are and whatever you decide, your baby will be getting the best possible care with the physicians at Mount Sinai. They are some of the top doctors in the country."

In a foggy blur, semi-induced by morphine, I somehow managed to communicate to Dr. Lorel that, yes, I would be going with her to Mount Sinai. Of course I would be going.

The nurses, who had been hovering outside the door while we

spoke to Dr. Lorel, quickly entered the recovery room to start preparing me for transfer and then wheeled me to the Labour and Delivery entrance doors. Both ambulances were already there, one in front of the other.

The nurses stopped my rolling bed to let Ella pass. Warmed and protected by a small transport incubator, our precious angel and her entourage of transfer team specialists flew by us at a frightening speed. My heart collapsed as I took in Ella's transfer device and all of its complicated gadgets, including a ventilator, various beeping monitors and a bunch of attachments that looked like itty-bitty baby pumps. The hurricane of activity — with our daughter in the middle like the eye of the storm — disappeared into the first ambulance.

I was next.

My own team of nurses and the paramedics who had been standing by transferred me onto the waiting ambulance gurney and, within moments, I had also been swallowed up. I watched from the inside as my tear-streaked mother pulled at her neck. My panic-stricken husband looked blank and absent.

"Are you coming?" I asked Eric who seemed to be frozen to the ground.

"I . . . uh . . . I . . . I can't. I can't. I'm sorry. I'm so sorry. But I can't. I can't."

I felt all the blood drain out of my already panicked body. This wasn't happening. My mother stepped up. "I'll go. Eric, you stay here with your parents. We'll call as soon as we know anything." Dumbfounded, I watched as my mother — *not* my husband — climbed into the ambulance and took my hand.

My mother and I said nothing to each other the entire ride to Mount Sinai. But she never let go of my hand. Not once during the entire ride.

Three hours later, Eric walked into the private Mount Sinai hospital room where my mom and I were waiting. His eyes remained focused on the ground, his hands jammed into his jean pockets. I could see through the door that his parents were with him, but had waited in the hall.

My mother was still at my bedside, holding my hand. She had spent the past few hours crying with me while we impatiently waited for updates from the doctors. None had come, and they were still taking tests and trying to figure out what was wrong with Ella.

"You decided to come?" I said, more sarcastically than I intended.

"Nicky, I . . . uh . . . I don't know what to say. Everything happened so fast, and I panicked. Is she . . . is she okay? Is Ella going to be okay?"

"We don't know yet. The doctors are still examining her and taking more tests. I haven't been allowed to even see her yet. No doctor has come by. We're just going on what the nurses are telling us." I refused to waste my energy on him. My focus needed to be on Ella.

Eric awkwardly stood next to the bed, looking as though he was near tears. Neither of us knew what to do or say. The spiral of complicated emotions seemed to encircle the room at increased speed with each passing minute. The morphine I had been given after my C-section was beginning to wear off and I needed to remain perfectly still to avoid the searing jabs from tearing through my lower abdomen.

"Why don't I give you two some privacy?" my mother asked, standing from her chair. "Nic, will you be okay if I take a walk and get some coffee? I'll bring you back a latte."

"Yes, thanks Mom. That would be great. And I'll be okay. Thanks for being here and staying with me." I failed at my attempt to smile at her, but wanted her to know I was grateful for her support. Plus, I was unable to prevent myself from throwing a verbal dagger Eric's way.

When exiting the room, my mother patted Eric on the shoulder, as if to tell him that it was okay. I knew she understood everyone reacts differently in tragic situations. She had been handed some doozies in her lifetime and had come to believe that it is not possible to know how you will react in a bad situation. That is, until you are in it.

I was not as understanding. I was devastated by all that had happened, and insurmountable panic was consuming every inch of my body. I was scared, oh so scared, about what lay in our path. And like the cherry on top of our squashed cupcake, my husband had crushed me when he had abandoned Ella and me at a time when we needed him the most.

Eric and I sat in silence. We said nothing to each other. The agonizing minutes crawled by at a pace slower than dial-up internet. I didn't trust myself to speak. I didn't even trust myself to look at him. He had taken my pain to a higher, more explosive level, and I was worried about what would come rushing out of my mouth if I began to talk.

Forty minutes later, after my mom had returned with my father, Eric's parents and six lattes, an exhausted and visibly upset doctor came into the room. He didn't introduce himself, but his badge read Dr. McKinnon.

After confirming we were Ella's parents, he cleared his throat and stated, "I'm sorry to tell you that your daughter is very sick. We've been running tests all afternoon, and we suspect she has something called neonatal hemochromatosis. It is a very rare condition in which toxic levels of iron accumulate in the liver and other tissues of a fetus. It occurs while the baby is developing in the womb and occasionally, but not often, can be detected in utero by ultrasound."

Dr. McKinnon paused, and let us take in what he was saying. I could hear Eric's mother crying softly in the corner and my mother went to her side to comfort her as she wiped away her own tears.

"What does it mean?" Eric asked, suddenly seeming more angry than afraid.

"She has liver failure and now her other organs are shutting down. She doesn't have much time," Dr. McKinnon said gently. "You should come and spend time with her in the NICU. I suspect she has only a few days. We are doing everything we can for your daughter. We have the pediatric liver specialists from SickKids Hospital suggesting experimental treatments for us to try, but so far she is not responding to our resuscitative measures."

My breath left me. I struggled to move. I needed to get out of the bed and go to her. But I was tied to the bed by catheter and IV. Dr. McKinnon gently guided me back down, and explained that I would be able to see her as soon as the nurses cleared me to go in a wheelchair — probably within an hour or two. Dr. McKinnon turned to Eric and told him he could visit the NICU with him if he would like as he was returning there immediately.

"Can you bring Ella here to the room?" Eric demanded, squishing his face into an expression I didn't recognize. His eyes seemed both disturbing and new — even to me — his wife and partner of almost fifteen years.

"We need to support her breathing and organs right now, and I think it's best if she stays in the NICU. An entire team is doing everything we can for your daughter."

"Will she . . . can she . . . is there a chance this might get better?" I was clinging to hope.

"Occasionally, but not often, some newborns have been known to overcome the effects of neonatal hemochromatosis. But you need to know that Ella's condition is severe — the worst we have ever seen. You need to prepare yourselves. . . ." He paused, almost at a loss for words. "I'm so sorry."

"When will you be back?" I asked, desperate for the doctor to stay, yet knowing it was better if he was with Ella.

"One of our team members will bring you updates. I will try and come back later this evening, but the nurses are also here whenever you need them." Dr. McKinnon paused, his gaze shifting from Eric to me as an empathetic sadness filled his eyes. "I'll ask a nurse to see if we can get Nicky into a wheelchair soon. So you can both come together and see Ella in the NICU." He quickly left, seemingly uncomfortable and anxious to exit the room.

"Thank you, doctor," Eric replied, barely above a whisper. He sank into the chair at the end of my hospital bed, and buried his head in his hands, shoulders shaking with his sobs.

My mother came to my side and sat gently on the bed to make sure she didn't tug at my catheter or cause pain to my fresh C-section wound. Gingerly, she pulled me into a warm hug so we could cry together.

Yet my tears didn't come. I was numb. In shock. Denying everything the doctor had told us. For some reason, at that moment, I felt absolutely nothing.

Brian stood awkwardly in the corner, moving his hands from his pockets to his side, while Amelia sat on the arm of Eric's chair, her hand placed firmly on his shoulder. Brian muttered something about needing air and quickly left the room, shooting his wife an apologetic look before he disappeared, promising he would be back soon.

From my bed, I could hear Amelia's soft words, whispered through her sniffles. "Go to her, Eric. She needs you. You need each other."

Slowly, Eric stood to full height and crossed the room. He stood beside my bed, and awkwardly patted my back in a way that reminded me more of a proud father congratulating his son after scoring a goal than a husband consoling his wife in a tragic time of grief.

I turned from my mother and held my arms up to Eric, as though I was a toddler wanting to be picked up. I was desperate for him. I needed him.

When Eric finally kneeled beside my bed and opened his arms to me, I buried my head in his chest, my arms clinging to his neck. His strong arms wrapped themselves around me in an embrace that felt more familiar to me than anything I had ever known.

I collapsed into him. And then the tears came.

A short while later, Dr. McKinnon reappeared at my bedside. He gently placed a hand on my shoulder, and said the words I would never, ever, forget, in a voice that was filled with softness and compassion. "I'm so . . . I'm very sorry to tell you this, but Ella has taken a turn for the worse." The doctor paused, almost as though he were waiting for something, or someone. Then, he cleared his throat and continued, "We're going to bring her to you now so you can be with her in the short time that she has left."

I stared at him, letting the silence fill the room. Panic pulsed into my throat, threatening to suffocate me.

"How long do we have?" I croaked, unsure of where my words had come from. I recognized my own voice as much as I did Eric's eyes, which seemed to have adopted a foggy glaze.

"Maybe an hour or so," Dr. McKinnon replied softly, his voice barely above a whisper.

"Shouldn't you be keeping her in the NICU? You said that was where she needed to be — that you need to support her. . . ." Eric questioned. The doctor shook his head sadly and, from behind him, a nurse appeared, carrying a tiny baby wrapped in a pink blanket and a knit hat. My baby. My Ella.

The nurse handed me our beautiful angel, and my heart went through emotions that were so mixed I somehow felt numb. It was as though I had managed to sleep on every part of my body in the wrong way, and every limb and tip was asleep with pins and needles.

I held our baby girl, and forced my memory to snap the picture that I would hold forever in my mind and heart. No one said a word as tears slid down my cheeks, anointing our baby girl and all of her beauty.

I begged God for help. Begged Him to make her better. To turn Ella into a healthy newborn with glowing pink cheeks and a little smile that took over her face when gas bubbles formed in her tummy.

But my prayers went unanswered.

It happened quickly. Eric was at my side, holding her entire hand with his pinky finger, and all four grandparents were cuddling in.

Ella's eyes fluttered open, only for a moment, as if she was greeting us, and taking in our faces before moving on.

And then our precious baby girl took one final breath, and she was gone.

6

I walked through the motions of the next three weeks in a semi-
comatose fog. My mother appeared at every meal with brown grocery
bags filled with whatever homemade soup or stuffed chicken that
she had whipped up the night before. Despite her constant efforts, I
couldn't seem to choke down more than three bites per meal, let alone
the plateful she continually begged me to eat.

"You're recovering from major surgery, honey," my mother said
gently. "You need to keep up your strength so that your body can heal."

I would shake my head, no, and she would crawl into my bed.
Tenderly, she raised the soup spoon to my lips, just as she had done so

many times when I was a baby. Like a little bird, I opened my mouth
to take the tiny bites my mother offered. When I could take no more, I
turned my head, still silent, and my mother would stop pushing me. At
least until the next meal.

The three times daily Meals on Wheels delivery from my mother
was matched by tuna casseroles and lasagnas brought forward by
friends and neighbours. Everyone wanted to help, but no one knew
how. No one even knew what to say. So, instead, people cooked.

Two days after we lost Ella, Eric shocked us all by announcing he was
going back to work. He claimed there were several time-sensitive cases
that needed his attention, and he didn't want to let down his clients.

"But *work*, Eric? Really, honey?! *Work*?" Amelia cried, covering
her pursed lips with an open hand when she found out the news. She
and Brian had come over to see how we were doing, and my mother
was serving them tea and the fresh scones she had picked up from a
bakery earlier that morning. I was still upstairs in bed, but could hear
the group discussing Eric's work plans through my open bedroom door.

"I know it seems a bit soon, Ma, but I'm not doing any good here.
And I just . . . I can't . . . I can't be here. It hurts too much." I could
sense the uncomfortable pause all the way upstairs. "And my cases
aren't going to wait for me. I need to get back. There's nothing I need
to stay home for."

"What about your *wife*?" Brian asked gently. I could hear the surprise and disappointment in his voice.

"I'll be here with Nicky at night, and there are lots of people here
during the day to help take care of her, including all of you guys. Plus
Maggie is flying in tomorrow, so she'll be able to help too."

"And what about the memorial service on Thursday?" Amelia
asked.

"Of course, I will be there."

The awkward silence that followed Eric's answer was obvious even to me, one floor up. I pulled the covers up over my ears and wished they would all just go away.

As I wrapped my arms around myself, I was greeted with new pain as my tender breasts reminded me that my milk had come in. My doctor had told me to get a really good bra and, other than that, I just needed to wait out the unfairness of my body wanting to breastfeed the baby I didn't have.

Eric came up ten minutes later and got in the shower. When he finished, he barely looked at me as he got dressed in our walk-in closet.

"So you're going back to work, Eric? Today? Were you planning on telling me?" I asked quietly from our bed when he came near me to get his watch from the bedside table.

"It's what I need right now, Nic."

"I see. Okay, then." I didn't have the energy to protest or even try to understand how he could just pick life back up so quickly after going through such heartbreaking loss. Or why he wasn't holding on to me as I drifted, listless, in my complicated veil of grief.

Then Eric kissed me quickly on the cheek and was gone.

---

When my father picked Maggie up at the airport early the following morning, she came directly over. My mother let them in, and Maggie walked straight upstairs and crawled into bed with me.

"Oh, Nicky. I'm so, *so* sorry." My sister crawled right under the covers and hugged me in a way that only a sister can. She said nothing more, but continued hugging me as I sobbed into her shoulder, letting the tears flow. I could smell the familiar scent of her hand cream and, for a moment, it took me back to a happy place from long ago.

"Can I get you anything? Are you hungry? Thirsty?" Maggie asked. "Mom said you haven't eaten today yet."

I shook my head. I didn't want anything. I wanted nothing but Ella.

"Have you been sleeping?"

I shook my head again. I dozed on and off throughout the day and night, but hadn't had a solid stretch of sleep since I had returned home from Mount Sinai.

"How did this happen, Maggie? *Why* did it happen?" Fresh tears slid down my face, hot and burning as they formed trails on my cheeks. Maggie pulled me back into her hug.

"*Shhh shhh* . . . Nicky. I don't know, big sister, I really don't. It's not fair. It's really so very unfair."

"You didn't even get to meet her!"

"I know, Nicky. I'm so sorry. I wish I would have come home earlier. I had no idea that you'd go into labour so early."

"You couldn't have known that. Or what was going to happen. I just wish you could have held her. I wish she could have met her Aunt Maggie!"

"I hold her in my heart. And I *feel* like I know her." Maggie's eyes lined with tears. She grabbed the box of tissues from my bedside table.

"Well, I feel like I'm in a nightmare." I sobbed into the tissue she handed me. I hiccupped, then coughed, my breaths struggling to keep up with my sobs. Slight twinges deep within my C-section incision burned, and I silently thanked my mother for ensuring I routinely took the heavy cocktail of meds that masked the majority of my post-surgery pain. "I just can't believe this is happening. I need to wake up from this awful dream, Mags. Please, please help me wake up! Help me feel better."

"*Shhh*, Nicky," Maggie soothed; stroking my hair as she held me like a baby. "I wish I could do that for you. I really do."

"I miss Ella so much and I can't make the pain stop. I need it to go away. I can't take how much it hurts. Please. Make it stop."

"I know, Nic. I know. Let it all out. Let it all go." My sister clung to me even tighter. Hugged me harder, until the sobs that emerged from somewhere deep within me shook my body in a way that almost scared me. I could feel drool lacing its way out the sides of my mouth, down my chin and onto my sister's shirt, but I didn't care. I wept until my choked sobs turned into a howl-like sound coming from my throat. I wept and sobbed into my sister's chest until, finally, I had no more tears to give, and I fell asleep in her arms.

The memorial service was small and quick. Only our parents, Maggie, Eric and I attended. Eric's brothers and their wives wanted to come, but I couldn't face anyone other than the small group. I knew they would understand. And if they didn't, I didn't care.

My mother choked back a sob as the minister read from Ecclesiastes, *"There is a time for everything, And a season for every activity under heaven: A time to be born and a time to die . . ."*

Surprisingly, no tears fell from my eyes. I felt numb, like I was watching the service from afar instead of attending. I reached for Eric, who was sitting beside me, still and quiet. His hand felt like cold stone. I squeezed it, but was given nothing back. He stared straight ahead, never glancing at me or acknowledging that I was even there.

When the service was over, we all returned to our house and my mother took over hostess duties. She put on a pot of coffee and pulled out freshly baked banana bread. I wondered when she had found the time to bake.

"It was a lovely service," Amelia said awkwardly, breaking the silence. "Didn't you think so, Eric?"

He shrugged, then nodded yes, before grabbing himself a beer from the fridge and sitting at the kitchen table, staring only at its surface. I could feel his pain. I sensed it in everything he was doing. Or wasn't doing, as the case might be. I was desperate to hold him. To console him. But he wouldn't let me in. I was being barricaded by his grief and I struggled to understand the best way to knock down his wall of sorrow.

My mother asked what I would like to drink and put a plate of warmed banana bread in front of me. I shook my head, telling her I wanted nothing. The banana bread sat before me, untouched. Eventually it got cold.

"I think I'll go upstairs for a rest," I told the group, unsure of what else to say or do. "Stay for as long as you'd like."

"Want me to come with you?" Maggie asked, standing from the kitchen chair she was sitting on.

"No. Thanks, Mags. I'll be okay on my own."

I slowly walked the stairs and climbed into bed, still fully clothed in my black pant suit. Tears, and then sobs, finally greeted me, and I bit into my pillow, not sure if I wanted to let them out or force them to stop.

I heard movement in our hall, and was certain that Eric was coming to check on me. To take me into his arms and tell me everything was going to be okay. I strained to listen and heard him enter the office. He shut the door and it sounded like his muffled voice was on a conference call.

Anger snapped through me as I sat straight up, mascara clumping my eyelashes together and leaving stains on the white pillow case I had been hugging. I got off the bed too quickly, causing pain to snake through the site of my incision, and I burst through the door to our office.

"Seriously, Eric? *Seriously*?! You're doing work? *Today*? Ten *minutes* after we said goodbye to Ella? Are you seriously that cold?"

"Tim? I'm going to have to call you back." Eric clicked his BlackBerry off and turned to face me, his eyes pierced and angered, yet lined in devastation and sorrow. "Nic, you knew I was on a work call. You can't come in here like that, yelling at me. . . ."

I cut him off. "We just had the *memorial service*. For our *daughter*. How could you? How could you even think about work?"

"The Stevens case is going to trial tomorrow and I had to talk to Tim about some last-minute details. I can't help it if the world isn't stopping for us."

"Let someone else at your firm deal with your fucking case. I don't give a shit about it, and neither should you, Eric."

"Nicky, please, you need to calm down. Our family is right downstairs. . . ."

I knew he was right, but I didn't care. I was beyond furious. He had pushed me too far, and newly formed anger coursed through my veins like pulsing blood. I no longer cared — about anything or anyone.

I stared him straight in the eye, and heard the silence of our families sitting downstairs, uncomfortable to be with each other and unsure of what to do or say. "Maybe we should go?" I overheard Amelia say quietly. Then, a moment later, the soft click of our front door being pulled shut.

"Are you happy? Now our family is gone and they think we're crazy."

"You *are* crazy, Eric! You don't even want to deal with what's going on. You just want to pick up where you left off and pretend that nothing happened. We had a *daughter*. She *died*."

"You think I don't know that, Nicky? You think I *don't know that?*"

"Well, you sure as hell aren't acting like it."

Eric threw his BlackBerry across the room, leaving a chipped divot where it bounced off the painted wall. "Fuck," he grunted, his frustration reaching a new height. He crossed the room and picked up his BlackBerry to inspect it. Made sure it was still working. "I'm getting out of here for a while, Nicky. I can't deal with you, or this, right now. I'll be back in a few hours."

"Fine. Whatever, Eric." My husband squeezed past me and exited the room. He didn't bother to look back to see that my legs had buckled under the weight of my grief and that I was curled up, sobbing, in a ball on the floor.

7

Somewhere over the next few weeks, our marriage also died. We tried to fix it, of course, but we were at a complete loss on how to make our marriage work after experiencing such unequivocal tragedy.

The social worker assigned to us by Mount Sinai referred us to a local therapist who specialized in working with parents who experienced the death of an infant. But it seemed that even *she* couldn't do anything, or even suggest something, to help us repair our relationship.

She recommended that we also join a local grievance group that helped parents who had lost a baby. I had hoped there was truth in the old adage that misery loves company. It doesn't. At least not for Eric, who wanted to shut the world out and never speak of Ella again.

"Would anyone else like to say anything? Tell us how they are feeling?" Shannon, the group leader, asked towards the end of the first — and last — meeting Eric and I attended together. Shannon glanced at Eric, who had been the only one in the room to not say anything during the hour we had been at the meeting. Eric remained silent and looked down at his feet, shrugging his shoulders and looking defeated.

"You didn't even say *anything*. Not one word!" I said to him after the meeting on our car ride home. It had started snowing, which Eric was completely disregarding as he drove too quickly through the dusted streets. My mind was taken back to the last time I had been in a car with Eric when he was driving too quickly. I clung to the memory.

"I told you that I didn't want to go. You forced me into it. *Remember?* You said that it would be good for us. Well, it wasn't. I hated it. Every minute of it." Eric's words were quiet. Bitter.

"Fine, then. Don't go anymore. I'll go by myself."

Eric never joined me again at the grievance group meetings, and even missed our next session with our therapist, Dr. Covert. Eric messaged me on my BlackBerry ten minutes into our appointment, saying that something had come up at work and he wouldn't be able to make it on time. He didn't even apologize.

Upon seeing the frustrated tears welling in my eyes, Dr. Covert handed me a tissue, saying simply, "Well, Nicky, hopefully Eric will be able to come next time. For now, this gives us a chance to talk about you. What *you're* going through."

I shrugged. Blew my nose. I wanted to be with Dr. Covert — I was desperate for her to find a way to make me feel better — but I needed Eric to be there, *with* me. "I miss Ella, of course. Like crazy. But I miss

Eric too. He just feels gone to me, Dr. Covert. It's like his soul died with her and all I have left is this empty shell that looks like him."

"I hear that a lot when I work with grieving parents. Men often deal with death differently than women. Innately, many men feel that they are the stereotypical strong protectors who should not freely show their emotions. This is one of the reasons there seems to be a struggle between mothers and fathers after a child dies. Wives are looking to their husbands for support and understanding, but many times, their husbands can't — or won't — show the same sympathy."

"But it's like he doesn't even care that she's gone!"

"We know that isn't true, Nicky. Eric is just showing his grief in a different way," Dr. Covert answered gently. "In most cases that I have seen, and Eric seems to be included in this, men *act* instead of dwell on the situation. They put their feelings into actions and experience grief physically, not emotionally. Instead of talking about their feelings, they focus more on completing specific tasks."

"Like going back to work?"

"Yes, like going back to work."

"But what about me? What about what I need? What about the fact that I need *him*? My husband."

"That's what we're working on, Nicky. You have to remember that this will take time."

But Eric's non-stop work ethic in response to what we had been through never seemed to change. And it clashed horrifically against my need to constantly talk of Ella and the few moments we had with her. Eventually, our brutal fights at home entered into the territory of how much we could even say her name out loud.

"I can't take hearing you say her name!" Eric would say to me, quietly at first but with an increasingly raised voice that ultimately reached screaming. His words scraped at my eardrums like a death metal song being turned up on the stereo. His face would be bright red by that point, his eyes lined in tears that refused to fall. He was shutting Ella out. And subsequently me as well.

"I'm scared I will forget her," I would retort back. I was obsessed with her memory and craved — no, needed, with every ounce of my soul — to be grieving with my husband. But he couldn't give that to me. He couldn't talk about what we had been through. Or *her*.

"Where are you, Eric? It's like you're standing there, but you're not even here with me. Can't you see I need you? That *you* need *me*?"

"I'm right here. I haven't gone anywhere, although sometimes I want to."

"What?! Fine. If you're so miserable, then why don't you just go?"

Eric looked straight into my eyes, his gaze hovering somewhere between misery and madness. "I don't *want* to go, but you're making me feel like it's my only chance at escape. The only way I'll be able to breathe again."

"Escape from *what*, Eric? From me? Our life together? The new world that we've been given? The one that doesn't include Ella?"

"Stop, Nicky. Just stop. I don't know anything anymore. I'm struggling to just move forward. But you constantly bringing up her name isn't helping, because it only reminds me that she isn't here anymore."

I searched his eyes, waiting for him to continue, the bitter rage encircling us and closing in.

"But what about me? I miss her. I need her. I don't want to just forget her, like you want to do."

"I don't want to forget her, Nicky. It hurts so much to talk about her. It just hurts too much. So, seriously, just *stop* talking about her."

I stopped, as he asked, and stared straight into his eyes. And then I delivered the blow that I knew neither of us would ever forget. "It's like you didn't even *love* Ella! Why do you want to forget her so badly? She was our daughter!" I hissed the words, seething and hurting. I had lost control of my emotions and my actions. My soul had collapsed when Ella's heart had stopped beating.

The callous insinuation having shot through the air like a bolt of lightning, I couldn't take it back. He took two giant steps towards where I stood. Closed in on me, fists raised, and then punched a hole through our kitchen wall. He paused then, and hung his head, his shoulders slumping under the pain of my accusation. Eric said nothing, but it was the closest he had ever come to hitting me, and it scared both of us.

Eric couldn't look at me before grabbing his keys and screeching out of the driveway in his BMW M3, a recently made purchase my mother swore was designed to make him feel better.

He disappeared for four days after that. I didn't know where he was or what he was doing. Our conversations were forced and uncomfortable when he returned, ultimately reverting back to screaming matches when we couldn't take the strain. It was as if we no longer knew how to talk to each other and occasionally yelled just to break the silence.

We couldn't even manage to be in the same room together. I didn't recognize Eric or who he had become; the man I married was simply gone. I knew he felt the same way about me. To be honest, I didn't recognize myself either.

By the middle of the summer, we were no longer sleeping in the same bed. By fall, we were officially separated. The papers were signed almost nine months to the date of Ella's birth and death.

Neither of us wanted to keep our home, so we sold it to the first buyers to make us an offer. Belinda, our real estate agent, assured us it was a fair purchase price, with a reasonable closing date.

"Do they have kids?" I asked her, as we signed the papers at our kitchen table. My heart was breaking as I asked the words, but I couldn't help myself. For some reason, I needed to know.

"Two," she said softly. "A little girl who is six and a son who is two."

I nodded, blinking back tears as I continued to sign the paper-work. From under the table, I felt Eric reach over and gently squeeze my knee. It was all I needed for the tears to fall on the paper, smudging my signature.

"It's okay," Belinda jumped in, dabbing the sale agreement with a napkin from the table, trying to save the signature. Eric's hand left my knee. "I'll dry this up, and we'll just white it out and sign overtop. It will be *fine*."

Our time in the house officially ended with the ring of our door-bell on a crisp Saturday morning in October. I opened the front door to find three burly men, standing side-by-side in sweat-stained clothes that seemed to have been washed but permanently marked by too many long days of lugging boxes and furniture.

"You Nicky?" the largest of the three men asked. "We're here to move your stuff."

I opened the door wider, just as Eric came down the stairs, his hair still damp from his morning shower. His crisp, clean jeans and button-down shirt stood in stark contrast to the movers' faded T-shirts and sweats. As Eric passed me to shake hands and introduce himself to the movers, I breathed in the smell of his shampoo. It smelled of familiarity, mixed with a blend of lavender and mint.

As the men got to work, they took turns glancing at me in a way that seemed to inherently suggest they all knew it was one of those sad moving situations. Maybe it was just me being paranoid, or perhaps it was because the boxes were clearly marked with an *E* or an *N*, and the movers were instructed to carry each box to the appropriately identi-fied van, both of which were parked on our street.

"His versus hers," I heard one of the movers mutter underneath his breath as he carried an oversized box down our stairs, leaving a smudge of back sweat against the wall as he went.

And that's exactly how it had been for the previous month as we divided our belongings. Wedding china for me, flat-screen TV for him. Couch for me, dining room table for him.

It had actually been relatively easy dividing up our assets. Much easier than I had heard so many people complain about in the movies. Maybe it was because Eric and I had somehow remained cordial in our last few months together. Or maybe it was because neither of us really gave a shit about the possessions that had found their way into our home. After all, it was just stuff.

When the last boxes were loaded, we took turns saying goodbye to the empty house and, finally, each other. As hard as it was, we agreed to no contact. I knew that seeing Eric again, talking to him — well, it would just make it harder. I needed a clean break. A new start. A world without him.

I used my half of the money we made on the sale of our house to purchase a small, one-bedroom condo in the heart of downtown. I needed to get out of suburbia and my new home came with the city buzz I was craving, and the promise of watching baseball games and concerts from my balcony when the stadium roof was open. It was the start of my new normal.

Except my new normal was lined with insomnia. I lay awake all night, every night, and wondered why I couldn't keep a classroom of Grade 3 kids in check the next day. Every time I closed my eyes, I had hospital room nightmares that led to crying fits into my pillow.

Each new day, I would drag myself through the morning motions of getting ready, and hoped that under-eye concealer would be that day's secret weapon. It never worked and I knew I wasn't fooling anyone.

Eventually, my principal called me on it, saying that she could be somewhat lenient given the circumstances, but that I needed to focus on pulling myself together. Soon.

I tried sleeping pills. Three different kinds, in fact. But I lay awake right through them. Night after night, I got up, frustrated and tired of crying, to surf through any mindless internet sites that would prevent Eric and Ella memories from sinking in.

I scoured Facebook, but was bombarded with recently posted pictures of the gorgeous, smiling faces of my friends' children. I left the site, turning to Perez Hilton and certain I would be granted mindless, numbing entertainment. The first article I read was on John Travolta and his daughter Ella Bleu. Bye-bye Perez.

One night, over my token dinner for one, I picked up the phone to call Eric; he was the only person who knew exactly how I was feeling, and I craved his touch and understanding. I needed him.

I made it through all of the numbers but one before I forced myself to hang up. The Eric I knew was gone to me. He had been replaced by a stranger, and there was nothing I could do to get him back. We were finished. It was over.

I clicked the phone off. Then on again. Off. On. Off. On.

Numb, I listened to the dial tone fill the silence of the empty room. Eventually it was replaced by the loud alarm bursts designed to tell you the phone is off the hook. The sound hurt my brain.

I scraped my untouched food into the garbage and climbed into bed without brushing my teeth or washing my face. I stared into the darkness, waiting for sleep to find me. It didn't come.

The following Tuesday I fell asleep at my desk while my students were writing in their journals. Unfortunately for me, my principal walked by at that precise moment. She requested an end-of-the-day meeting, which ended up marking the end of my time at the school. At least temporarily. I was strongly encouraged to take a semester leave of absence, and was assured the position would be mine to retrieve come the following fall. "Go to the beach, Nicky. Take the vacation you've always wanted. Climb a mountain. Go skydiving. Whatever you need to clear your head," my principal encouraged. Deep down I knew she was right. I wasn't the same teacher she had hired, and it wasn't fair to the students.

The problem was I didn't want to do any of those things she had suggested. It wasn't that I didn't have dreams, it was just that every line item on my bucket list had included Eric. We had talked about seeing the glowworms in the Waitomo Caves in Auckland *together*. He was going to be my dive buddy when we learned to scuba dive on the Great Barrier Reef. I had always imagined holding *his* hand as I took in the awesomeness of Egypt's Great Pyramid of Giza. And we had always planned on hiking the tiny paths of the Inca Trail, one following the *other*. Our life list was long, and was too quickly cut short by the unde-featable heartbreak that was out of our control.

In the middle of the night after my principal had delivered her blow, I was having a typical 2 A.M. date with my computer. I abandoned my meaningless night surfing and googled: *how teachers can help in other parts of the world*.

My computer was flooded with options, but eventually the online path I followed took me to a company that was recruiting teacher volunteers for small towns in Africa. I got sucked into the details, reading everything I could find on what it would be like to actually leave my current depressing world and enter a brand new one — one without any memories of Eric or the tragedy we had experienced together.

The company was searching for qualified teachers who could help support African teachers in the orphanage classrooms of small towns on a volunteer basis. They would stay with screened and approved host families who would provide safety, shelter and food to their home stays. Commitment times were variable and could be flexible based on the volunteer teacher's willingness and availability. I made a mental note to call the volunteer company the next day to find out more details about what I needed to do before leaving.

For the first time in over a year, I felt a sense of hope. I needed to be freed of everything encircling my world that emphasized what I no longer had — and would never have again. I needed to be as far away from Eric as I could imagine. Being within a drivable distance of him was too painful, too distracting and too tempting.

Most of all, I needed to find a way to stop feeling the pain I had been going through since Ella's death. I needed to feel other things. Happy things.

I knew that by giving back — by giving what I could to the world's most unfortunate children — I would somehow find some sense of reward, even if just a little bit. I would do something that I could feel *good* about doing.

It was the only way; I would drown in sorrow unless I did something completely opposite of the world I knew. Best of all, I could do it while staying true to the one thing I loved — teaching.

That night, for the first time in months, I slept like a baby.

PART TWO

## 8

The iron gate heavily clanked shut. Behind it, an armed guard with a face as black as the star-filled night sky around him stood still as a stone, his face exuding boredom and his camouflaged uniform failing to hide his oversized torso. His index finger rested on the gun's trigger, leaving me uncertain about whether I felt sheer terror or gratefully safe.

The guard continued to stare right through me as I ungracefully juggled my bags and watched the private *matatu* that I had taken from the Nairobi airport drive away. A voice inside me screamed for the van to stay, and my lungs seemed to buckle as utter panic took over a very tired travel body that suddenly felt heavier than my own.

I somehow managed to take hold of my two bulging suitcases, duffle bag and backpack. It had been so much easier at the airport when my teary-eyed mother and father had been there to help carry the load. I walked towards the home where I would be staying during my post of teaching the children at the orphanage. Just as I thought I had it figured out, my oversized pink duffle bag fell off my shoulder, directly punching into the tender, bruised area where I had received my last round of vaccinations.

"Damn it!" I said out loud. There was no one to hear me except a black and white stray cat that had slinked in from the dry grass beside me. Tired tears filled my eyes and I suddenly yearned for my king-sized bed more than anything else. I kept shuffling forward, wondering why there was no one there to greet me. Or help me. I dropped my bags to take a rest, and strained to see the new world around me. Given the late hour, I couldn't see much except for dim lights coming from the home in front of me.

Due to obsessive pre-trip planning, I knew that I was about forty-five minutes outside of Nairobi in a secure villa neighbourhood called Ngong (or "Gong" as pronounced by the locals) and that the mean-looking man I had left behind at the gate really did have my best interest at heart. My host family lived in one of the safer neighbour-hoods, the pamphlets had said, which was largely made possible by the night guard wearing a gun.

Slinging my backpack and duffle bag over my shoulder, I pulled my two suitcases across the dirt path. Clouds of red powdery dust pillowed around me in the still night. I sneezed.

In front of me, a brighter light went on at the front of my host family's home, signalling that they were awake and waiting. Seeing the light, I gained new energy, and forced a smile as the entire family stepped out from inside. They waved to greet me.

"Welcome, *rafiki*!" my host father greeted me, using the Swahili word for *friend*. He and a boy about sixteen years old darted forward to help carry my bags. "We are so happy to finally meet you. And we are pleased to have you stay in our home. I am Kiano, and this is our youngest child, Petar. We have four other sons, but they are grown and live in homes with their own families." Kiano paused and turned to the woman standing behind him. "And this is my beautiful wife, Abuya."

Relieved of my bags, my arms became free for obligatory, yet very warm and welcoming, hugs from each family member. Kiano squeezed me tightly, gently slapping my back, while Petar offered a shy hug.

"*Karibu*, Nicole," Abuya said. Welcome, Nicole. She had warm, brown eyes that flickered in the light, and skin that looked like molasses. "We are so happy to have you stay in our home," Abuya continued in near-perfect English. She immediately took my hand in hers; it was rough to the touch and she had short, brittle nails that were yellowing — an obvious sign of constant hard work.

"Thank you, Abuya. And, please, call me Nicky." I smiled, grateful to be speaking with friendly faces. "I'm so relieved to be here, and very thankful that you are willing to take me in while I stay in Kenya."

"Nonsense. It is we who should be grateful," Kiano responded. "You are here to help the children and while you do that you need a place to stay. If we can provide a place for you to eat and rest your head, then we are called to do it. It is our . . . how do you say . . . our *duty*? And it is our pleasure."

"Please, come in, come in," Abuya said as she ushered me into her home. She wore a belted, dark blue dress that buttoned all the way down the front, reminding me of an African version of June Cleaver. Her shoulder-length hair matched the colour of the espresso beans Eric had ground each morning for our daily cappuccinos, and she held it back with a thick red hair band. "It is getting cold outside, *rafiki*.

Come in, where it is warm." Abuya smiled then, showing the whiteness of slightly crooked teeth against black skin; instantly she conveyed a warmth and maternal dependability that comforted me.

I stepped through the front door, directly into a small living room the size of Amelia and Brian's cottage bathroom. Three oversized, worn couches were stuffed into the room, all with frayed fabric and noticeable holes. In the far corner, there was a small chair that I later realized wobbled too much to actually sit on and, beside it, there was a small black and white television sitting on a rickety card table.

"You have a TV?" I asked, failing miserably at my attempt to hide my surprise.

"Yes, Nicky," Kiano replied, smiling through a toothy grin that was more crooked than Abuya's. "We have television. What did you expect?"

"I'm not sure," I replied, hesitating to tell them the truth. "I guess I thought there might not be electronics of any type. The orientation book said that many Kenyan homes don't even have electricity."

"I am only teasing you, *rafiki*. You are the third person who has lived with us while staying in Ngong — and everyone who comes here is surprised to see our television. We also have a kitchen with a microwave, which often seems to be a surprise as well. We have an oven too, but that stopped working about a year ago, and we cannot get it fixed right now." Kiano pointed to a small room beside the living room. "Here, let me show you the kitchen."

I followed Kiano into the kitchen. It was obvious the room had received a vigorous scrub shortly before I arrived, but I couldn't help but notice two cockroaches run into the plywood wall when Kiano turned on the kitchen light. I somehow managed to stifle a scream, and shifted my glance in an effort to pretend I hadn't noticed.

Beside the broken oven was an open window, which mosquitoes were using as their own private entrance into the house. "No screens?"

I asked, pointing to the window. Instead of any sort of netting that might prevent malaria from entering, there were steel bars. Once again, I wasn't sure if I felt safer to see the bars or more afraid given the reasons the family might need them.

"You notice the steel bars, I see?" Kiano said, nodding his head towards the window. "They are here to protect us."

I smiled at Kiano, offering him a hint of thanks, but inwardly said a quick prayer for safety. The house, which Kiano and Abuya had proudly boasted about building themselves, was made of thin plywood, and I didn't have the heart to point out that if someone wanted in, they could easily get in — bars or no bars.

"Would you like to see the rest of the house? I will have Abuya show you to your room, which I know she is preparing now."

I nodded my head. I was exhausted and desperately wanted to sleep.

"Bu, come please," Kiano called to his wife, barely raising his voice. When she instantly appeared, I realized just how easily sound travelled throughout the home. The entire house was small, about the size of two rooms back home, but, more than that, the noise could be heard everywhere because *all* of the internal walls were about two feet too short. Not one of them touched the ceiling, and the open structure reminded me of the cubicles Eric had worked in when he first started at his law firm.

"Follow me, Nicky. I will show you to your room." Abuya once again took my hand, and guided me to a tiny room directly off the living room.

In one corner was a small bed. At the top of it was a lumpy, white pillow with no case, and covering the bed was a fraying orange and grey quilt that had obviously been handmade. Despite its wear and tear, the thinning blanket was still beautiful and I had to stop myself from getting cozy underneath it right then and there.

"Petar has brought your things in here. I hope you will find your stay in this room enjoyable," Abuya said, pointing to the pile of bags in the corner. My suitcases, duffle bag and backpack created a luggage teepee in the only spare space in the room.

Just as I was about to tell Abuya that I wanted to call it a night, she offered me some chai. "We have been looking forward to your arrival for so long and we are excited to get to know you, Nicky. We made some chai in preparation for your arrival. Would you like some?"

I looked into the enthusiasm of her warm eyes and didn't have the heart to say no. I nodded, and hoped the Kenyan version of my long-time Starbucks favourite had as much caffeine as a double espresso.

Once in the living room, I sank into a worn and tattered couch. Abuya poured the tea, and explained its tradition over the kitchen's six-foot wall. "Chai is a daily tradition in our country and an ongoing excuse to sit and discuss the day. We all drink it every day, and all day. Each family has a slightly different recipe, but we all serve it with milk and sugar. My own recipe is one that was passed down from my Grandma Hamisi and it is a favourite among many people in Ngong. I have managed to keep the recipe a secret for many years but, if you like it, I will tell it to you before you return home."

"I'm intrigued," I said, taking the gigantic mug of steaming tea Abuya offered to me. By Starbucks standards, the mug would have been bigger than a venti.

"I do hope you like it, Nicky. I make the tea each morning, and then again each evening. It is kept in our kitchen thermos. Please feel free to help yourself whenever you would like some."

"It's delicious," I replied honestly after I had taken my first sip. "I can see why so many people here love it so much."

As I sipped at my tea, Abuya hovered beside the couch I was sitting on, and Petar rose to give his mother his seat; his gesture didn't go unnoticed by Kiano, who gave his son a nod of approval as Abuya took her spot directly beside me.

Sitting, my host mother patted my knee, "So, my dear Nicky, please do tell us about you. We are so curious to get to know you."

"Okay, Abuya . . ."

My host mother quickly cut me off. "Please, Nicky, call me Mama Bu. That is what all of our house stays call me. The kids at the Kidaai orphanage too."

"Okay, then. Let's see, where should I start? I'm thirty-three years old, and I've always lived in the suburbs, the area outside of Toronto. I was born and raised there, and then went off to university and teachers' college." My host family nodded their heads, listening to every word I spoke. "Hmmm, I guess you already know that I'm a teacher. I really love it, and am looking forward to working with the children at Kidaai as well."

"The organization sent a description on you a few weeks ago. They said many good things about what a wonderful teacher you are," Mama Bu commented, her eyes meeting mine over the brim of her mug.

"Thank you." I blushed lightly at the compliment and looked down at the cement floor.

"And what about your family?"

"My parents are both well, and I also have a sister, Maggie. She's a permanent global traveller, it seems, and is always in some faraway place. Her most recent adventure has taken her to Australia. The last I heard she was in a place called Byron Bay, but leaving shortly to make her way down to Sydney."

"It seems that your mother has two world travellers. Look where *you* are!" Kiano pointed out, still smiling through his pearly, crooked whites.

"Hmm, I guess I *have* caught a bit of the travel bug myself. This is my first time to Africa though."

"And what about your other family, Nicky? The organization said that you are married?" Mama Bu pressed on, although gently. "Was it hard to leave your husband?"

I paused, unsure of how to answer Mama Bu's question, or how much of it I wanted to tell them. The mention of Eric drove a sharp pain through my heart and my entire body felt rigid. "Yes, I was married," I said softly, taking a deep breath. "But it is a very long and sad story. The short version is that my husband, Eric, and I were dealt some really crummy hands. Unfortunately, we weren't able to make our marriage work."

"What do you mean 'dealt some really crummy hands'? I do not understand the translation?" Mama Bu looked confused, and I forced a smile, grateful for a break in the conversation.

"Oh, it's an expression referring to what life brings you. I guess it compares the uncontrollable things that happen in a game of cards, and most often the expression is used when someone is unlucky in life. I'm pretty sure it's based on the game of poker," I explained, wanting to change the subject from the questions Mama Bu and Kiano were asking. "Do you play poker here, or any game of cards?"

Just as Kiano was about to answer, the room went dark. Pitch black. I was instantly scared.

"It is okay, Nicky," Mama Bu said soothingly, her voice carrying through the dark room. "This happens often, unfortunately. The electricity has gone out. Petar? Kiano? Please. Get the lanterns."

I heard scrambling. Fumbling through the dark. Within a minute, Petar and Kiano had lit the kerosene lanterns. They brought them into the sitting area where Mama Bu and I were still sitting on the couches.

"There! That is better." Mama Bu smiled over the lamplight.

"Why did the electricity go out?" I asked, puzzled. There was no storm to affect the power; the calm night was still and quiet.

"It is the government. They control the electricity and have the authority to decide when it goes on — and when it goes off. We have no command of this and do not know when it will happen. We just light candles and hope that the electricity comes back on soon."

I tried to wrap my mind around what Mama Bu had just said. The Kenyan government just turned off electricity *whenever* they wanted to? I couldn't imagine living in a country where external authorities had such direct control over the everyday light in my living room.

"How long is it out for?" I asked, still bewildered.

"Sometimes it is for a few hours, and sometimes it lasts for days. Last month the power was out for six days. It was not fun, as you can imagine. We missed the nightly Kenyan news for almost a week!" I could see Mama Bu shaking her head in the shadows of the lamplight.

"We can give you the big lantern for your bedroom if the power does not come back on," Petar piped up. "We are used to the dark so you can have it."

I smiled at his generosity. "Thank you, Petar, but I brought a small flashlight with me. I can use that until the power goes back on. Are there any plans for tomorrow?" I asked, changing the subject. I was enjoying getting to know my host family, but serious jet lag had taken over and I was about to fall asleep on Mama Bu's lap.

"Well, since tomorrow is Saturday, I told the orphanage director that we would not be arriving until early Monday morning. That is the first day of school for the week. Kiano and Petar have chores to do around the house, but I was thinking I could show you around Ngong. How does that sound to you, Nicky?"

"I would love that," I replied, forcing a smile through my exhaustion. I wanted to learn everything I could about Kenya. Sadly, other than the research I had done in the weeks leading up to my trip, the only thing I really knew about Africa was what I learned while watching *The Lion King* with Eric's nieces and nephews.

"How wonderful. I will be honoured to teach you," Mama Bu responded, finishing her last sip of tea. Then, looking straight into my eyes, she hospitably continued, "I can see that you are very tired and need a good night's rest, my dear Nicky. Let us retire for the night, shall we? We will see you in the morning, and we will have breakfast together before leaving for your first real journey into Kenya."

"Thank you, Mama Bu." I stood up and realized I didn't know where the bathroom was. "I would love to wash my face and brush my teeth before going to bed. And I *really* need to go to the bathroom after all of your delicious chai."

"Yes, I will show you where it is." Mama Bu rose from her chair and pointed to a closed door. "We are thankful to have a toilet, as many of our friends only have squats, but unfortunately there is no sink to wash your face or brush your teeth. I will bring you some warm water, which I still have from dinner. You can take it into the bathroom to use it there."

"Here, Nicky, take the big lantern so you can see. It will be very dark in there. The smaller lanterns will be enough light for Bu," Kiano said, insisting that I take the biggest lantern with me.

I thanked them for the light, and got my toothbrush and tooth-paste from my backpack. Stepping into the closet-sized washroom, I was shocked by what the lantern light *didn't* reveal. After Mama Bu's explanation, I hadn't expected to find a sink, but there was also *no* bathtub and *no* shower. Not even a mirror.

I squatted over the seatless toilet, and made a mental note to dig out some of the sanitizer I had brought with me in my suitcase. Relieved to see a handle, I flushed the toilet.

Mama Bu lightly tapped on the door and handed me a tin cup filled with water, and a tattered face cloth. Using my index finger, I tested the temperature; the water wasn't cold, although it certainly wasn't warm by Canadian standards.

I thanked Mama Bu for the water and said good night to my host mother.

"Good night, Nicky. We will see you in the morning." I could see Mama Bu smiling in the dim light. She squeezed my arm and then turned towards her bedroom.

I shut the bathroom door and used the lukewarm water to wash my face. I scrubbed my teeth — vigorously — and tried to free myself from the dirty feeling that airplanes always brought me. Without a sink to use, I spit into the toilet.

Once finished in the bathroom, I made my way to the tiny bed; I shivered in the cold, my bare feet curling against the icy cement floor as I walked.

Finally, after twenty-four hours of travel, it was time to sleep.

—

The bed was as hard as it looked, and the pillow was frayed and damp. Darkness like I had never experienced flooded the room and I grew scared of the unknown around me. I clutched my small flashlight, which I had brought into bed with me and tried to resist the temptation to turn it on to look around. I had no idea where to get new batteries if they died, and I didn't want my host family to see the beam of light over their six-foot walls.

Mosquitoes buzzed in my ear and I swatted them away in the dark. I had forgotten to retrieve the netting that I had brought in one of my suitcases and knew it would be impossible to find it blind in the tower of bags. Instead, I pulled the quilt high over my ears and prayed for malaria to stay away. That, plus the two cockroaches I had seen earlier in the kitchen.

In the near distance, I could hear a dog barking and the occasional truck driving by the house. Farther away, I could make out the sound of bongo drums, which Kiano had earlier explained was the *Mijikenda* (literally, the nine tribes) performing percussion-based music that was as beautiful as it was complex. Accompanying the bongos was singing and the occasional howl of laughter.

Closer to home, Petar sneezed in the room directly beside me. Mama Bu sighed in the room she shared with her husband and, later, I heard Kiano fart in his sleep. I could hear *everything*.

The deep sleep that I had been promised while falling asleep in the sitting room escaped me and, suddenly, my body felt electric. The black room combined with my inability to sleep (and probably some caffeine kicking in) created a mind-racing hotspot, and I was afraid of where my brain would take me. Remembering Ella hurt too much, and thinking of Eric was just as painful.

I didn't want to go there.

Yet, after about an hour of lying in the darkest of black, long after the *Mijikenda* had quieted down, I was no longer able to distract my mind, and my thoughts crept to our beautiful Ella.

I could still feel the light weight of her peaceful body that I held in my arms for so many minutes after she left us. Her long eyelashes, a mirror of her father's, were etched in my mind. The feeling of desperation as I begged God to reopen her eyes came flooding back to me.

I clung to my pillow, biting into it as I tried to mask my cries. I buried my sobs, hopeful that no one in the house would hear me.

An image of Eric appeared in my mind, bright-eyed and smiling. I missed him in a way that I didn't know was possible. I thought of the way he would tickle my ear when we were lying on the couch, watching a movie. I remembered how he would always brush the snow off my car after a storm had hit — just so that I wouldn't have to do it.

I needed Eric. My lungs constricted from the sobs, and my heart screamed, *"Why are we half a world away from each other . . . without our beautiful baby and without each other?"*

When the tears seemed to finally dry up, my thoughts turned to what Eric would be doing at that very minute. Was he also sobbing? No, that wasn't him. But what was he thinking? Was his mind on me, so many miles away? Did he even know that I was in Africa?

In an attempt to feel a little less pain — even a smidgen — I turned on my imagination. I shut my eyes and pretended it was a long-ago Saturday morning, and I was still there with Eric. I imagined it was as it had been on so many other weekend mornings, and we were just waking up to the bright sunshine streaming through the shutters. We would make love, and then Eric would bring his freshly made cappuccinos and the morning newspaper to our bed. After catching up on the daily headlines, it would be a double shower . . . I smiled, remembering Eric's never-ending joke about us needing to conserve water.

Finally, somewhere in the deep night, I fell asleep.

9

Within a few hours, I was shaken back to reality by a rooster crowing right outside my window bars. I was confused at first, given the last thought before I fell asleep was of a happy hubby and the perfect marriage, but the shrill cackle of the morning alarm clock quickly proved that I was, in fact, not in Canada anymore.

I could hear Mama Bu clinking pans in the kitchen, and realized that catching up on my sleep would need to wait. I changed into a clean pair of yoga pants and a red T-shirt, then realized it was still quite cold in the house. I grabbed a hooded grey sweatshirt and threw it over my T-shirt.

"Good morning, Mama Bu," I said, joining my host mother in the kitchen. I eyed the counter for the duo of beady-eyed cockroaches I had seen the night before, holding my breath and hoping they had left the building. My disgust of the repulsive critters formed a temporary sense of guilt for not being more appreciative of the family who had taken me in, but I disregarded the feeling knowing that Mama Bu, or any woman in her right mind, would agree there was nothing overly *rafiki*-like about vermin.

"Good morning to you as well, Nicky," Mama Bu replied hospitably, giving me a friendly hug. I thought again how much I liked the warmth of her voice — it was comforting, mellow, and made me feel safe. "Would you like some chai? I just finished brewing it."

"Yes, thank you. That would be great. I'm definitely in need of some more caffeine. I'm afraid I'll still be terribly jet lagged today."

"There is an endless pot of chai for you, dear, which will help with your tiredness. Help yourself to as much as you wish. I also have some eggs and toast — it is a good thing the power went back on through the night so I could make our breakfast. Would you like some?" Mama Bu offered me the plate she was holding, which contained one egg. A square piece of toast sat alongside the single egg, coated in bright red jam.

I nodded, taking the plate from Mama Bu. I mustered a smile of appreciation; the kitchen did not have a refrigerator in it, and I had no idea where the egg would have been stored. Saying a silent prayer for health, I hoped my body would be okay with cupboard-stored eggs.

"Let us take our breakfast to the sitting area. We usually eat around the table in there, sitting on our couches, as we do not have room for a kitchen table."

"I noticed your many couches last night. Do you have a lot of people visit?"

"That is the Kenyan way, my child. You will see that family and friends will be always dropping by, just as we always drop by their homes. Kiano and I have many couches so that people will have room to sit."

"Makes sense. I look forward to meeting your family and friends," I replied, taking a bite of my toast. It tasted like sweet cardboard.

"Good morning, Nicky," Kiano greeted me warmly, coming into the sitting area. "Bu, have you made some breakfast for me?"

"Yes, Kiano. I will get it." Mama Bu left her half-eaten egg and went to the kitchen to retrieve another plate for her husband.

"You slept well, yes?" Kiano asked.

"I did, thank you, although I was just saying to Mama Bu that I'm still very tired."

"I suspect that will be with you for a day or two yet. By your first or second day in the Kidaai classroom, you should be good as new!"

Mama Bu returned with a plate mirroring ours, and handed it to her husband.

"Thank you for breakfast. It's delicious," I said through bites of toast. My rumbling stomach was happy to be eating again. Gaining confidence, I attempted the egg. I took a bite, small at first, then larger. The egg was creamy and tasted like home.

"Petar is sorry to have missed you, but he is already out tending to his chores. You will see him later today, once you and Bu are back from your travels." Kiano inhaled his breakfast, speaking through his bites.

"Speaking of our plans, we will leave in half an hour," Mama Bu said as she took Kiano's empty plate from him and carried it into the kitchen to wash the dishes. She filled the sink with cold, soapy water. I jumped up to help her.

"We will start by showing you around our land. Then we will walk into Ngong town. Does that sound alright with you?" Mama Bu said, scrubbing the dishes, which she handed to me to dry. She pointed to the various spots in the open cupboard where each dish went. "I will show you where Kidaai is, as well as the market. And later I will take you to the slums. It is always sad to see, but I think it is needed for you — many of the children you will be teaching are from the slums. You need to see the reality of where they come from."

"Is Kidaai in the slums?" I asked, anxious to learn more about where I would be working, and suddenly nervous about having to go into the slums of Ngong every day.

"No, Nicky. Kidaai is very close. It is about ten minutes up the road, near Ngong town. The slums, well, they are about twenty minutes past that by foot," Mama Bu answered. She scrubbed the thin plastic kitchen counter with vigour, careful to wipe every inch before hanging the cloth over the sink. "The little ones who need help get taken from the slums, or other places, and put into orphanage care. They are the ones you will be teaching."

"How long have the kids been in the orphanage?"

"It really all depends. Some have been there for only a few months, while others have been there for years. I think the youngest Jebet has right now is three. The oldest is about eleven, or so." Mama Bu took a pot from the sink and put it away in a cupboard. "The biggest problem Kidaai has right now is that the kids do not stick around past that age. They all seem to run away when they reach the age of eleven or twelve. It is really very sad — they almost always end up back in the slums."

Puzzled, I wondered why kids would leave the comfort of an orphanage, only to return to the devastation they came from. "Why would they do that?"

"Oh, many different reasons, I guess. Some are acting out and . . . how do you say it . . . *rebelling*? Others think they can take care of themselves. Many do not like Jebet — she is the orphanage director — so

I wonder if they do it to get away from her. Others have family back in the slums, and they leave to go and find them. But mostly the older kids don't want to stick around because they don't like caring for the younger kids all the time. It's too much work for them."

I nodded, wondering how much work they were actually doing. "And why don't they like Jebet?"

"She is pretty tough on some of the kids," Mama Bu said sadly. She wiped her hands on a tea cloth, then smiled, clearly wanting to change the subject. "Now, shall we go? Let's walk around our land and I will show you some of our trees and gardens. We have got plenty of it, compared to most."

"Sure. Sounds great!" I grabbed my backpack from my bedroom and stuffed it with things I'd need that day, including a granola bar, hand sanitizer and a bottle of water from the plane. Plus one of the three big bottles of sunscreen I'd stuffed in my suitcase. My fair skin had always burned easily and I was paranoid of turning into a lobster after a few minutes in the African sun. I knew I'd be slathering on the thick sunscreen many times per day and I hoped no one would make fun of me.

The brochure I read at the airport warned visitors to carry their backpack on their front, so I slipped my arms through the straps and carried it like I was a kangaroo and it was my joey.

"Ready?" Mama Bu asked, when she saw me.

"Definitely! Let's go." I was ready to take on the world. Or, at the very least, my new part of the world.

—

Walking out the front door, I shielded my eyes from the sun and took in my first daylight view of Africa. The ground was covered with red dirt, and dustier than I was expecting; every surface had been covered with a russet-coloured dry, powdery film. It tickled my nose. I sneezed.

Taking two more steps out the door, I was greeted by a burning stench that was so strong it made me gag. I covered my mouth. "Mama Bu? What is that? What's burning?"

"That is garbage smoke, Nicky. We have got nothing to do with our garbage but burn it," Mama Bu replied. She shut the warped door behind her. The door was decaying and about the same width as a thick pad of paper. "You'll get used to it. Everyone does."

I hoped so, but wasn't sure. With each new breath I took, the thick smoke choked at my throat and threatened to launch a wheezy cough from deep within my chest.

"Now, Nicky, let us check out the fruit trees we have growing." Mama Bu led me up a patchy grass hill, dried out and thirsty, directly behind their house. When we got to the top, we found a grove of trees littered in fruit.

"We have mostly mango and papaya. Have you had them before?"

"Oh yes! They're two of my favourites. We don't have any trees growing in our backyards though. We have to buy fruit at the grocery store." I touched the smooth surface of one of the mangoes that had fallen from the tree; it was cool from being in the shade. "What a sweet treat to have it right at your doorstep."

"You are right about that, chicka. We do not have a lot, but God is a good God and He blessed us with these trees on our property . . . and a backyard filled with *sweet treats*," Mama Bu answered, laughing at the expression. "Here, now I will show you our garden." My host mother led me through the patch of trees and over another hill to a hidden vegetable garden, which was filled with rows of brightly coloured vegetables. "This is what we use to make our meals. All of it is grown by us."

"Wow! Look at it all. You've got *so* much!"

"Thank you, Nicky. This year we have grown some snow peas, bobby beans, sweet potatoes, okra and maize."

"Maize? I haven't heard that term since I was in elementary school and we were learning about the pioneers." I paused, admiring the perfect, weed-free rows of the garden, which had clearly enjoyed a lot of farming TLC. "Back home, we now call that corn."

"Yes, one of the past volunteers who stayed with us talked about corn. But here we call it maize."

"I love to hear about what you call things. And I'd love to pick up a bit of Swahili while I'm here as well, if you'd help me?"

"Of course, *rafiki*. I will teach you about life in Africa and you can teach me more about North America." Mama Bu gave my hand another firm squeeze. Her affectionate touch made me feel so grounded and safe, almost as though I was a child again. I welcomed the feeling and relished how it made me feel warm and protected.

"We have also got some rice wheat and sugar cane, though I would like to grow more." Mama Bu began walking again, to another section of the garden. "We started having a good year, but the dry season is coming, so our crops might turn soon. They are already not doing as well as in previous weeks."

"Oh, I hope that doesn't happen. What you've got now is very impressive."

"Thank you, Nicky. I agree, but only God knows what is in store for us." Mama Bu paused, shielding her eyes from the blazing sun and looking past the garden. "You can see in the distance where the chickens are. We will not go there right now, because Kiano and Petar are tending to the eggs. We do not want to disrupt them." Mama Bu tugged gently at my arm, and started walking in the other direction, past where the night guard had been standing.

"The guard doesn't stay in the day?" I asked.

"No, he leaves at six o'clock. You have got no worries in Ngong town during the day, dolly. You can wear that backsack on your stomach if it makes you feel better, but it is safe in daylight. It is the night that you have to worry about." Mama Bu stopped in her tracks and turned to look straight at me. "No matter what, Nicky, you absolutely cannot be out after dark. You have to plan your travel around the sun schedule, do you hear me? Because if the snatch-and-run thieves do not get you, it will be Kiano who has your hide when you get back to the house. We worry about our home stays, and it is our job to keep you safe!"

I listened to Mama Bu's words, taking them seriously. Fear of being targeted by violence obviously didn't sit well with me and I vowed to never be out after dark — no matter what.

"Are you okay with a quick stop? My neighbour, Barika, has been going on about wanting to meet you for days now. I can't wait for you to meet her." Mama Bu beckoned me to follow.

"Of course."

"Wonderful. You will like her . . . just be prepared for her to talk. *A lot*." Mama Bu tugged at my hand once again and guided me down the path to the red dirt road where I comfortably fell into step alongside her.

## 10

*"Karibu*, Miss Nicole!" Mama Bu's plump neighbour squealed when she saw me. Barika greeted me with a big smile and a handshake so firm she crushed my hand. She pulled me in and squeezed me until I struggled for breath. "We sure have been waiting for you! Welcome to Ngong."

"Thank you. It's a pleasure to meet you," I replied, trying to remove myself from her overbearing embrace as tactfully as I could. Barika dropped the hug, but quickly grasped my hand and pumped it firmly in her own.

"I am Barika, Bu's neighbour — and her very good friend. We've been like family for many years and anyone staying with Kiano and Bu is family of mine." Barika opened the door and waved us inside. "Please, won't you come in for some chai so we can talk and get to know one another?"

"We have only got a bit of time, Barika," Mama Bu warned. Then, turning to me, she said, "Barika is one of my closest friends but, like I said, the woman is a talker. If she had her way, we would stay here until nightfall, drinking chai and talking about everything under the sun." I chuckled softly as Barika waved her hands in protest and my host mother deepened her grin. It was clear to me that the two women were more like sisters than just friends.

"Sit, sit, Miss Nicole." Barika pointed to the couches before bouncing from the living room to get us our tea. She called out from the kitchen, "So, tell me, Nicole, do you *like* Africa?"

"Well, from what I've seen so far, I like it very much. But I've only been here for about twelve hours, although I did read a lot about Ngong before I came. It sounds like a great place."

"You will see it all today, Nicky," Mama Bu said. "We will walk through town and I will show you where everything is. We will hit the market and I will show you where you can find the internet spot."

"You have internet here? I didn't realize I'd be able to access it so easily," I said, relieved. I thought there would be internet in Nairobi, but not Ngong.

"Yes, chicka, we have got the internet right in Ngong. Are you surprised? All of us can connect to the rest of the world from our very own town. And you can too."

"Is it expensive here?"

"About one shilling per minute, dolly," Mama Bu replied. I did the quick math in my head and realized it would cost about sixty Canadian cents per hour. I suddenly felt closer to home.

"And what about the orphanage? Will you go there today?" Barika called out from the kitchen.

"No, not today, Barika. I told Jebet we would be by on Monday. She did not want us stopping in on the weekend," Mama Bu answered.

Barika's reply came at lightning speed, only this time in complete Swahili, *"Bu, umeambia Nicole kuhusu Jebet? Yeye ni mkali na Nicole anahitaji kujua."* There was an edge to Barika's voice as she spoke.

Surprised by Barika's sudden clipped tone, I wondered what she was saying about Jebet. And why she had mentioned my name — *twice.* I considered asking Bu about it, but didn't want to seem rude.

"She is asking about Jebet, the *mkuu,* or orphanage director," Mama Bu explained, patting my knee. It was as though she could read my mind. "Jebet is . . . hmm . . . not the nicest person in the world. Barika thinks you deserve to know that before you meet her."

"Is Jebet really that bad?" I asked, a pit growing in my stomach.

"Others think so, such as Barika. I am more understanding. I believe that, somewhere deep inside of her, Jebet still has a nice heart. But she has gone through . . . *uchungu* . . . and it has changed her. She has always been a fairly strict *mkuu* but, lately, well, it almost seems like she has become a different person." I could tell Mama Bu didn't want me to judge Jebet prior to meeting her, but that she was concerned enough to say a few words of warning.

"In English, *uchungu* means grief . . . or pain," Barika explained, carrying in a thermos of chai and three mugs that were as large as the ones we had used the night before. "But I don't think that matters. We've all gone through hardship here in Kenya. Who is Jebet to stick the children at the orphanage just because she has gone through some sorrow? If she wants to see pain, she should visit the slums."

"She is *from* the slums, Barika. You know that. And she has been back many, many times. The children in her orphanage are from the slums. And she is the only one taking them in." Mama Bu shook her head, clearly frustrated with Barika. I sensed that it was not the first time the two friends had discussed Jebet.

Mama Bu continued, "I am not saying Jebet is an angel. She is far from it. And I agree that she should not be so hard on the children. But you know she is not the same woman who started at the orphanage so many years ago. She has been through much. It is not her fault."

"Not her fault, Bu? Hmmph." Barika crossed her chubby arms and turned up her nose.

"Let us just say that we need to give her a break," Mama Bu answered, responding to Barika. It was obvious that Mama Bu wanted to say more about Jebet but felt it wasn't her place. She knew more, that much was clear, but I was unsure if she was keeping quiet because I was there or because she didn't want Barika to know. Perhaps it was both.

"But she hurts the children?" I asked, my eyes going from Mama Bu to Barika, in search of an answer. "She uses a stick on them?" I was sickened by the thought.

"Not really, dolly. At least, she does not *really* hurt them," Mama Bu said gently. "Here in Kenya, sticking is an accepted way of discipline. I know in your country people frown on it, but here it is okay. Jebet has her stick, and uses it when one of the children misbehaves."

"The girl's shocked already. Hmmph. Didn't those orientation books you read tell you about all of *this*?" Barika asked, taking a long slurpy sip of her tea. When not talking, Barika gulped at her tea and then licked her lips like a lion finishing up his prey.

"No, I haven't heard or read anything about it," I replied honestly.

"Sticking doesn't just happen at orphanages. It happens every-where 'round here. And to lots of people. Rather than go to the police, citizens take matters into their own hands, and give beatings when someone crosses them."

"But why does it happen so much? Can't the police stop it?" I asked, suddenly nervous about what I might see while in Africa.

"It's called *mob justice*, chicka. And, no, the police can't stop it. Or they don't, anyway. They are *corrupt*. Our government too. All people care about 'round here is getting money. So the police don't do what's right — they do what pays. Even when people are guilty of doing something wrong, the police won't do anything if they are bribed." Barika almost looked pleased with the fact that she was clearly shocking me with her speech.

"Surely they can't all be like that," I searched Mama Bu and Barika's eyes. "*Can* they?"

"The police and government don't help like they do where you're from. It's not the same here, Nicole. You asked about the police? They've got hungry children to feed. They will do whatever they need to for more shillings." Barika shook her head, still slurping. "The problem is, sometimes the beatings are deserved . . . and sometimes they are not. You just never know. And it's sad, because we've seen it *a lot*. And we've got lots of friends who have been beaten. Some to a pulp, and others to death."

Horrified, I sucked in air.

Barika continued, "Just last month, our friend Milka, she lives up north, well, her son died from a beating. He was accused of stealing. Milka swears he didn't do it. I believe her, but, either way, Milka's son is now dead because of it."

I looked at Mama Bu in shock. All she did was shake her head, saying softly, "Unfortunately, Nicky, what Barika is saying is true. Violence is a part of Kenya. I am sorry to say that the beatings do happen often."

Barika interjected, "Sometimes they get way out of hand, like in the case of poor Milka's son, but there's nothing you can do to stop it. And if you see one while you're here, which you might, Nicole, you can't be offended. And you can't try to stop it, or you will get hurt. You just need to put your head down and keep walking. You have to mind your own business."

"I knew there was crime here, but I had no idea Kenya was so violent. This all sounds so awful."

Barika was about to jump back into the conversation but was cut off by a ringing phone. Surprised, I watched as she retrieved a cell phone from her kitchen. *"Mambo? Hujambo! Sijambo!"* Barika paused, listening to the person on the phone. She tsked lightly before replying at a clipped speed in Swahili.

"I am not sure who she is speaking to, but she has told them to come over for a visit. It sounds like they will be here soon," Mama Bu said, translating for me.

"You have cell phones?" I asked, clearly surprised.

"Yes, dolly. We have all got them. They are not really that expensive here. We can pick one up for you when we get to town, if you would like one too?"

"Definitely! I had no idea I'd be able to have a phone," I replied excitedly. While the news of having the internet so close made me feel instantly more connected to home, hearing that I could buy a cell phone made me feel almost like I was still there.

"It is a plan, then. I know the best place to pick one up."

Barika continued chattering in the kitchen, prattling into her cell phone at lightning speed. Mama Bu stood and walked to the kitchen to motion to Barika that we were leaving.

"One minute, Bu." Barika raised her index finger, telling us to wait.

Mama Bu shook her head and whispered loudly to her friend, "Thank you for the chai, but we must carry on. We will come again soon for a longer visit. You finish talking to whoever you are talking to and we will see ourselves out."

I stood and waved to Barika. Still holding her phone, she took three giant steps towards me and embraced me with the same strength she had delivered with my welcome hug.

"It was a pleasure to meet you, Barika," I said, my words muffled in the woman's shoulder. She was much bigger than I was, and about six inches taller.

Barika released me, raising her index finger one more time before saying suddenly into the phone, "*Kwaheri.*" Goodbye.

"You didn't have to get off for us, Barika," I said. I knew Mama Bu thought we could take advantage of her being on the phone and exit quietly and quickly.

"Nonsense. I was being rude." Barika waved her hands in the air. "Plus, I wanted to say that I didn't mean to scare you about Kenya. Here in Ngong, the beatings don't happen very much. It's not like Nairobi. And we've got a beautiful countryside. Despite the hardships, God is good to us here in Africa. We have lots that we are proud of, and so much for you to see and experience that is great. I have no doubt you will love it here."

I nodded, showing that I understood what Barika was telling me.

"It's just that in this country it's about survival," Barika continued. "People do what they need to to stay alive. Sometimes that means beatings. Other times it means doing what is needed to make sure you live. You'll see what I mean when you get to the slums with Mama Bu."

"We need to go, dolly," Mama Bu said, cutting Barika off. "The market has been open for quite some time now. I want to get there before it is too busy, so you can take it all in."

"Okay, okay Bu . . . I get it. I will see you both later." Barika gave me one final bear hug, and waved from the door step until we could no longer see her.

The smell of garbage smoke had strengthened since we had left Mama Bu's house earlier that morning. I sneezed.

The ditches along both sides of the road were filled with unburned garbage; the rotting piles were everywhere and contributed to the stink of the land. "Why don't they burn that too, Mama Bu?"

"We can only do so much, dolly."

As we walked, I watched all of the people we passed. We hadn't seen any other people when we first left Mama Bu's house, but the road had become busier, with many Kenyans bustling about. People in bright colours passed us, or strolled behind us as we trekked towards town.

Mama Bu called out and greeted many of them, shaking hands and even hugging some as they passed. They spoke in quick Swahili, which Mama Bu always translated for me. Many of them promised to visit, while others told her to stop by as soon as she could. Every one of them eyed me, even after Mama Bu introduced me, and I became very aware of how much my whiteness stuck out.

Children were walking everywhere, many of them without adults. All of them were oblivious to the sharp rocks and dirt underneath their bare feet — *none* of them wore shoes. "*Mzungu! Mzungu!*" they called loudly, pointing directly at me. They wouldn't stop staring.

"What are they saying?" I whispered to Mama Bu.

"They are saying, 'White person! White person!' You will hear it often, I am sure."

We passed three more shoeless children playing on the side of the road, three feet from the garbage ditch. They used twigs and rocks in some sort of game. One of them called out to me, saying in a thick Kenyan accent, "*Mzungu*, how are you?"

"I am well, thank you. How are you?" I smiled deeply at the child, her chocolate brown eyes warm and curious.

"Fine."

"Are you playing a game?" I asked, wondering if the little girl would be in my classroom. She looked about eight.

"Fine," she replied again.

"She doesn't speak English, Nicky. It is just the English words the children have come to know. They know to ask 'how are you?' because you are white. And they will answer 'fine' no matter what you say to them in return." Mama Bu pulled at my hand and encouraged me to keep walking.

I followed my host mother, but looked behind me and waved at the little girl. She smiled, raising her own hand, and then turned back to her friends to continue their friendly game of sticks and stones.

## 11

The energy at the Ngong market was contagious. Crowded and colourful. Hectic rows of little stands filled with fruits and vegetables were flooded with Kenyans pushing up into each other, shaking hands or slapping each other on the back. Each person seemed to talk over the other, using Swahili expressions I didn't yet know.

Bright yellow bananas and mangoes were everywhere, with a few stalls offering shoppers unrefrigerated meats and eggs. Fire-engine red tomatoes were piled high into pyramid shapes, and oversized woven baskets were filled with the same bobby beans I had seen in Mama Bu's garden. Purple eggplant lay beside various greens of cabbage, limes and snow peas, and the smell of spices wafted from the food stalls offering nutmeg, cloves and cinnamon.

I paused to run my fingers along the silky skin of the eggplant, instantly transported to the first time Eric had cooked for me. We'd been out on two dates by that point — once for coffee and once to the movies. Eric's parents were out of town, taking a trip to the Bahamas — something about needing to reignite the flame. Too much information for a son to know, in my opinion, but Brian had always been overly descriptive with his children.

"Do you like veal parmagiana?" Eric had asked me when I arrived on his doorstep holding a cheesecake. It was cherry, and I'd purchased it at my mother's favourite bakery minutes before I had arrived. Eric was wearing jeans and a navy golf shirt. Flour handprints decorated his thighs.

"Er . . . well, I used to. But I, uh, I stopped eating meat in my first year of university." I followed Eric into his parents' kitchen and was greeted by a chaotic array of dishes, pots and food. Veal parmagiana bubbled in hot oil on the stove, marking the countertop with polka-dot oil stains. I tried to mask my embarrassment. "I'm so sorry, I should have told you. But it's not a problem. I'll eat the veal. I'm sure it will be fine just this once. It smells delicious."

Eric acted quickly, ignoring my offer to eat what he had prepared. He flicked the stove off, and handed me a beer from the fridge. "I'll be back in five minutes. Don't move a muscle." Eric grabbed his keys from the counter and, true to his word, returned five minutes later with two bright purple eggplants he had purchased at the small grocery store down the street. An hour later, he chose to eat the eggplant parmigiana with me, telling me he wanted to save the veal he had made for his lunch the next day. The eggplant tasted like heaven, and I'll never forget him smiling at me from across the table, his blue eyes . . .

Laughing shoppers snapped me back to reality, passing shillings to vendors and thanking them for the exchange. They stuffed their purchases into personal potato sacks and carried bigger items away on their heads.

"How do you like it, Nicky?"

"It's . . . wonderful!" I replied quickly, trying to return to the present moment.

"It is busiest today, given that it is Saturday market. But each day is like this," Mama Bu replied, taking my hand and guiding me to a food stall selling maize, bread and various grains. "Here, I want to introduce you to Moses, a friend of our family who sells at the market every day of the week."

Upon seeing us, Moses threw his hands up in the air and stepped from behind his food stall. He shook my hand, smiling broadly at me, "*Karibu! Karibu!* I like meet you." Concentration filled his eyes as he focused on trying to choose the right words in his choppy English sentence.

"Thank you, Moses. It's nice to meet you."

"How are you?" Moses asked. I smiled, remembering what Mama Bu had told me about the common expression asked of white people.

"Fine," I responded, choosing the word he knew.

"You eat? I have bread." Moses took the largest loaf of bread from his stall, and gave it me. "This bread gift for you."

I looked at Mama Bu, and took the bread after reading her expression, which silently communicated that I should take the offering.

"How do I say 'thank you' in Swahili?" I asked.

"You say *ahsante* when you want to thank someone," Mama Bu explained.

"Well, *ahsante*, Moses. This is very nice of you." I repeated my new word over in my head a few times to commit it to memory.

"Here, here. I have banana." Moses went behind his stall and retrieved two bananas, which he gave to Mama Bu and me.

"*Ahsante*," I repeated, taking the banana. "You are very kind."

Mama Bu and Moses chatted quickly in Swahili as I peeled my banana and took a big bite. I knew food with a peel was safe, and my rumbling stomach was grateful for something I could eat without worry.

The fruit's flavour took me by surprise; the taste was different from the bananas I picked up during my weekly grocery shop. It was sweeter. More bold. Like it was picked when it was actually ready, instead of having ripened on a transport truck driving along the highway.

"You like?" Moses asked me, noticing the smile on my face.

"Very much so. Thank you. *Ahsante*."

Moses nodded, and then pointed to my neck. He started speaking quickly to Mama Bu, and looked concerned. I wondered what he was saying about me.

"Moses thinks you should remove the necklace from around your neck. I told him I was taking you to the slums, and he fears that it might make you a target for theft." My fingers flew up to the cross necklace that Eric had given me. Despite all that had happened, I hadn't been able to part with it. With my wedding rings now gone, it was the only reminder I had of him. I couldn't bear to lose it.

"Do you agree?" I asked Mama Bu. When she nodded yes, I gently undid the clasp, and tucked it into the front pocket of my jeans.

"Now, come with me, Nicky. We will go and get you that cell phone so that you may call your worried parents."

We waved goodbye to Moses and Mama Bu led me to the outskirts of the market and onto a dirt street filled with little shops. As we crossed the road, *matatu* drivers waved their arms out the window, screaming Swahili at us.

"What are they saying?"

"They are telling us to *get on their ride*. They want to drive us somewhere for a fare," Mama Bu explained. We ignored them and the *matatu* drivers sped past us, leaving us to breathe in the red dust stirred up by their spinning wheels.

We walked past a row of little stores and restaurants and Mama Bu pointed to an open door. "That is where you can use the internet," she explained. I peeked inside and saw six or seven computers. Locals typed furiously on the keyboards. Outside the internet café, two teenage boys about Petar's age sucked on cigarettes, staring at me. I had never felt so self-conscious about my pale skin.

We walked into a small store with a sign out front that read *foni*. Mama Bu explained that I needed a cell phone with a plan that would allow me to call home. The shop owner went to a back room behind the counter and, within ten minutes, I was the new owner of a Motorola flip phone. It wasn't a sexy smartphone with all the bells and whistles, but I had never even carried one of those before I left for Kenya. This wonderful device would connect me to my family. And that was all I cared about.

"How much is it to call home?" I asked. Mama Bu translated, then listened to the shop owner's Swahili answer.

"He says it is 140 shillings a minute to call during peak times. And calls within Kenya are free." I did the easy conversion in my mind and realized it would take about $1.40 per minute to call home.

I nodded and dropped my new phone into the front pocket of my backpack. I'd call my parents later, when Mama Bu didn't have to wait for me. "So? What's next?"

"We head to the slum. It is not pretty, Nicky, but you should see it while you are here. You need to know where the children come from that you are teaching."

I nodded again. I wanted to go, but I knew I wouldn't like what I was about to see.

"You can keep your backsack on your front if you want to, but there is no need to worry. The slum is a safe place during the sun hours because the slum crowds will protect you. If there are people out, no one will mug you. Snatch-and-run thieves have been known to be killed by a crowd. The people of the slum look after their own. And visitors too. But do not be forgetting what I told you about being out at night."

"You got it, Mama Bu. I can promise you that it will never happen." I followed her down the dirt road, which was growing more and more decrepit by the footstep.

When we approached a small river, which we needed to cross to get into the slum, I began to see slum dwellers everywhere. They were walking in all directions, or hanging out in small groups, *"Mzungu! Mzungu!"*

"There are so many of them!" I said quietly in Mama Bu's ear. "I had no idea."

"We are not even there yet, dolly. You just wait. The slum has thousands of people living in it," Mama Bu looked directly forward as she answered me, not even glancing at me as she spoke. Her walk seemed to become more focused and purposeful.

The slum dwellers continued to stare as we passed. They cranked their heads to watch us, and some even started to follow; the more cautious sauntered sheepishly behind, while the more extroverted made no qualms about following directly in our footsteps.

*"Mzungu! Mzungu!"*

About five minutes outside of the slum, a little girl ran up beside me and took my hand. She appeared to be about six or seven, and wore a tattered blue baby doll dress with a frayed butterfly collar. Her head was shaved short and, like all the other children, her feet were bare.

Snot ran down her face, and it was obvious her dress sleeves had been used as her Kleenex for many days. Yet, despite all of this, I wanted to do nothing more than whisk the little girl up into my arms. I looked down at her bright shining eyes and let her hold my hand. She held on tight. Beside us, I could sense that Mama Bu was smiling.

When we got to the slums, the entourage we had accumulated spanned about twenty people wide. Children flocked to us, "*Mzungu! Mzungu!*"

From the back of the crowd that had formed around us, a man who looked about seventy years old stepped forward and gave me the global sign for food, using a phantom fork and pretending to eat. Mama Bu acted more quickly than I could react and passed the elderly man the banana that Moses had given to her earlier that day. The man took the fruit from Mama Bu, nodding his head and expressing complete gratitude in a way that I would never forget.

Seeing the banana reminded me of the granola bar I had tucked away in my backpack. I retrieved it and gave it to the little girl in blue, whose hand I was still holding. She took it gratefully, smiling up at me and squinting in the sun. She opened the wrapper, then sniffed at the granola before eating the bar so quickly I was afraid she would choke. When finished, she picked my hand back up and squeezed.

A swarm of Kenyans closed in on us. Mama Bu shook her head, apologizing repeatedly in Swahili for having nothing more to give. The circle thinned as they realized we had no more food, and I began to see the inner slum through the holes in the crowd.

The main road that led us to the slum was wide, but the offshoots were narrow and filled with garbage, sewage and stink. Small vendor stalls lined the main road but, unlike the market Mama Bu and I had visited that morning, very few offered food. Instead, the majority of items were second-hand and dirty. And no one was buying them.

Undersized donkeys and stray dogs so thin you could see their rib cages nosed their way into the rubbish piles lining the street, looking for any piece of scrap food they could find. Unfortunately for them, the people of the slum had gotten to the garbage first and no scraps remained.

Flocks of people were everywhere around us and, despite Mama Bu's warnings, I was shocked to see living conditions that were more jam-packed than a five o'clock subway car headed towards Union Station.

Small homes made of corrugated tin were smacked up against each other and Mama Bu explained that more than one family lived in each of the one-room shacks. None of the steel huts had doors, although some had curtains hanging in the entrances to provide a sense of privacy. Through the entryways that remained open, I could see clothing hung on nails that had been pounded into the walls. None of the homes had running water or electricity.

Behind some of the dilapidated shacks were squat toilets shared by multiple families. In front of the huts, women were cooking pots of mush over charcoal campfires, oblivious to the paralyzing stench of rotting garbage and decomposing human waste that was all around them.

As we continued walking, we ran into the old man who had taken Mama Bu's banana when we had first gotten to the slums. He waved, and Mama Bu started to speak to him in Swahili.

"He says that he shares one room with his wife and eight grandchildren. The single room is used as their bedroom, kitchen and sitting room."

I shook my head, fighting tears.

"His house is collapsing," Mama Bu continued, translating as the man spoke. "And his family does not have space for a squat, so they have to share one paper bag and throw it out at night."

The tears I had been fighting fell down my cheeks.

Mama Bu took both of the man's hands in her own. Together, they prayed, and Mama Bu asked God to give him more food and better days ahead.

"*Ashante kwa enu hisani*," the man said. Thank you for your kindness. He turned and walked away, waving a skinny arm as he went.

Mama Bu and I kept walking.

Mile after mile of wreckage filled my eyes and hurt my heart. I wondered how human beings could actually *live* in such disgusting devastation. The pictures I had always seen on TV were nothing compared to the reality around me. The sick. The hungry. The unimaginable poverty.

At one point, the stench and heartbreak became too much for me. I threw up on the side of the dirt road, embarrassed, and conscious of those watching me.

It was the first time I let go of the hand of the little girl in blue, yet I sensed that she didn't move as I hurled the little bit of food I had in my stomach into the ditch. And I was well aware of the irony when it was she who patted my back in an attempt to make me feel better.

## 12

When Mama Bu and I returned home a few hours before dinner, I excused myself and went to my host family's backyard to call my parents. It was only ten o'clock there, and I knew they would be awake and watching the last period of *Hockey Night in Canada*.

"Mom?! It's me!" I cried over the slightly crackly reception when she answered the phone.

"Oh, honey! It's so wonderful to hear your voice. We've been so worried! We didn't know when we would hear from you and I've just been sick over not knowing when we'd talk to you. How are you?! How is everything? Are you safe? Are you liking Africa? Is your host family taking care of you?"

"Mom? Mom! Slow down," I interrupted her, laughing. I was over-joyed to be talking to her. I told her about my host family, my first day in Kenya and all that Mama Bu had shown me. I could hear my mom sighing on the other end of the phone as I described the conditions of the slum.

"Oh, honey, that sounds awful. Really heartbreaking."

"It was. But I'm glad I went. I needed to see what it is really like here." Then, out of nowhere, I asked, "Have you heard from Eric?"

The question surprised even me. I had no idea where it came from; I had promised myself before the call that I wouldn't ask about him. He was no longer my husband and we had both moved on.

"No, sweetie, I haven't," my mom said sadly. I knew her heart was broken for both Eric and me.

"Well, uh, I guess that makes sense," I said, stumbling. "After all, why would you hear from him? We're over and nothing will change that."

"We could call him for you, if you'd like?" my father offered. He had picked up another extension and had been listening in.

"No, no. Don't do that, Dad. I just thought that if you had heard from him . . . well, uh, I guess I just wanted to know how he is coping." I blinked back tears, desperate to not cry while speaking to my parents. "But, please, don't call him. It would be humiliating. We're . . . well, you know . . . officially separated and all, so there really isn't a point anymore."

"Oh, honey, of course. We'll do whatever you want. You tell us what you need and we'll do whatever we can for you. You know that. If you want us to get on a plane tomorrow and join you in Kenya, we're there. You just let us know what it is you want us to do — or not do," my mom responded, her voice filled with concern. I knew she was grasping for a way to make me feel better and — considering it was over a cell phone, halfway across the world — she was actually doing a pretty good job.

"Thanks, Mom. I appreciate that," I answered, stalling for more time but knowing I had to hang up. "I hate to do this, Mom and Dad, I really do, but I need to hang up now. It's really expensive to call you, but I wanted to make sure that you knew I was okay. But I'll be able to access email really cheaply, so send me as many emails as you want. I'm going to try to check often."

"We love you, Nicole."

"I know. And I love you too. I miss you!"

When I hung up the phone, I sat silently by myself for a few minutes, thinking of them. Three months was a long time, and I already missed them more than ever.

———

I left the backyard and walked into the kitchen to see if I could help. "Wow, something smells fantastic in here! What can I do?"

"I would love some help, *rafiki*. Thank you for offering," Mama Bu answered. She gave me her toothy grin. "For your first dinner with us, we are having *chapati na sukuma wiki*. It is like collard greens, and we boil them with tomatoes and onions. We will have it with chapatis."

"Sounds great," I said. After a long day full of walking and eating very little, I was starving and would eat anything. "What is chapatis?"

"A flat and round bread. Thick, and good for scooping. We use it to pick up the *sukuma wiki* instead of a spoon or fork."

"I can't wait to taste it," I said, genuinely interested in trying authentic Kenyan food. I was also secretly relieved that there was no mention of meat.

"You shall, except that we will not eat for several more hours.

Dinner is not until 7:30, and you can help me then. What do you think of going now and taking a nap? I sense that you did not sleep well last night." Mama Bu gave me a look and I knew, then, that she had heard me crying. "I have got everything covered until dinner, and you need to rest."

I nodded, completely exhausted. I couldn't have refused a nap even if I wanted to. I agreed to take a rest, and went to my bedroom to lie down. With my eyes already closing, I stuck my hand in my jeans pocket to remove the cross necklace so that I could tuck it somewhere safe.

It was gone.

I dug deeper, but found nothing — except for total panic.

I tore my room apart, hopeful it had fallen out and I would find it. I didn't. With the family's help, we searched every corner of the tiny house but came up with nothing.

"I am so sorry!" Mama Bu said, guilt taking over her face. "I told you to remove it, and now it is gone! I feel terrible. I wish I had seen it before we left as I would have told you to leave it at home, but you were wearing a sweatshirt. . . ."

"Oh, it's okay, Mama Bu. Really. It's not your fault. I should have been more careful. I knew it was silly to even bring it to Kenya . . . but, well, it reminded me of home, and I couldn't seem to part with it." My throat was closing, and I knew I was near tears, so I excused myself and left to take my nap.

On the hard bed, I bit into my pillow to try to mask the gut-wrenching sobs that took over. I was disappointed to have lost the necklace, but I knew my tears were bigger than that; I was devastated to lose the final connection I had to Ella and Eric.

Eventually, I forced myself to stop crying. It was over. They were gone, and so was my necklace. Perhaps it was a sign: I needed to accept the truth. Neither Eric nor Ella were coming back, and the sooner I realized it, the sooner I could heal.

When I woke up two hours later, new smells greeted me from the kitchen and my stomach grumbled. It was dark out and the cold air had started to seep back into the house through my window bars.

I jumped out of bed, hopeful that I hadn't slept through dinner — or the preparations. I wanted to help Mama Bu and was interested to see how she would be cooking our dinner. But when I got to the kitchen, I realized that dinner was already ready.

"It is okay, Nicky," Mama Bu said when I apologized for sleeping so long. "We will have many more dinners together with lots of opportunities to help. For now, you can put these plates on the coffee table and get ready to wash your hands."

"Do I do that here?" I asked, pointing to the kitchen sink.

"No, you just need to take a seat, dolly. On one of the couches. We eat in the sitting room. I will be bringing you what you need to wash your hands."

Mama Bu called Kiano and Petar for dinner and I took my seat on my own tattered couch. Mama Bu followed, carrying a pitcher of slightly warmed water, along with a plastic bowl, bar of soap and towel.

"We always wash our hands together. Even in restaurants," Petar said. "There is a sink with a bar of soap and towel — right where you eat. It is considered to be bad manners if you don't."

"Petar!" Mama Bu warned, glaring at her son. "Let us not tell Nicky what is rude, for that is rude."

"His intentions are good, Bu," Kiano interjected, patting his son on the knee. "Let him be."

"That's okay, Mama Bu, I'm glad Petar told me about it. I like knowing all about your customs. Better to hear about it now than embarrass myself later!" I smiled at Petar who grinned back. I finished washing my hands and watched as Mama Bu took the water, soap and towel to Kiano. Then she served Petar. Lastly, herself.

We all joined hands as Kiano led us in grace. It was longer than I was used to, and spoken in Swahili, but I enjoyed listening to the words of another language. When he finished, Kiano added, in English, "We thank you, dear God, for bringing us our new *rafiki*, Nicky. Please keep her safe during her travels here and help her find strength and wisdom as she works with the children at Kidaai. Amen."

"Amen," I added, smiling warmly at Kiano and feeling like I was part of the family.

"Here you are, Nicky. Your first supper in Kenya." Mama Bu first served everyone a mug of chai from her oversized thermos, and then she handed me the bowl of food. "Use the chapati to pick it up. Like a fork."

As I started to scoop, a flash of worry took over as I remembered the stories of Canadians getting sick after eating African food. Montezuma's revenge in a house with six-foot walls and sounds that bounced around like the Grand Canyon's echo would be, to say the very least, embarrassing for everyone. Most especially me.

I forced myself to push the thought to the back of my mind. To stop worrying, and start tasting.

I took a bite.

It was delicious. The warm flavours from the spices Mama Bu had used made the collard greens taste tender and savory. And the chapati was served warm — soft and buttery with a flaky middle — but still great for scooping. It tasted like a warmed, thick tortilla, but heartier and more flavourful.

After dinner, Mama Bu and I cleared the plates and placed them in the kitchen. I cut up mango, while she prepared the chai.

I bit into the fruit and savoured the juicy sweetness. "It almost tastes like honey!"

"Well it should, Nicky. Remember, it is our backyard sweet treat!" Mama Bu teased me. "Would you like some more?"

"Thank you, but this is plenty." I did want more, but didn't want to seem gluttonous in a country so damaged by famine.

"So, Nicky, Bu tells me you visited the slums this afternoon. Not a nice sight, is it?" Kiano said, stretching out on the couch as his wife took his fruit plate away. She returned to stir his tea with some milk and sugar.

"It was pretty shocking. And devastating. I wish I could do more to help everyone who lives in the slum," I admitted, thinking of the elderly man who didn't have enough food to feed his grandchildren — and the little girl in blue who was so loving, despite having so little.

"Ah, but you already are, Nicky. By being here and taking the steps to teach the children of Kidaai. You are already doing so much for the people of Kenya. You will see." Kiano blew on his tea. Took a sip.

"I'm looking forward to meeting them on Monday. And I'm excited to get working," I said.

"I could see in your eyes today, Nicky, that you are a born healer and teacher. I know you will do great things for our people," Mama Bu jumped in, returning from finishing up in the kitchen. "I have no doubt that you will help them greatly. You will teach them, and love them, that is for sure. But I am also certain that *they* will give *you* even more back."

Kiano set his empty cup on the table, and Mama Bu took it to the kitchen. Calling behind her, she said, "We have church tomorrow, Nicky. We do not have many rules in this house, but one rule that must not be broken is church. Anyone staying here always joins us so that we can go together, as a family. It starts at nine. We leave at eight."

"I'd love to join you for church. I'm not much of a rule breaker, after all," I teased.

"That is great to hear," Kiano replied, grinning.

I took a long sip of tea. "I feel like I've spent a lot of time telling you about me. I'd love to know more about you. You work in a bank?"

"Yes, that is right. I am a teller that helps people with deposits and getting their money out. Like you might have where you live," Kiano described.

"In Ngong?"

"No, unfortunately not. I work at the Buru Buru branch in Nairobi."

"How do you get there?"

"By *matatu*. There and back."

Mama Bu came back into the room and joined us on the couch. "Kiano works very hard, Nicky. Long hours and he is very committed to his job. He leaves the house very early in the morning and is not home until dinner time," Mama Bu said. Pride filled her cheeks.

"And what about you Mama Bu? I know you often help out at Kidaai. Are you there every day?"

"No, not every day. Usually just when Jebet needs me to help out with the cooking or the cleaning. But she recently hired some house help, so I have not been going very much."

"Ah, it's time for the news to come on," Kiano interrupted, snapping on the television. "We watch the news as a family together every night."

Kiano flipped the station. The news anchor was just starting the headline story about a thirty-year-old man who had been accused of trying to steal a tire. The cameras panned to crowds narrowing in on the man; he was beaten, stripped and mocked by a jeering group of people. The man was left to waddle around the city streets of Nairobi, naked and trying to escape the laughing onlookers.

"Just like we were talking about at Barika's house," Mama Bu whispered in my ear. "Public humiliation is common. It is considered to be appropriate."

"The idiot! Serves him right for stealing." Kiano pumped a fist in the air and mocked the man for his crime. "People ought to know not to steal."

I bit my lip, wanting to ask Kiano how he knew the man had actually stolen the tire when it hadn't been proven. I hoped the next story was better.

No such luck. With Mama Bu translating quietly in my ear so that I could understand, the news anchor described a horrific encounter between a wife's husband and her lover. As the camera crew panned the scene of the bloody aftermath, the anchor reported on the husband who, after finding his wife in bed with another man, locked the two lovers in his house and left to grab a few friends. Returning to his house, the man brought his brooding friends and a crowd that egged them on. The husband pulled his wife's lover out of the house, and caned him until his face was unrecognizable with blood. I had to turn away from the TV.

"*Naam! Naam!*" Kiano cried, jumping up and cheering for the man beating the other.

I choked back words and realized that I couldn't watch the stories any longer. One of two things was going to inevitably occur — either awkward tears on my end, or a heated, argumentative discussion with Kiano, who was not only undisturbed by the stories but excited about them.

I thanked my host family for dinner and announced that jet lag was taking over.

"Good night, *rafiki*," Kiano said. Mama Bu rose out of her seat to give me a hug. "Tomorrow, we will walk to church as a family."

"Sure, sounds good," I replied. The concrete was cold, even on my sock feet, as I left the sitting room to get ready for bed.

As I changed into my pyjamas, I couldn't help but note the irony of a Christian who mandated family worship on the morning after a hardhearted reaction to another man's beating.

Outside my room, Kiano continued to cheer on the men he watched on TV.

## 13

"Are you ready, *rafiki*?" Mama Bu asked. We had just finished our
Sunday breakfast: one egg, one piece of toast.

"Yes, definitely. Do you think what I'm wearing is okay?" I asked,
slightly uneasy that I would wear something that would stick out. This
was comical, of course, given I knew my skin colour would stand out
more. I turned to show Mama Bu my simple black skirt, short-sleeved
red shirt with capped sleeves, and black ballerina flats.

"Oh yes, dolly, you look nice. Really nice. But it does not matter
what you wear to church. God will love you no matter what," Mama Bu
answered, tugging on her own skirt. It was thick and yellow, hanging

down to her ankles, with a matching untucked long-sleeve top that buttoned down her front. She had on the same thick beige sandals I had noticed on our walk to the slum the day before. "Now, let's get Kiano and Petar and be on our way."

Our walk started on the dirt road that Mama Bu and I had taken the day before, but that was quickly abandoned for a dusty trail through a field that I would have missed had I been travelling on my own. We walked two by two, given the narrow width of the path, with Petar and Kiano leading the way. Mama Bu and I fell into a comfortable walk beside each other.

The parched grass under our feet was turning brown; the trampled blades morphing into the dried up dirt patches they were anchored to. The stench of garbage smoke lingered, making itself comfortable in our noses, and thick clouds of dust formed as we walked.

"Here in Kenya, we are very spiritual," Mama Bu said simply, breaking the silence as she began telling me about African religion. "Life is tough in Africa. Very hard. And often it is too short. Sometimes the only real thing that makes sense to us is believing in something bigger. To know there is something else, with more meaning that explains what we go through."

I nodded, clearing my throat as the dust around me tickled it.

"Do you think that too, Nicky?"

I shrugged. "I'm not sure what I believe."

"Do you believe in God?"

I shrugged again. It was a forward question, one that normally would have made me feel uncomfortable. But for some reason, it seemed to make sense coming from Mama Bu. "I thought so, at one point. Now I'm not sure. I don't know what I believe."

"I see." Mama Bu didn't push. Instead, she shielded her eyes from the sun, and continued, "Well, our beliefs are based on the spirit world

. . . how we connect with them. In times of great danger, we appeal to God directly. But in other times, we call on lesser divinities."

"Lesser divinities?"

"Yes, like the spirits of natural objects. We hold them in awe. Things like the spirits of the sun, or moon, or sky. We believe they have all been created by God as intermediaries."

I nodded.

"We believe the spirits hold a hidden mystical power that they received from our supreme God. We all participate in daily prayer, and often pray to these spirits for things like healing or rainmaking. But when troubles are really big, we pray to God directly."

I nodded again, feeling a strange sense of déjà vu as the memory of a third-year global religion class set in. It was a night class many students took as an easy-credit course, three hours long, and in the coldest lecture hall on campus. On some nights, Eric would meet me at the double doors when class was over, and I'd imitate my professor as he walked me home. "It is the *deities* and *dimensions* of African religion that make it *so interesting*. . . ." I'd sing, mocking my professor and pretending to comb over the bit of hair that perpetually fell in his eyes. "The people of Africa *thrive* on it. Religion is *life*, and life is *religion*. . . ."

Mama Bu paused, lifting her foot. She extended one arm out to maintain balance, and stuck the pudgy fingers of her other hand into her shoe. Her lip curled, and she held up a rock to show me she got it. "We are Christian folk in Africa, and many people around here are Maasai. You will see some of them today in church."

"I remember learning a bit about the Maasai in school, but I don't really know very much," I admitted. My calf was starting to cramp from walking so far in ballerina flats. It had been over forty-five minutes.

"I can teach you, if you are interested. Let us start with today's church service." Mama Bu pointed in front of her, and I could see a wooden church in the distance. It had been painted white, and was sitting on top of a hill of brown grass. Churchgoers milled about, shaking hands and burying themselves in friendly conversations as they waited for the service to begin while children of all ages ran about the yard.

"Come on, *rafiki*," Kiano called out from in front of me. He waved Mama Bu and me forward. "Bu, I want to introduce Nicky to our priest."

Kiano tapped a slender man on the shoulder. The man turned and immediately greeted my host father with a handshake and a grin. "*Marahaba!*" the man said. Hello, good day!

"Wambua, this is Nicole. She will be staying with us for three months while she volunteers at Kidaai."

Wambua turned to greet me and gave me a gummy, toothless grin. He took both hands in mine and gave them a little squeeze. "*Karibu*, Nicole. Welcome to our village, to our church and to this morning's service. It is a pleasure to meet you."

"Thank you, Wambua. And it is so nice to speak with you. I'm glad to hear you speak English."

Wambua chuckled and shook his head. "Well, of course! Didn't Kiano and Mama Bu tell you that this is the English service? We have two — one in Swahili and the other in English."

"Oh, I didn't know," I said. My cheeks flushed lightly.

"We usually go to the Swahili service, but wanted you to understand what was going on," Mama Bu said warmly.

"Wambua is our priest, and also our rainmaker," Kiano jumped in, interrupting Mama Bu. "He is an important man to us for many reasons, and the person who will stop our drought."

"A rainmaker?" I asked.

"We must pray for the rains to come and save us. I'm sure you have noticed how dry it is here, yes, Nicky? The drought is starting to be so severe that we are facing hunger and starvation due to crop failure,"

Wambua explained. "Today's service will focus on bringing the rains, and we will pray to the Lord for Him to take care of us until they arrive."

This guy would have fascinated Eric. Not typically one to veer in any direction other than the straight and narrow path he lived his life on, Eric had become wrapped up in the natural side of our fertility treatments. I'd spend hours telling him about *everything* Bib said and did during my reiki treatments, or exactly what I remembered from my hypnotherapy sessions.

"Come, Kiano, and bring your family and new friend. I'd love for you all to have a special seat at the front of the church." Wambua pointed to the church stairs, and signalled for us to follow him.

Wambua ushered us deep into the sanctuary and instructed us to take our seats. Instead of pews, the church rows were made of white lawn chairs that reminded me of the patio furniture my university roommates and I had purchased at a garage sale in the summer before our final year.

"*I love you, Nic. . . .*" Eric had whispered to me one night, leaning sideways in the rickety white lawn chair. It was about 2 A.M. on a warm September night, and we had just smoked an after-bar joint. My roommates were sleeping upstairs, passed out after a night of hard drinking at the university pub, when Eric pulled the chair I was sitting on towards him. Two of my chair legs lifted and we lost balance, landing in a heap on the floor and laughing uncontrollably in the dark. We stayed there, Eric and I, gazing at the sea of stars overhead before making love. We didn't move until we were hit by the early morning dew. . . .

I looked around me and took in the simplicity of the sanctuary. The concrete walls were cold and corroded with grey paint peeling and chipped. The altar at the front of the church was raised about eight inches, as if to create a small stage, and a lightly coloured wooden pulpit was placed in the centre, a microphone resting on its ledge.

Within minutes, the white, wobbly chairs were completely filled with the congregation who had been waiting outside when we had arrived. I looked around, smiling hello when my eyes met others, and admiring the layers of coloured clothing the Kenyans had dressed up in. Babies were cradled in mothers' arms and small toddlers held older children's hands as we waited for the service to begin.

I felt a tug on my arm and was brought to my feet by Mama Bu. The peekaboo speakers I had noticed behind layers of blue and gold curtains started crackling, which was quickly replaced by the beats of Sunday sound. Even before the first note, the congregation was on their feet. Clapping, singing, dancing. Some stayed near their seats, while others formed lines and locomotioned their way through the sanctuary, tapping and clapping to the sweet beat of gospel.

*"Ujesu ungowethu . . . siya vuma . . . ungo wethu ngempela."* Kenyan voices surrounding me sang loud and proud.

"I thought this service was in English?" I asked Mama Bu above the music.

"It will be. The speaking and message will all be in English for you, but most songs are in Swahili."

*"Siya vuma — sithi amen, amen, siya vuma. . . ."*

Feeling like a stiff pole amid dancing flags, I awkwardly started to move my hips and get into the beat of the music. When no one outwardly laughed at me, I gained confidence. By the end of the song, I had fully joined my new friends in their energy.

"Good morning, and welcome to our English Sunday service," Wambua began once the singing had quieted and people had taken their seats. "I'd like to put forth a very warm and special welcome to our new friend, Nicky, who will be staying with Kiano and Abuya for the next few months. Nicky is here to help teach the children of Kidaai, and we thank God for her selfless contributions."

Mama Bu gave my knee a squeeze and everyone around me smiled and gestured hello.

Wambua continued, "Every Sunday we focus our messages on real-life issues. We want you to be able to say that what we talked about on Sunday gave you something that could help you on Monday, whether it is in your family, at your work or in another area of your life. It's not about pretending that we're perfect. It's about God, who is willing to give His grace to grow us," Wambua said loudly. He used his hands as he spoke, waving them in the air until sweat marks lined his underarms.

"He is very good," Mama Bu whispered in my ear, nodding her head. "We are lucky to have him."

"Today we will focus on what we need in the coming week — the raaaaaaains!" Wambua continued.

The congregation broke out in cheers, clapping and raising their hands, singing, "Praise the Lord! Hallelujah!"

"*Aisifuye mvua imemnyea*," Wambua thundered. He who praises rain has been rained on.

"Praise the Lord! Hallelujah!"

"The earth is our female deity, a mother-goddess who rules *all* of us and is the mother of *all* of our creatures. She lives and gives birth to ever new generations of beings. She will make the grass grow when heaven gives Her rain." Wambua paused. He looked up and lifted his arms towards the ceiling.

The congregation answered him. "Praise the Lord! Hallelujah!"

"Without the rain, She will withdraw into Her own depths, waiting for better times to come. Bring us rain, dear Lord, so our grass will sprout, flowers will open and frogs will croak. As soon as the new rains come, life will once again begin miraculously."

"Praise the Lord! Hallelujah!"

*"Dalili ya mvua ni mawingu,"* Wambua cried. Clouds are the sign of the rains. Bring us the clouds, and bring us the rains!

"Praise the Lord! Hallelujah!"

"From waters of the heavens, to waters of the sea, I ask of the spirits to bring rain to thee!"

"Praise the Lord! Hallelujah!"

Wambua paused again. Inhaled deep breaths, and looked around before continuing. "We have many children here with us this morning. Many who like to sing. Please, choir, come forward and sing 'Where Is the Rain?'"

The pastor beckoned with his hands, and brightly clothed children wearing their Sunday best joined him at the altar. They formed two lines — little ones at the front — and started singing and clapping.

Mama Bu leaned over and said, almost proudly, "The small children wanted to learn an English song, so the older children decided to teach this one to them. They taught the little ones how to sing it all on their own."

> *The giraffe and the elephant went for a walk,*
> *They stopped in some shade and started to talk;*
> *"I wish it would rain," said the giraffe with a sigh.*
> *"I'm tired of watching the clouds pass us by!"*

> *"Yes," said the elephant, "Where is the rain?*
> *I wish I could eat fresh green leaves again.*
> *The sun is so hot and the land is so dry,*
> *When will the rain fall from the sky?"*

> *Later in the day the sky turned grey,*
> *The flying ants flew out to say,*

*"The rain is coming! We smell it in the air!*
*And in the distance, thunder we hear!"*

*The giraffe and the elephant looked up at the sky,*
*And heard the black eagle give forth his cry,*
*"The rain has come, The rivers will flow,*
*The dry season is over; now the green grass will grow!"*

The kids' choir finished with broad smiles. Some bowed as we clapped and cheered, and then the children walked back to their seats.

"This morning I want to remind you that the window shall be opened," Wambua said, starting his morning message. "It is easy to forget, in times like this, but we must all remember that our Lord will not shut the door on us without opening a window. The rains will come — and our hearts and our fields and our crops will be open to receive it."

I shifted in my seat.

"Sometimes life isn't what we think we would plan for ourselves. The rains do not come, and our crops go dry and our children go hungry. Drought causes jobs to be lost, and illness develops throughout the land. Our nation ends up being even more impoverished, and starvation and malnutrition become extremely prevalent. We do not always get what we want or hope for. Life, sometimes, is a big letdown. And when this happens, it is easy to give up."

I shifted again, the seat suddenly uncomfortable.

"A young woman knocked on my door very early in the morning about a month ago. We'll call her Gathoni. She was hungry and very weak as she had been without food or water for several days. She was also pregnant and had lost her job because of it. She had been a virgin before she was raped."

I heard a woman tsk behind me. Mama Bu looked down.

"When she came to see me, the woman had been without food and water for days, and she had nowhere to sleep. Her family died a long time ago, she was not married and her friends seemed to disappear once she became illegitimately pregnant. When I sat down to speak with her, the woman's options had run out and she had no one to help her. The hunger pains she was experiencing were agonizing, she was becoming extremely malnourished and dehydrated — she had not had a drop to drink in days. Gathoni's will to fight was starting to run out and she was afraid of the feelings she was experiencing. Afraid she would take her own life as her only way out."

Around me, murmured voices expressed sympathy. A woman sitting five chairs from me silently wiped away tears.

Wambua continued, "Before Jesus' death, He was forced to carry his cross from Golgotha to Calvary as a public spectacle. When Jesus was carrying the cross to the place of His crucifixion, the weight of the cross became excessive. The Roman authorities grabbed a man who was simply passing by and had him carry the cross for the remainder of the journey to Calvary. The man's name was Simon."

Wambua looked around him. Everyone was glued to Wambua's face, hanging onto the conviction and magnetism of his words.

"For those of you who remember Simon's story, you know that the cross weighed well over a hundred pounds. Imagine that weight being forcefully hoisted onto your back. It would certainly be an incredible load to carry, particularly for someone you didn't even know. Simon was just passing through. Matthew and Mark say that Simon was forced to carry it, and Luke says that Simon was seized and the cross was put on his back. Regardless, the situation was forced onto Simon, no matter what he wanted. Simon didn't know Jesus and he didn't volunteer to carry the heavy cross. He was forced into it. He had no say in the matter — the same way that we are sometimes forced into situations that we don't want or ask for.

"Unfortunately, in this world, bad things happen to good people all the time. The Bible is full of situations where people are persecuted, harmed, killed, mocked and suffer unjustly. Life is complex and often goes in directions that we do not want and, as a result, devastation, or frustration, or hunger or perhaps even something worse occurs. No matter how loudly you wail or how strongly you protest against it, there is nothing you can do or say to change it. And that can be extremely hurtful and very frustrating."

Wambua took another pause, and I started to feel a tingle bubble down my spine. I knew Wambua was a rainmaker, which must have made him a very powerful man, but I was starting to feel as though his supremacy went beyond that. Although it was just the morning message, the way he spoke made me feel as though he was able to look deep into my mind and heart and know exactly what I was going through and feeling. It felt like he was speaking directly about me. And directly to me.

Wambua cleared his throat and continued, "You can't always control what happens to you, but you *can* control your response and how you react to it. Simon could have given up. He could have fallen and said that he couldn't do it anymore. He could have faked not being capable of moving any further. The Roman authorities wouldn't have thought twice about it, and they would have simply grabbed someone else from the crowd and made him carry it for the rest of the distance. Somewhere on that long journey, when Simon was willingly carrying a one-hundred-pound cross for someone he didn't know, he turned from being a victim to a *victor*. No longer was a miserable fate that he didn't choose being thrown at him but, instead, he participated in his ultimate destiny and, as a result, ended up following Christ, both literally and figuratively.

"Like Simon, the young girl who came to see me a month ago ended up choosing her destiny, despite how much had gone wrong and how many things were against her. Gathoni could have given in to her suicidal thoughts, killing both herself and her baby. But she didn't. Instead, she responded to her horrific situation by getting the help she needed. She took all of the bad luck and awful circumstances that had been thrown at her and gained strength through choosing a path that led to recovery. And when she did, we were able to find her a new job with an employer who was willing to overlook her pregnancy and give her room and board as payment. Gathoni still doesn't have much, but she does have a safe place to sleep, as well as food and drink for both her and her baby."

I fanned myself with a piece of paper that had been tucked into a hymn book. The sanctuary had become stuffy and hot throughout Wambua's message.

"When we find ourselves knocked down and in situations that we don't ask to be in and when the pains of life are overwhelming . . . we are not out of control. We are always in control of how we respond, and we need to respond like Simon. And like Gathoni. Genuine faith develops from times of trial and pain and, as Paul tells us, we need to rejoice in our sufferings because they are an opportunity to put our faith into action. No longer think of carrying the cross as a burden, but as something that will ultimately lead you to a greater place. And when you take *control*, despite the fact that a door may have been shut on you, I am quite certain that God will be right there beside you to *open a window*."

As Wambua finished the last words of his sermon, he held my gaze for many seconds before turning away. And it was then that I became convinced he *was* speaking directly to me.

14

After we had returned from church, Mama Bu made us a lunch of rice and beans. I was hungry given our long walk, and inhaled the food.

"What did you think of church, Nicky?" Petar asked me, diving into his portion of the mango, which we were having for dessert again.

"I thought it was great," I said honestly. "I loved the energy and the passion. The singing and dancing is so much fun. And the little kids who sang in the choir were so adorable, even if a little off-key."

Kiano laughed, "You noticed that too, huh? Good thing our Petar here has always sung like a cherub."

"I was a bit surprised at how long it was though. Is it usually over two hours?"

Kiano fought a yawn as he answered, and stretched out on the couch, "Depends on the day, but usually the services are about that long . . . sometimes two and a half hours."

"It is not time to get comfortable, Kiano," Mama Bu gently scolded her husband as she piled the dishes up on the coffee table. "It is just about time for you and Petar to get out of here."

"*Mwenda pole hajikwai*," Kiano answered with a smile. He stood up and affectionately poked his wife.

"That, Nicky, is an old Swahili expression meaning, 'He who moves forward slowly does not trip,'" Mama Bu translated for me. Then, with a friendly poke back at him, she smiled and said, "But really, Kiano is just procrastinating."

"Ah, *Baba* is just teasing you, *Mama*. He is running on Kenya time. We're only about fifteen minutes late," Petar said.

"Fifteen minutes! It will be half an hour by the time you get there. Now . . . *kugo, kugo*! Go, go! Or you will embarrass our family."

"We're going, *Mama*. Thanks for lunch. We'll be back soon." Petar stood to join his father, and kissed his mother on the cheek before leaving. After only a few short days with my host family, I could already tell how much Petar adored his *mama*.

"Where are they going?" I asked Mama Bu after they shut the door.

"To Kiano's sister's house, who lives about fifteen minutes from here. They have gone through some great hardships in the past year, and Kiano and Petar are going to help out." Mama Bu shook her head, lost in thought.

"Hardships? What kind?"

"Lucy, Kiano's sister, lost her husband about a year ago when he was beaten on the side of the road by a gang of strangers."

"No!"

"Sadly, yes. No one knows exactly why it happened, but it was after nightfall and he was late returning home from work."

"Why was he late?"

"I do not know. It is not really important now, I guess. There was a gang of men who attacked him on his walk home. Poor Chege, he did not have a chance. Gossip followed his death, which made it worse for Lucy and the children. . . . Garbage stories floated around about him stealing a chicken from the home of one of the men who beat him, but Kiano and I do not believe that for one second. Chege was a good and honourable man. I do not know what happened that night, but I do know that he did not steal a chicken!"

"Poor Lucy. And their *children*! It must have been devastating for them."

"Yes, and she has five of them, all under the age of six."

I couldn't believe it. Eric's and my next door neighbour had had five children — three boys followed by twin girls — and we had watched her constantly struggle to parent so many kids, even with the help of her very involved husband *and* a nanny named Renee. And Lucy was raising five all on her own?

"Lucy was a teacher before she had children, but then stayed at home to raise her children. She was forced to get a job when Chege died. Teaching did not pay enough so she now works seven days a week as a maid so that she can support her family. She rarely sees her children anymore and we hardly ever see her." Mama Bu stopped talking and quietly clucked her tongue.

"Who watches the children?" I asked sadly.

"Chege's mother. She moved in to help. She had lost her own husband a few years back, so it was natural she would take care of the kids. But their property and gardens are big and take a lot of care, which

Lucy cannot do any longer because she is working so much. Chege's mother is old and frail and cannot tend to the yard and fix what is broken around the house."

"So Kiano and Petar help with the yardwork?"

"That is right. They have been going there once a week on Sunday afternoons for the past few months or so. It was Kiano's idea to help. He says he and Petar will do it until the children are old enough to take over."

"Do you ever go with Kiano and Petar?"

"I have been a few times. But mostly I stay here to try and get some weekly chores done."

"Well, I'm free on Sundays. I can help you out."

Mama Bu smiled. "In Kenya we have an expression that says, 'Mgeni siku ya kwanza, siku ya pili mpe jembe akalime.' In English it means, 'A visitor is only a visitor on the first day. On the second day give him a hoe so he can cultivate your field.' Does that make sense to you, Nicky?"

I nodded my head yes, knowing that the expectation was for me to help as much as needed.

"That is how it is in Kenya so, yes, you can help me soon. But only when we are good and ready." Mama Bu winked at me before walking to the kitchen, calling out behind her. "First, before we start our chores, we will drink some chai."

Mama Bu and I settled on the coziest of the three couches, side by side, and drank from our oversized steaming mugs of chai. We were still both wearing our Sunday church clothes, and Mama Bu folded her long skirt beneath her legs. She curled her calloused bare feet underneath her and blew on her tea.

"I feel a bit guilty about having a mid-afternoon chai as soon as Kiano and Petar leave for Lucy's house, but I really need the break. My days are long with work and I need a few moments to myself at the end of the weekend to sit by myself and have a quiet cup of chai."

"Oh, I hope I'm not intruding!"

"No, goodness, no. I am glad you are here. My quiet time can include you. I just do not want the men around me on Sunday afternoons. When they are here, my work *never* seems to end."

"Do you do all of the work at home?"

"Mmm-hmm," Mama Bu answered, sipping her tea and closing her eyes.

"Do Kiano and Petar help you?"

"They tend to the chickens and do some outdoor work, but anything that is needed for the inside — fetching water, cooking, cleaning — that is what I do. It is our custom for the men to work outside the home, so they can make money to put food on the table, and for the woman to take care of everything else."

"Do any women work?"

"Oh yes. Some because they want to, and others because they need to. Such as Lucy."

"In my house, growing up, it was like that as well. My mother did the majority of the work, although she had a job as well."

"Outside of the house?"

"Yes, she was dental assistant. She's retired now."

"And your *baba*?"

"He is now also retired. But he was the principal at one of the local high schools for thirty-five years."

"Where you get the love of teaching, yes, Nicky?"

"You're probably right. Especially because my father was a teacher before he became a principal." I laughed then, suddenly remembering myself as a child. "When I was really little, I used to line up my stuffed animals and pretend that I was just like him. For my sixth birthday, when the majority of my friends were asking for new bikes, I asked for a classroom-sized chalkboard. To this day, I think it was my favourite birthday yet. I still remember how excited I was when I woke up and found it hanging on the wall of my playroom."

"Teaching is in you, clearly. That is nice."

"I guess so, yes." I took a sip of tea. It was still too hot. "How about you? Any special birthdays that you can remember?"

"I do not know when my birthday is, Nicky."

"You don't know when your *birthday* is?" I said, shocked to hear Mama Bu's response. I suspected she probably didn't have elaborate birthdays, but how could someone not know when their birthday was?

"*Siyo*," Mama Bu replied. No. "Kiano either. Birthdays are not a big deal in Africa. We never celebrate them — we do not have extra money for presents, so what is the point of knowing the date? My *mama* and *baba* never told me, even when I asked. They said they forgot the exact day, but had memories of it being during the rainy season."

My mind flew to my own last birthday. I had been pregnant with Ella, and Eric had surprised me with dinner at Auberge du Pommier and a diamond bracelet. "Baby diamonds," he had said, smiling over the candlelight. "Anyone who pushes out a baby deserves some baby diamonds. . . ."

"Do you know the year, Mama Bu?"

"No, I do not," Mama Bu responded simply. "You need to understand, Nicky . . . I was the second youngest of twelve children. My parents simply could not keep track, because they were too busy taking care of us and making sure we all had enough to eat. But I do know how old I am. I am fifty-three. Or fifty-four. One of the two."

"Do you know when Petar was born?"

"Yes, we made sure to keep track of all of our kids' birthdays. Petar has a really easy birthday to remember. He was born on the first day in June, which is also Madaraka Day."

"Madaraka Day?"

"It is a holiday here. It remembers the day we were finally able to rule ourselves. Before that, it was Britain."

"Do you do anything for Petar's birthday?"

"We do not celebrate in any special way. Not like you would do. We never get gifts, but we do try to have meat for dinner on Petar's birthday, which makes him happy. A special occasion usually calls for a special dinner around here. For us, it is usually that night and Christmas that we get our meat."

I felt relieved, knowing then that it was unlikely I would find myself in a situation where I was expected to eat the unrefrigerated meat I had seen hanging at the market. I hadn't eaten meat in years, and knew refrigerated meat would do a number on my insides, let alone the meat Kenyans ate.

"So, what do you think I should expect tomorrow?" I asked, changing the subject. "I have to admit I'm a bit nervous. I feel like I have a rock in my stomach."

"You will do great work here, *rafiki*. I am quite sure of it. There is a permanent Kenyan teacher that you will be working with. She has the name of Hasina. She is a wonderful woman, and has been teaching at Kidaai for a couple of years. She speaks fluent Swahili and English, so you will be able to speak directly with her. Some of the pupils, especially the older ones, speak English, but the younger ones only speak Swahili."

"You mentioned the oldest kids will be thirteen or so. What about the youngest?"

"The youngest are in pre-unit, which I believe you call kinder-garten. Schools here are based on standards, which run from Standard

1 to Standard 8. Thanks to our President Kibaki, primary education was reintroduced a few years back for all children. They just need a desk, a uniform and books. That part needs to get paid for by the parents."

"How does Kidaai get those things, with no parents?"

"Donations, mostly."

"I see. And what standard does Hasina teach?" I asked, interested to know what room I would be in and which level of students I would be teaching.

"Ah, Nicky, Hasina teaches all of them."

My face clearly showed surprise, for Mama Bu further explained. "There is only one room, dolly. All thirty-five pupils are in the same classroom and they all learn from Hasina. They range from Standard 1 to Standard 8."

Suddenly, the rock in my stomach grew larger.

15

On the morning of my first day of volunteer teaching, I rose early. There was no way to deny it: I was nervous. And my nervousness had created insomnia. I had been a teacher for almost ten years by that point, yet my nerves were experiencing a new kind of jumpiness I had never felt before. I was concerned about the language barrier. I was anxious about fitting in, particularly given that I would be the odd white person standing out in a room of thirty-five black faces. And I was downright scared about how two teachers could successfully manage (and teach!) thirty-five students of all different ages.

I grabbed my last granola bar and headed out early. On our

Saturday tour, Mama Bu had pointed out where Kidaai was and told me that she would probably see me there later in the day. She had planned on taking me to introduce me to Jebet, but Kiano had returned the night before saying that Lucy's eldest daughter had developed a high fever. Mama Bu had spent the night tending to her.

I was expected to arrive at seven o'clock and had been instructed to ask for Jebet, who would show me to the single-room school. The orphan children would have eaten their breakfast at that point and would be playing in the yard, waiting for their first lesson to begin.

I walked ten minutes up the road, choking back garbage smoke and sneezing from the dust. As the orphanage drew nearer, I saw beside the dilapidated building uniformed children running about an open field, skipping and smiling as they played. They didn't see me at first, so I took advantage of the few moments of solitude to soak up the authentic world of Kenyan children.

The children seemed happy, chasing each other on the dried grass and falling to the ground in bubbly giggles. It reminded me of the count-less recess periods I had supervised over the years — with the exception of hopscotch courts, swings and slides. Instead of playground equip-ment, these shoeless students used feathers, sticks and discarded trash as centrepieces for their imaginative games. I silently applauded the endless innovation that I knew only children could muster.

A young girl about ten years old was the first to spot me watching them play and she ran up to me shouting the now-expected "*Mzungu! Mzungu!*" She pointed at me for all of her friends to see. Within moments, every child that had been playing in the field trampled over the dirty, dried-out ground to throw themselves at my feet. I had about twenty children — all of them in school uniform but none of them in shoes — pulling at my hands and shirt and pants and hair in greetings filled with joy.

The kids took turns shaking my hand and, as I greeted each one of them in turn, I noticed that almost all of their school uniforms were torn and ratty. The shorts and shirts on the majority of the children didn't fit correctly; some needed to roll sleeves and others were barely able to squeeze into their undersized uniforms.

The stench of the group was overwhelming and I forced myself to avoid covering my nose. The children smelled as though they hadn't bathed in months and the majority of them had filthy faces and noses that were both crusty and running with snot.

They all had matching shaved heads that were as identical as the uniforms they wore, and I found it difficult to tell the difference between boys and girls. Later, I found out that the children had their heads shaved to keep things as easy and clean as possible—but, because of this, the only real thing that I could distinguish between them was their ages. The youngest was close to five, and the oldest, fourteen.

One of the smaller children took my hand and said, "Me Gracie. How are you?"

"I am great," I answered, exaggerating a big smile with my mouth and hands. I chose a different word in hopes of teaching them an answer other than *fine*. "How are you, Gracie?"

"Fine!" the children echoed.

"Do any of you speak English?" I asked, still holding two of their hands.

"We do!" a few of the older kids answered, sticking their hands in the air. One of them asked, "Are you teacher?"

"Yes, I am. My name is Nicky. What are your names?"

"I am Nadia and this is my brother, Ita. We speak English."

"It is nice to meet you both. Can you please tell me where I can find Jebet?"

Wide-eyed, Nadia and Ita both pointed to the second floor of the large and decrepit orphanage. Just as I was about to ask which door I should go in to find the *mkuu*, I noticed piercing eyes so pointed they looked like slits staring down at me from the largest of the upstairs windows. I instantly knew it was Jebet. She held the sheer curtain to the right side of the window with a thick, oversized stick. Through the barred opening, the woman looked stern and ominous as she cast her browbeating stare onto the group of us standing in the field. She shook her head slowly from side to side and I could practically hear her hissing insults.

I raised my hand in what I hoped was a welcoming wave, but the woman darted to the side of the window and out of my line of sight, marking her departure with the clash of her stick against the metal-barred window.

———

"Hello?" I called, entering the orphanage through the red front door. As I pushed it open, paint peeled off and fell to the floor.

"*Ndiyo?*" A voice called back. Yes? A skinny woman wearing a dark blue apron emerged from what I could only imagine was the kitchen, wiping her hands on a tea towel filled with holes. "Oh! *Karibu!* You Nicole?"

"Yes, I am Nicole. I am here to volunteer in the classroom and help teach. Are you Hasina?"

"Oh no, Hasina no help in kitchen. She teach in classroom," the woman replied. "I am Johanna. I help with cooking and cleaning for orphanage. Jebet told me that you coming this morning to help teach." Johanna smiled at me and pumped my hand up and down energetically as she introduced herself. After the chilly stare of Jebet, I was grateful to meet a smiling face.

"Do you know where I can find Jebet? I was told to meet her here this morning."

"She not down yet. Still sleeping in her room. But I can show you to class if you'd like?"

"Yes, thank you. That would be great!" I knew I couldn't avoid Jebet forever, but was admittedly relieved to have postponed my first face-to-face encounter.

Johanna took me on a route through the orphanage and out the back door. As we passed through the crumbling kitchen, its stone walls decaying and in desperate need of repair, I noticed a stack of dirty plates piled high in an oversized, square sink. In the centre of the room, a bulky pot with a cinched waist held a round bowl-like top. Upon eyeing it, Johanna pointed to the ceramic pot and told me it was called a *jiko*. "We use it to prepare food. It make cooking easy and cheap."

I followed Johanna through the back door. It swung awkwardly outward on two broken bottom hinges.

We continued through a dusty backyard passageway to a separate, self-standing building with a shingled red roof. We walked through the open door frame of the school into a single classroom where a short black woman passed out papers to a row of empty desks.

Watching the woman, I was transfixed by how much the scene reminded me of my own classroom: a teacher passing out papers in an empty room in hopes that proactive preparation would help create focused learning once the kids came in from playing. Yet the differences were as glaring. No kids' paintings hung on the crumbling cement walls, the thick globs of bright red and purple brushstrokes still drying from that morning's art lesson. There was no seasonal bulletin board filled with influences from that month's traditions and festivities, and no sand or water stations littered the classroom. No chalkboard hung at the front of the room, and there certainly was no bookcase filled with Dr. Seuss and Robert Munsch.

It was simply a dirty, bare room. Squished together rows of rectangle tables were used as desks. Lining the tables were benches, some broken and some not. All were scrunched together in an attempt to ensure that as many students as possible could fit into the classroom. At the front of the room was a small desk with three drawers lining each side of the chair. I assumed it was Hasina's. The top of the desk was bare with the exception of a tub of chewed pencils and nubby erasers.

The petite woman looked up from distributing the papers and smiled at me, her almond-shaped eyes crinkling in the corners. "Hello there. Might you be Nicole? I've been expecting you. And I'm so glad you're here to help."

"Yes, Hasina, I am Nicole, but please call me Nicky. I'm excited to be here. Can I help you pass out the papers?"

Johanna gave a little wave and quietly exited out the door we had come through, her English not strong enough to keep up with the conversation.

I took the stack of blank papers Hasina handed to me and placed them side by side along the front tables, mirroring the Kenyan teacher's squished spacing.

When we were finished, Hasina retrieved a handheld bell, reminiscent of what my mother would give us to ring when we were in bed with the flu and needed her attention. Hasina motioned for me to follow her outside where she rang the bell high and loud. Within seconds, the children I had seen playing in the field came stampeding by us like the running of the bulls. Shrieks of laughter trailed behind them as they took their seats.

Hasina rapped a flat stick at the front of the classroom to get the students' attention. I looked around, wincing at how mashed together the students were, sitting side by side on the benches. For the most part, the older kids sat together at the back of the classroom and the younger ones gathered at the front.

"*Sabalheri wanafunzi*," Hasina opened the day, bidding her students good morning. Thankfully, I was standing beside an English-speaking preteen who took one look at me before whispering the translations in my ear. The girl looked to be about twelve with breast buds revealing the onset of puberty. I smiled, quietly thanking her.

Hasina continued by giving the pupils the *habari za asubuhi* — in English, the morning news and messages. She explained that school would let out early that day because she had to leave to attend a meeting. I waited for the children to jump up and down, clapping and cheering at the prospect of trading in school lessons for playtime, just as they would have back home.

But not one of them responded the way I was expecting. If anything, some of them looked a bit disappointed. Even more surprising, complete silence continued to fill the room as Hasina went over the morning announcements. Somehow, the teacher was able to continue to hold the undivided attention of all thirty-five students. I admired her proficiency; classroom management was a skill that I constantly worked at mastering.

I wondered if Hasina was going to introduce me next, but instead she updated the class on one of the younger students, who was absent from school. Iman would not be returning to school on that day, or in the future. Johanna, who had shown me through the school, would tell me later, in confidence, that Iman had been with the orphanage for two years, but that his uncle had unexpectedly visited Kidaai and retrieved his nephew to work on his land. The uncle hadn't wanted Iman until he was old enough to tend to farm work; he had no use for his nephew when he was young and weak, but wanted him back now that the child was old enough for man's work. At seven years old.

Now Hasina waved for me to join her at the front of the class. I stepped forward and waved at the class, bidding them hello in Swahili. They smiled and waved, but still remained perfectly behaved.

"This is *Mwalimu* Nicky," Hasina said, "Teacher Nicky. She will be with us for the next little while, helping you to learn." Hasina bounced back and forth between English and Swahili, wanting to make sure both the younger children and I understood.

"Now, let's begin our studies," Hasina continued. "We will start this morning by continuing our social studies discussion on the countries of Africa. Yesterday we spoke of Kenya, and learned all about what surrounds us, including our location within the African continent, our cultures and what animals roam throughout our land. Today we will look at other African countries."

I took a seat at the back of the class and observed the children. Hasina seemed to connect directly with the seven- to nine-year-old students, their eager faces nodding and taking in what she was saying. But the youngest students looked lost. And the older students, bored.

The twelve-year-old that had translated for me earlier ignored what Hasina was saying, silently rolling the sides of the blank paper sitting in front of her, shutting out her surroundings. I suspected it was because she already knew what was being taught.

Hasina crossed to her own desk and removed a small stack of thin textbooks, almost all of them falling apart at the seams. "We share the books as we only have eleven," Hasina said to me in English, handing ten of them to me so that I could randomly distribute the books throughout the class. I passed them out and the children quickly clustered together to share the book closest to them.

Turning to address the entire group, Hasina held up the book opened to page seventeen and explained that it showed a map of Africa. She pointed out where Kenya was in relation to the other countries, and traced its boundaries.

I watched the students in front of me each take a long look at one of the textbooks and then pass it to their neighbours. From what I could see of the pages, the textbooks looked to be at about a Grade 1 level.

When everyone had their chance to take a look at the map, Hasina went through the entire exercise again, but this time pointed out the Republic of Somalia, explaining that it was the country that fell to Kenya's northeast.

"Now, please take your pencils and use the piece of paper in front of you to write down everything that you already know about Somalia. You will have fifteen minutes to complete the activity, and then we will share our answers as a group."

Once Hasina was convinced the students were buried in their assignment, she came to the back of the classroom to talk quietly with me. I was in the first hour of my volunteer work and already I had enough questions to last the rest of the day. Her multi-age approach was interesting, yet I sensed the students falling at the extremes of the age range weren't absorbing what they could be. I was eager to learn more about the curriculum that Hasina had been given, and how she adapted it to such a broad range of ages.

"The curriculum?" Hasina scoffed. She shook her head, pursing her lips. "There *isn't* a curriculum, Nicky."

As a teacher, what I learned shocked me. Hasina had to do much more than any other teacher, but with so much less. She had no guidance, given that Kidaai only had a makeshift classroom within an orphanage school that was not validated, or even regarded, in the eyes of the Kenyan government. Any school supplies Hasina had to use were donations from previous volunteers and a few warm-hearted families from Mombasa. The government had simply disregarded these children because they were orphans.

The majority of donations went towards basic survival, which never included schooling. The children first needed to eat, drink and have access to medicine when they were sick. The academics part of growing up — getting an education that would teach the children to read and write — was considered a bonus. On most days, Hasina and her class went without.

As the kids finished their activity, the room started to stir. The younger children had long since been bored with the activity, many of them writing nothing but scribbles on their papers. Some even still had blank pages.

Hasina asked for a volunteer and I watched as a few of the kids raised their hands, offering to share what they had written down with the class. I quietly strolled around the sides of the classroom and tried to peek at the students' papers. The majority had five or six things written down, but one eager student had an entire page of Swahili writing; she was sitting on the edge of her seat, anxiously fluttering her hand in an effort to be picked.

Hasina pointed at the girl, who stood up and started reciting facts about Somalia. She spoke only in Swahili.

As the eager student droned on, I noticed a boy about thirteen at the very back of the class, off to one side. He was by himself, sitting perfectly still, but twisting his hands in his lap. I walked behind him and noticed his page of paper remained completely blank. The pencil he had been given was sitting perfectly vertical on top of it.

"Do you speak English?" I asked quietly.

"Yes, *Mwalimu* Nicky. A bit."

"Do you want to write down what you know about Somalia?"

"Yes, me *really* do." The boy looked at me with wide, round eyes as he nodded his head.

"Okay, well there's still a bit of time. Why don't you quickly list what you know about the country?"

"Because, *Mwalimu* Nicky, me not know how to read or write."

## 16

The next morning, I was anxious to speak with Hasina. The day before had been busy. Given Hasina had to leave the classroom early, I hadn't had a chance to thoroughly speak with her and I was anxious to continue our conversation about teaching the children. I wanted to learn more about the lessons she was using and ask about my role to understand how she thought I could help.

I stuffed my backpack with a few of the supplies I had brought with me from home — markers, activity books, construction paper, stickers, a few rulers, some Play-Doh, a package of pipe cleaners and four bottles of glue. I didn't know where Petar or Kiano were and I hadn't seen

Mama Bu since Sunday as she was still nursing her niece back to health, so I grabbed some fruit from the kitchen and headed out the door.

When I got to school, I walked into an empty classroom. I was hoping Hasina would be there, since she had arrived so early the day before, but the classroom was still and quiet. The shared textbooks we had used throughout Hasina's lessons the day before were piled neatly on her desk. The dusty wooden floor the classroom had been built upon was still marked with the prints of shoeless children.

Not knowing what lessons we would be covering that day, I wasn't sure how I should set up the classroom. Instead, I took my seat on one of the unbroken benches and waited for Hasina's arrival.

Forty minutes later, I was still waiting. I could hear the children playing in the field and I wondered if it was typical for Hasina to be late. I had heard Petar joke about "Kenya time," which coined the consistent way Kenyans showed up late for everything, yet Hasina didn't strike me as the type of teacher who would approach the classroom in such a lackadaisical manner.

I left the classroom and wandered through the orphanage back door to find Johanna finishing up the dishes.

"Good morning, Johanna. Have you seen Hasina? She isn't in the classroom and I expected her to be here by now."

"No, no, Miss Nicky. Me not know. Here, I get Jebet." Johanna wiped her hands on the tea towel that was hanging off her shoulder. Her eyes seemed weary, yet she forced a wobbly smile onto her face, revealing a large gap between her two front teeth. When she smiled, her nose turned even more upwards than it already was, giving her an almost cartoonlike quality, yet she was still pretty in her own way. Beautiful, even.

I clasped my hands together and tried not to be nervous about meeting Jebet. She was just the orphanage director, after all. What did she have over *me*?

But when Jebet and Johanna walked into the kitchen, the room turned icy cold. The orphanage director's persona instantly juxtaposed Johanna's calm and gentle demeanour, and the pair looked like Dr. Jekyll and Mr. Hyde standing next to each other. Sweet and sour.

Jebet's craggy face served as the backdrop to her flat and wide nose with nostrils flaring into perfectly matching circles as she breathed. The orphanage director still carried the stick that I had seen the day before. She ungraciously barked her way through our first conversation.

"Hasina's not here. She won't be back today." Jebet's words were quick and irritated, despite the fact I hadn't yet said two words to her.

"Hello, Jebet. I'm Nicky. It's a pleasure to meet you," I said in the warmest tone I could muster. I held out my hand, determined to, at a minimum, comfortably coexist with the orphanage director during my days in Kenya. After five seconds of my hand hanging empty in the air, I returned it to my side. "Do you know when Hasina might return?"

"Who knows? There's another teachers' strike, so now none of them are working. Hasina is probably off screaming at the government with all of the other teachers, asking for more money. Like they need it! All I know is that now these damn children have *nothing* to do all day. And *I* am *stuck* with them, you hear? Hmmph. I need to have the dirty monsters around me all day like I need a bullet in my brain."

Did she say . . . a *teachers' strike*? An actual *strike*?

There had been no talk of it. And nothing on the news, which I had continued to watch every night.

I was sad for the children who would be pulled out of school, particularly those who needed it most. And I was disappointed to have spent only one day in the classroom with the children before the strike rolled in.

I wondered what else I could do in Kenya; I wasn't scheduled to go home for three months. Maybe work at Kiano's bank? No, that wouldn't work; I was terrible at math and never accurate when I counted money. Take care of Lucy's children? They had Chege's mother. Teaching was my *passion*. I had no other skills, and nothing else to offer. Nor did I want to spend three months volunteering in some other way.

Jebet started eyeing me suspiciously, and took a step closer. I could smell the faint trace of alcohol on her breath. "Unless . . . unless *you* want to take over? We need a teacher, and I'm sure you can figure all that classroom stuff out. Yes?"

I couldn't believe how Jebet's mood could swing so drastically from one minute to the next. She went from barking at me to asking me for a favour.

I glanced at Johanna and watched her nod encouragingly at the orphanage director's suggestion. Despite it being obvious that Jebet's offer stemmed from not wanting to deal with the children herself, I was intrigued and interested at the thought of taking over the classroom. At least until the teachers' strike was over, at which point I would happily hand the reins back to Hasina.

The challenges of so many kids in one classroom was intimidating, particularly given the broad age range, but my mind hadn't stopped racing with ideas of ways to teach them since the day before.

"I'll do it!" I exclaimed. I was surprised to hear my voice, and my confident tone surprised me even more.

"Well . . . good. There, it's settled. Now, go and get the dirty brats and start teaching them. *Out* of my *sight* already!" Jebet picked up her stick and turned, leaving the kitchen as quickly as she could.

"You be good teacher. Hasina tell me that she like you," Johanna said as she scratched at her chin. Her left hand rested on her lower abdomen, which she rubbed lightly as if her stomach was aching. I wondered if Johanna was hungry.

"I guess I should get the kids and tell them what's going on," I responded timidly. Out of nowhere, I became incredibly nervous. My stomach curled in knots and I suddenly wondered if I had spoken too quickly. I didn't even speak the language the majority of them knew best. And I certainly had no clue how to effectively teach thirty-five children who ranged from age four to fourteen.

"You be good," Johanna said again, as though she was reading my thoughts.

I smiled and took a deep breath before leaving for the classroom, where I grabbed the little bell from the desk to call the kids to class. Within moments, all thirty-five of them were mashed back together and sitting in the exact seats that they had sat in the day before.

"*Hujambo*," I started, clearing my throat. I inhaled the musty air of the classroom and watched as wide eyes waited for me to continue. Several of the students blinked repeatedly, their eyes looking almost mechanical. "Would any of you who speak English like to help me out? I have an announcement to make and I would like for everyone to understand it."

No one moved an inch. No one put up their hands or even offered to help. All thirty-five children sat staring at me.

"Okay, I need you to listen then, and understand as best as you can. Hasina won't be here today, but I will be teaching you. I would really like for one of you to translate for me. It would really help me out."

The girl who had translated Hasina's lessons for me the day before timidly raised her hand, looking sheepish and afraid. I smiled in relief, grateful to have a volunteer, and motioned for the girl to join me at the front of the class.

"Thank you for volunteering," I said to her quietly. "What is your name?"

"It is Esther. And I am happy to help you."

I spoke slowly, so that Esther had time to translate my English into Swahili. For the most part she did really well, although I had to give her a few synonyms for the English words she didn't recognize.

"*Mwalimu* Hasina won't be with us for the next little while. She and the other teachers in Kenya are working together to figure out solutions for some issues that have come up." I paused, letting Esther catch up. As the little girl spoke to the class in Swahili, the students looked sad — and a bit scared to learn their teacher would no longer be with them. "Until Hasina returns, I will be your teacher. I am excited to be here and I look forward to teaching you."

The scared faces softened. Slightly.

"We will need to figure some things out together," I said honestly. "The truth is that I wasn't prepared to be your only teacher today. I'm going to need to find out what supplies we have and what types of things we will be learning about over the next little while."

A young boy about seven sitting in the third row raised his hand timidly. "Yes?" I asked him.

"Our supplies that we have are in Miss Hasina's desk. They are all in her drawers," the little boy said, pointing to the desk.

"Thank you. What is your name?"

"John. My name is John." The little boy smiled and wiped his running nose on his sleeve.

"It's nice to meet you, John. And thank you for pointing me in the right direction." I walked to the desk and opened the drawers. Inside, I found a thick stack of blank papers, and some extra pencils and erasers.

I thumbed through the drawer, stalling for time. I had *no* idea where to start.

Given that I had just found out that I would be on my own, I hadn't had time to properly plan or come up with fleshed-out ideas. While it was true that my mind had been racing with teaching tactics since the day before, my inspiration consisted *only* of spiralling ideas. No concrete plans of attack.

I decided to start with the basics.

"There are many of you, and only one of me, so I hope that you will be patient with me as I learn your names," I started, taking the pipe cleaners, markers and construction paper out of my backpack. Esther continued to translate. "Let's begin with making name tags for each of us to wear. I will show you how to make one, and then you can all make your own."

I took a piece of yellow construction paper and cut out a large rectangular shape. I used a red marker to write *"Mwalimu* Nicky" in big, bold letters. To decorate it, I drew a few flowers with some of the other markers. Then, a few stickers.

Using one of the pencils, I poked a hole in the top centre of my name tag. I pushed a piece of blue pipe cleaner through it, threading it through one of my button holes. I secured the two ends tightly together to ensure my name tag wouldn't come off.

"There!" I said, showing my name tag to the students proudly. I started passing out the supplies I had used and encouraged the kids to make their own version of my name tag. "Now, it's your turn. Please be as creative as you like — it can be a rectangle like mine, or a heart or a star or a circle. And you can decorate it in whatever way you choose. The only thing I ask is that you write your name in big letters so that I can see it. I'm going to try to learn all of your names as quickly as possible."

The kids eagerly took the supplies and stared at the stickers in awe. Although I couldn't be certain, I suspected that some of them had never seen stickers before — particularly the ones that had googly eyes, which instantly became the number one pick among the group.

Many of the older kids jumped in right away, taking brightly coloured construction paper and a few markers and stickers back to their seats. Others took longer to choose their materials.

"*Mwalimu* Nicky? Can I use two colours of the long, fuzzy things?" one of the girls asked, referring to the pipe cleaners. I peered over her shoulder and saw that she had spelled out SADIKI on her name tag.

"Yes, of course, Sadiki. You may do whatever you would like with your name tag. Be as creative as possible so that yours is completely different from everyone else's."

I watched Sadiki light up as she chose yellow and orange pipe cleaners to create the hook for her name tag. Then, as though she was replaying my creative nudging over again in her mind, she twisted the top of the two-colour hook around and around until she had created a spiral. Looking pleased with herself, she fastened her completed name tag to the top button on her uniform.

As the rest of the children finished up their name tags, I racked my brain, trying to think of the best way to teach this particular classroom. I scoured my memory for concepts we had learned in teachers' college, or suggestions from other teachers that I had worked with.

But everything I knew of was specific to a particular age. Nothing in the curriculum I had used leveraged teaching methods for such a broad age range of kids. Multi-age methods simply didn't exist, because our classrooms didn't have a four-year-old sitting next to a fourteen-year-old.

And then it dawned on me. While the method of teaching wasn't created with a ten-year age span in mind, I remembered that Montessori schools purposely educate children in a multi-age group. The belief was that a mixed age of children would create an environment where students would spontaneously learn from one another. While the obvious insight is that older children would share their knowledge with younger ones, it made sense to me that the older children would *also* be learning, particularly given that teaching reinforces previously learned concepts. As I had quickly learned in my own career, a teacher needs to fully and completely understand the lesson before being able to *teach* it. For that teacher — whether a certified post-grad or a nine-year-old mentor — the full comprehension of the lesson they are teaching ultimately serves as an aid in the complete mastery of the concept.

With that thought, my own first lesson was learned: I needed to creatively leverage the more obscure ideas and methods I had heard about along my own learning path. Teaching these children couldn't be based on my previous years' experience in education. It simply wouldn't work.

I told the children they could go outside for an early break, and quickly got to work, setting up different learning stations throughout the classroom. I wanted each student to be able to choose whatever activity interested them.

I chewed a couple of pieces of gum that I found in the pocket of my backpack and, using it as sticky tack, set up an art station by creating "easels" along one wall, made from the blank paper.

I used different pages within the various subject textbooks to create information centres that students could individually choose to read about.

I created a craft corner with the leftover supplies I had brought with me from home, the brightly coloured pipe cleaners and markers calling out to the craftier students.

I constructed a shapes station by cutting out a triangle, circle, square, parallelogram, pentagon and hexagon, and labelled each with thick black marker.

I set up an alphabet-printing area where I wrote out each letter three times using dots that could be traced, and then left the rest of the space blank for the children to write out their own letters.

I slipped out of the classroom to ask Johanna if I could borrow two large bowls and the measuring cups I had eyed on the counter during my uncomfortable conversation with Jebet. On my way back to the classroom, I scooped up some of the dusty ground and set up a station where the children could learn to measure different amounts by transferring dirt back and forth between the bowls.

Finally, I developed an oversized multiplication square that I had recently used with my Grade 3 students. I drew a grid and placed an $X$ in the top left corner. I filled in the top row and left column with the numbers one through ten, and then inserted the correct multiplication answer in the box where each pair of numbers met. I made sure to write the even numbers in pink and the odd numbers in blue, and circled the square numbers with an orange circle.

When I was finished, I called the children back in and told them they were free to examine each activity centre and choose the one that interested them the most. Interestingly enough, they didn't all flock to the craft centre, which I had thought might happen. Instead, the kids curiously inspected a few of the different learning locations before dividing themselves between them.

"Can I go *here*? *Mwalimu* Nicky, can I draw on the *wall*?" a student named Gloria asked.

"Yes, of course. Go to whatever station you'd like." I answered.

Gloria retrieved a marker from the craft area and started drawing on the blank pages hanging on the wall. She was actually quite the artist.

A few of the children in the middle of the age group practised tracing their letters. Others played with the measuring cups, laughing as they transferred the dirt back and forth.

And then the real magic began. I started witnessing student-taught education happening between the children. The first time I noticed it was with the crafts; some of the older kids were showing the younger ones how to write their names on the back of their completed work.

Five-year-old Gracie curiously watched Ita trace out letters. When Ita finished, he encouraged Gracie to do the same, showing her how to hold the pencil with her right hand.

Esther pointed out one of the patterns she had proudly identified in the multiplication square to an onlooking friend. The curious schoolmate nodded her head in understanding of what Esther was showing her.

Elated, I felt a surge of victory.

17

When I got to school the next morning, ten of the children were waiting outside the door, clearly anxious to get in and start the day. Their faces lit up when they saw me walking towards the school and I waved animatedly at them as I got closer. I smiled as I realized just how happy I was to see them again. I laughed outwardly as I watched some of the older kids jump up and down, clapping their hands and calling out my name. Two of the younger students ran to greet me, each of them taking a hand as they pulled me towards the school. I had never experienced such a sense of eagerness to learn, nor had I ever seen children respond to a teacher in such an energetic way. I wondered if it was the learning and studies they craved, or simply the attention.

Either way, we filled the next two days with more group lessons, and I was overjoyed to realize how quickly the children absorbed everything that was put in front of them, whether direction came from me or another student. We fell quickly into a routine and by the end of our third day together it felt as though I had known them forever.

On Friday, I decided to kick the morning off with a music lesson. I knew how much rhythm and beats meant to the Kenyan culture and I was hopeful that a cadenced (and bilingual!) music lesson imitating a storm would, somehow, miraculously help to bring the rainfall that we were still so desperately in need of. The students told me that the skies had provided nothing but overbearingly hot sunshine for weeks, and the crops had grown increasingly barren.

I asked the students to help me move the desks, and then we sat in a crammed circle in the middle of the classroom. I told the children we were going to try to bring rain to the land by creating the sound of a storm on the wooden floor.

"So, what do you think comes before the rain?" I asked.

"Sunshine!" Samuel shouted out. I reminded the class that they needed to raise their hands before answering a question.

"Yes, you are right, Samuel. But something happens after the sunshine, and before the rain, to tell us a storm is coming. Does anyone know?"

Silence.

"How about the wind?" I asked the class. "It usually starts to pick up right before a storm." I showed the students how we could imitate the sound of wind by making circular motions on the floor. The kids smiled and laughed at the noise, realizing that thirty-six people rubbing a wooden floor actually created a pretty loud sound. One that really *did* resemble the wind.

"Then what follows the wind? I'm sure you know this one," I asked the class.

"Rain!" The outburst led to another reminder to raise their hands.

"That's right. The storm is on its way, and light rain is about to start." I pointed to one half of the circle and told them to keep making the sound of wind with their circular motions. Then, I instructed the other half of the class to hit their fingertips softly on the floor to elicit light rain — followed by striking it a little harder as the rain drops grew larger.

I motioned for the wind to build up, and the reverberations grew stronger. The wind and the rain overlapped, and I was impressed at just how much it sounded like a real storm.

"The rain is coming down harder! The raindrops are big, and it's coming down in buckets now," I shouted over the noise. I showed the children how to hit their fingers together on each hand to make it seem as though the rain was coming down louder, more quickly.

And, then, finally, we moved to pounding the palms of our hands together very quickly, the sound inside the classroom now deafening. The children seemed mesmerized at the loud, realistic sounds they were creating. It was as if they were all impressed by the show they were watching and didn't realize they were each contributing to its impact.

Just as I was about to reverse the order of the sounds to show the storm passing, Jebet walked into the classroom. She was using her stick as a walking stick, but raised it as she shouted, "What is *this*?! Do you call this *learning*? You are making a mockery of my school! Enough! Get up! Get up!"

The sounds of the storm instantly came to a halt as the children scurried from the circle and back to their seats. Because we had moved the desks to the sides of the room, there wasn't room for all of them and they were literally sitting on top of one another. Yet, despite how jam-packed they were, they each sat perfectly still, with their hands folded neatly in their laps. They all looked down.

"School is *done*, you hear! No more shenanigans today, *do you hear me*? Back to chores," Jebet bellowed. The deafening sounds of our hard rain and wind didn't compete with her ear-piercing volume. "The house needs to be cleaned from top to bottom. And *you*!" Jebet pointed to John and Ita, sitting side by side in the corner. "You two boys need to go and get the water. Now, *move*!"

Before I could say anything, the children fled the classroom and disappeared into the house. John and Ita remained behind, but started to walk away once the cranky orphanage director threw some shillings at them. I motioned for them to wait for one moment.

"Jebet? Why did you interrupt our lesson? I was teaching them some music. If you would like to speak with me about my methods, I would be happy to have that conversation with you. But, please, don't take it out on the children."

"Nonsense!" Jebet retorted, her nostrils flaring once again. "Work needs to be done. School comes second. Your self-made noises mean nothing compared to survival, which means getting the water and cleaning the kitchen. The house help can't do it all by herself, you hear? It's a *large* orphanage."

"I'm sorry, but I must have misunderstood something. I thought that you wanted me to spend the weekdays with the children teaching them school lessons?"

"Not when work needs to be done first! School comes second! We're out of government water and need some more, and that comes first. Don't you know that? Are you a *fool*? Now go back to Bu's house and don't come back until Monday!"

Confused, I watched Jebet turn and use her walking stick like a cane as she returned to the orphanage. John and Ita were still waiting, and listening. Once Jebet left, they shrugged their shoulders and started walking.

"May I come with you? Perhaps I can help," I said to the boys, not really sure what to do next. My plans for the day had collapsed with the irritating voice of Jebet's barked commands.

"If you want come, it okay," Ita said, smiling at me. He revealed a wide smile with two holes in the front, where his baby teeth had once been. "Stay here first. We get the bucket."

The boys ran into the house and returned holding an oversized water jug that reminded me of the containers we had used when my father decided he wanted to try camping. I remembered him retrieving the water from the closest tap and, even as a strong man, struggling to walk it back to our site. How were two little boys going to manage it?

I fell into stride beside the two boys who walked the path like they could do it in their sleep. When we exited the orphanage grounds, we turned right and climbed down a dusty hill so steep I had to dig my feet into the earth to prevent myself from slipping. All I could think about was how we'd manage to get the water jug back up when we could barely get down the hill *without* the water.

Through somewhat choppy English, I learned that the boys often walked to the private store in search of water. Once per week, the government opened up the pipelines into the homes of Africa to provide a rationed supply. The tanks were filled to the top but, once a home's water allotment was gone, it was *gone*.

Given the number of kids needing water at the orphanage, the reservoir never lasted a week and often ran out after four days. In constant need of extra, Jebet forced the kids to fetch more water so they had enough for dishes.

The walk to get water took only about fifteen minutes and I was happily surprised to have arrived at our destination so quickly. During our short walk, my mind had filled with images I had seen on World Vision commercials, where children and women were expected to walk for miles in search of water.

John took my hand and led me to a hose hooked up to two big tanks. We filled the jug, and then gave the money to a scrawny man who had been keeping a close watch over us. He smiled before pocketing the money, revealing a big grin with no teeth.

"Now that we got the water, we go back, *Mwalimu* Nicky. But this part of the walk much harder. But don't worry. We carry the water for you." My heart hurt. They were seven years old.

"No, no, I will help you too. We'll share." I smiled at him, taking the filled jug.

During the uphill walk back, the World Vision images returned when the fifteen-minute walk turned into an hour and a half of lugging. I insisted on spending the majority of our travel time carrying the jug on my back; I didn't have the heart to watch two small children struggle with a task that I didn't think they should be doing in the first place. The canteen weighed more than either one of them.

"It's okay, *Mwalimu* Nicky. We do it like this . . ." The boys showed me their innovative solution of each taking the jug with their inside hand, while using their outside hands to push against the other's shoulder so they wouldn't collapse into one another. I had to admit, it was pretty smart of them.

When they couldn't carry it for one more step, I attached the thick carrying straps to the jug, and another on my forehead; the heavy canteen hung behind me and rested on my back.

I learned some time later that I was giving a piggyback to fifty-five-pounds of water. I grew increasingly angry with each step I took;

it infuriated me to know that Jebet would expect two small children to carry such weight. Foot by foot, step by step, I became a sweaty, dusty ball of rage. By the time we reached the orphanage, my damp clothes were stuck to my aching *everything* and I was ready to tackle Jebet.

I dropped the water jug off in the kitchen and went to find the orphanage director; I was determined to find another solution to kids carrying such weighty water.

When I finally found Jebet in the common room, she was hovering over Gracie. Although Jebet's hunched back covered a lot of my view, I could see that Gracie was bundled in a ball on the floor and could hear that she was sobbing in a way that sounded more like a cat's wail than a crying little girl.

I took a step towards Gracie just as Jebet delivered a blow to the little girl's shoulder. She used the stick she had been carrying earlier that day.

*"No!"* I cried, now running towards them. I instinctively jumped on Jebet and tried to grab the stick from her grasp. "Please, *stop!* Right now. *Please!* Jebet, what could Gracie have done to deserve *this?*"

*"I said to leave!"* Jebet shouted, spitting through her teeth. "What part did you not understand when I said do not come back until Monday? *Get out! Get out!*"

"Jebet, I won't. I can't leave while you're hurting Gracie like this. She's just a little girl. *Please*, Jebet. Put the stick *down*. Tell me what she did to make you so angry." Afraid of Jebet hitting the little girl again, I held onto the stick with all of my might and looked Jebet straight in the eyes.

Realizing freedom from Jebet's stick, Gracie fled to a corner beside one of the couches. She stayed cowered in the corner, tears and thick snot running down her face and onto her chin. She continued to wail, although it was slowly turning into more of an agonized whimper.

None of the onlooking children went to help or comfort Gracie, and I recognized fear in all of their eyes as they stood still as stones and watched what was happening.

"That imbecile pissed her pants. I won't have it! She needs to learn to keep her legs shut or to piss in the squat, and *not* in her pants. Now we've got to wash her clothes, even though we have *no* extra water to wash clothes."

"We have some water, Jebet. I just carried it back," I explained to the fuming director, trying to calm her down and, most important, keep her away from Gracie. I had no idea what to do next and my wobbly legs matched Gracie's trembling body. It dawned on me that Jebet still held the stick and there was the chance she could turn it on me. From what I had seen, the woman was capable of anything.

"It doesn't matter. That girl is five years old. It's time for her to stop pissing in her pants. If she wants to learn the hard way, she's going to learn the hard way. Hmmph."

"It was an *accident*, Jebet. Gracie wouldn't have done it on purpose. I will clean her up and wash all of her clothes. Please, why don't you go and get the water I just carried back, for whatever you needed it for. I'll stay here and get Gracie all cleaned up."

Jebet snorted, and raised her stick in Gracie's direction, as if trying to threaten her. Then Jebet backed out of the room.

Once she was gone, I ran to Gracie's side and lifted her shaking frame out of the corner. She collapsed into my arms and I folded her into me, giving her a hug.

I was unconcerned that her soggy, stained pants were leaving marks on my own clothes. Every part of me needed to give the little girl comfort and love. I wanted to hug her harder, but I didn't know where she had been hit or if she was bruised. I didn't want to hurt her more.

"It's okay, Gracie. Shhh, shhh. It's okay, honey. It's okay," I whispered quietly into her ear. Her trembling wouldn't stop, so I continued to rub her back and kept trying to calm her with my voice and words.

As I comforted Gracie, I sensed the other children were still behind me, watching and afraid. An occasional sniffle and whimper came from the group, but other than that, complete silence. I turned and motioned for the kids to join me. They all sat at my feet as I hugged Gracie, rocking her back and forth.

Nadia closed in on us, starting a group hug, and the three of us sat together, hugging. After a moment, Ita joined us. Then Esther, followed by John. Runo and Shani. Maalik and his sister, Machelle. Macie and Paulo. Barongo, Hiuhu, Akello and Jomo. We all sat together, hugging as a group, and making each other feel safe.

When Gracie finally raised her head, she cautiously looked at me, and I saw a single welt along one cheek where Jebet had hit her. The line of raw skin dotted her cheek and stuck out in high contrast to her smooth, black skin. The edges were starting to puff up and I knew it would be a bruise within a few days.

I asked Esther to run and get Gracie some new clothes. With the other children also feeling better, I asked them to go outside to play. When it was just Gracie and me, I caressed her unharmed cheek with my hand.

"We're going to get you cleaned up now, Gracie. Okay?" I said gently. "It's okay that you had an accident. We all have accidents. I'll get you cleaned up and you will be good as new."

I didn't know how much Gracie understood, but I hoped she knew what I was telling her. I paused then, before gently removing her pee-soaked pants. When I took off Gracie's top, I found another stick gash across her back and a lighter pink mark on her shoulder where I had seen Jebet hit her.

I felt as if my heart had folded in on itself, and I gulped back the threatening tears that were sitting in my throat. I did not want Gracie to see me cry.

I folded up Gracie's soiled clothes and helped her into the new pants Esther had found for us. Taking the two girls by the hands, I led them into the kitchen in hopes of finding Johanna. I crossed my fingers that we wouldn't run into Jebet — both for Gracie's sake and her own. I was so angry that I didn't know what I would do to Jebet if I saw her at that moment.

Standing in the kitchen was Johanna, boiling that night's vegetables and beans in the ceramic *jiko*. Johanna looked up when we entered the room, her smile fading once she saw the welts on Gracie's body and face.

Johanna crossed the room and took the little girl into her arms. I couldn't understand the Swahili words that Johanna was saying, but I knew from the look on Gracie's face that the comforting hums coming from Johanna's mouth were making Gracie feel better.

"Run along, now, Esther," I said. "Thank you for getting Gracie some new clothes. Johanna and I will take care of her from here." I watched the little girl run from the kitchen, the broken door slamming behind her as she went. Turning to Johanna, I said, "Do you have a first aid kit? We should get those wounds cleaned up to prevent infection."

Johanna looked puzzled, so I found new words. "Bandages? Ointment? Gauze? We need to get her cuts cleaned." I pointed to the wounds on Gracie's body.

"We no got one," Johanna answered, shaking her head and looking very sad. "Old volunteer gave lots, but Jebet sold everything we got for money. She kept money for her."

Somehow, my blood began to boil even hotter. When I found Gracie, I thought I couldn't have been angrier. But less than twenty minutes after that, I had proven myself wrong. "Do you have soap, Johanna? We need to at least clean her cuts."

"*Eeh, eeh* . . . yes, yes . . . we do. I get it." Johanna picked Gracie up and retrieved some soap from a cupboard that had lost its door. She gingerly placed the girl on the counter beside the sink and proceeded to expertly clean out Gracie's wounds with the soap, along with some of the water the boys and I had carried less than an hour before.

As we worked, Johanna and I took turns singing to Gracie — Johanna in Swahili, and I in English. When I recognized the tune of one of Johanna's songs, I joined in, but in English.

"*Baa baa mbuzi una uzi. . . .*" Johanna sang, her voice sweet and strong. And me, singing, "*Baa baa black sheep have you any wool. . . .*"

By the time we were finished cleaning Gracie up, she was smiling and asking if she could go and find the other children. I took it as a good sign.

When she left, I picked up Gracie's dirty clothes and started washing them in the sink, careful to not use very much water. "Do you want to know what happened?" I asked Johanna.

"No. I already know," Johanna replied, in a sad and defeated way. "It happen more times. More and more. Jebet use stick on chil'n when they done bad. She mean, mean lady."

"Johanna, why didn't you tell me sooner?" I asked gently. I was upset that she hadn't mentioned it in our many conversations that week, but I didn't want to push her. "You know you can talk to me, right?"

Johanna slowly nodded, looking skeptical. "But if I say something, Jebet kick me out. I nowhere to go."

"I won't let that happen, Johanna. I'll make sure you always have somewhere safe to be." I looked directly into Johanna's eyes. "But we *have* to stop Jebet. This is crazy. We can't let her do this to the kids." My voice, now loud and clear, surprised even myself.

"*Shhh*. Jebet upstairs. We no talk now. We talk later." Johanna turned to the *jiko* and kept stirring. When I didn't respond, but also didn't leave, Johanna stopped stirring and came closer to me, whispering, "I no like it either. I want to stop it. I trust you, so I tell you some stuff. But not when Jebet home. We talk later. You should go. I'll watch out for the chil'n and I watch Gracie. "

When she finished speaking to me, Johanna picked up the long wooden spoon to continue stirring, only this time she didn't turn back around to talk to me. I was afraid to go, but afraid to stay. So I stalled, and waited a full minute for Johanna to say something more.

When she didn't, I took it as a sign that it was truly time for me to go. I could only trust that Johanna would stick to her word about watching out for the children and keeping an eye on Gracie.

## 18

By Saturday night, I was beside myself. I hadn't seen Mama Bu in almost a week. In my brief encounters with Kiano, he had told me that she was still tending to her very sick niece and didn't know when she would be back.

With Mama Bu gone, and Kiano and Petar often at work and school, I had come home from the orphanage to an empty house and was left on my own to make my own meals. For the most part, it had been a lot of granola bars, fresh fruit and bread. I could tell by how my pants were hanging on my waist that I had already lost weight.

On Sunday, I rose early and was relieved to hear dishes clinking in the kitchen; it meant Mama Bu had come home. I needed to see her. I scrambled to get ready as quickly as I could, throwing on the first outfit I found, and raced to the kitchen.

When Mama Bu saw my frantic face, she put her arms around me and asked what was wrong. I started to tell her, but Kiano and Petar joined us in the kitchen and asked what we were making them for breakfast.

Instinctively I knew not to continue talking about the orphanage in front of them, and Mama Bu whispered that I could tell her everything over chai after church. As they did each week, Kiano and Peter would be going to his sister's house, and we'd have all afternoon to talk about what was going on at the orphanage.

Once we had finished breakfast, we walked the same fifty-minute hike to church. I had thought the land couldn't be any drier than on our walk the previous week, yet, shockingly, everything seemed even more dehydrated and dusty than it had before. If the crops weren't already dead, they would be soon, leaving nothing to eat.

All through the morning, I tried hard to listen to Wambua's message, but I absorbed nothing of the two-hour service. I could think of nothing other than Gracie and all of the other vulnerable children in Jebet's reach. My mind raced with what I would say to Mama Bu and what we could do to help.

—

After our lunch, Kiano and Petar left for Lucy's house, and Mama Bu and I settled into her couches with our steaming mugs of chai. "Now, *rafiki*, what on earth could be the matter? Tell me everything you need to," she instructed, blowing on her tea. I could see genuine concern in her eyes, along with fatigue and exhaustion. I suspected it had been an equally long week for her.

I took a big breath and dove into the details. I recounted all that had happened during my first week at the orphanage, including the teachers' strike and me needing to take over for Hasina. I knew my story was coming out in nippy, stream-of-consciousness bursts, but I couldn't seem to tell Mama Bu quickly enough.

My host mother listened and nodded throughout my rambling chatter, telling me often to slow down so that she could understand my English.

When I was finished, Mama Bu set her mug down and pressed her fingers into her temples. In the slow and accented voice that I had so quickly come to love, she explained that she hadn't realized it had gotten so bad at the orphanage. "I am so very saddened to hear all of this. Jebet is not a warm person, or at least she has not been for a long time. And she has always been very strict with the children." Mama Bu looked at the ceiling. Studied it, and paused. She closed her eyes, squeezed them shut.

"In recent years, Jebet has disciplined in a way that some people might have questioned, but never with the force you are describing. That is not discipline, it is violence. I have not helped at the orphanage in a long while as the chores seemed to have been in control since Johanna started working there as the house help. It seems that might have been a mistake on my part."

"You couldn't have known, Mama Bu. Johanna seemed to imply that it has only gotten really bad recently. She said that it has just started happening more and more." Mama Bu nodded. I searched her face, trying to read it. "Why is she like this, Mama Bu? When we were speaking about it at Barika's house, I got the sense that you knew

Jebet's story. You said she hasn't always been that way, and I sensed something changed her. What did you mean?"

Mama Bu paused again, taking three long sips of her tea. She sank deeper into the couch, closing her eyes again. When she opened them, her eyes looked sad, as though they were somewhere far away. Gently, she began. . . .

Sometime around 1966, Jebet was born to an Ethiopian farmer named Antony and his wife, Susan. Although Jebet did not have any memories of the two bountiful years that followed her birth, she certainly remembered the vivid tales her *mama* and *baba* would tell her about how much rain fell after her arrival — and about how well their crops did. The family not only had enough food to eat themselves, but also copious amounts to sell to others and, as such, were considered wealthy — at least by Ethiopian standards.

Baba Antony believed that Jebet was his miracle baby who brought the prosperous rains to his farm within the first moments of her life. They believed this because, on the night Jebet was conceived, a rainmaker had visited their farm to pray with them; there had been a wicked drought and Baba Antony thought a rainmaker might be able to help.

That night, after the rainmaker left, and deep in the dark of their bedroom, Mama Susan swore that she felt herself become pregnant. And it was at that precise moment the rain started to fall over Baba Antony's crops, ensuring harvest viability and security from famine. The drought was over.

For the two years that followed, the rains came frequently and often. As Jebet grew, so did the success of Baba Antony's crops. It seemed that every time Jebet reached a milestone throughout her first years of life — sitting, crawling, walking — much rain would bless the earth and Baba Antony's farm. The plants arched towards the sky, opening themselves up to drink, and the growth that followed put abundant food on tables throughout the land.

When Jebet turned two and a half, her sister, Rita, was born — along with one of the most horrific droughts in recent world history. Later coined the 1968–1974 Sahel Drought, the deadly absence of rain was utterly destructive. During the six years it lasted, nearly a quarter of a million people perished and over five million were displaced — and the agricultural bases of five countries, including Ethiopia, crumbled.

Baba Antony did everything he could to protect his farm but, without rain, there was no food or money. When his final hope dried up with his last few crops, he packed up his family and fled for Kenya in search of a better life. He had heard that the drought hadn't impacted Kenyan agriculture in the same way as it had in Ethiopia, and Baba Antony had hopes for establishing another farm with the agricultural richness he once had.

When he failed to find agriculture prosperity, the family was forced into the slums of Rongai, where they lived in a dilapidated shack that had been left barely standing when its former family was wiped out by what was later assumed to be the AIDS virus. Rita and Jebet shared the one-room home with their parents and were forced to go days at a time with nothing to eat or drink.

Angry for his farm loss and the demoralizing way his family was living, Baba Antony needed someone to blame. Given the strong belief he had in his rainmaking miracle baby, Jebet, he became equally convinced that Rita was the second-born curse and was to be blamed for the poverty and famine that had fallen upon his family. Baba Antony, who was once known for his loving fatherly ways and how frequently he whisked Jebet up to give her adoring hugs and kisses, turned into a cold and harsh father, ultimately becoming both callous and unforgiving. He blamed Rita for all that had happened and also turned on Jebet for not being able to do anything to bring more rain and change the drought.

After one year in the Rongai slums, Baba Antony abandoned Mama Susan and his two daughters. Late in the night, when his daughters were fast asleep and holding the hands of his wife, he slinked out of the broken shack in the wee hours of the morning and was never heard from again.

With no father in the family, Mama Susan took on the role of both parents. She fought hard and was ultimately able to convince an orphanage to take her on as the house help. She and her two daughters moved into the orphanage where they were given food and shelter in exchange for Mama Susan scrubbing toilets, polishing floors, cleaning dishes, cooking food and making beds — thirteen hours a day, seven days a week.

Given the amount of time Mama Susan had to spend cooking and cleaning, the two daughters did not get to spend a lot of time with their mother, but they occasionally saw her during meal times or when they passed each other in the hall. But her daughters were warm, fed and educated.

Jebet thrived when it came to academics and was quickly identified as being extremely bright. A South African volunteer who had visited the orphanage took a great liking to Jebet and sponsored her to go to a private boarding school. Thrilled with the news, Jebet asked when she and Rita would be leaving and was heartbroken to learn that there was only money for one sibling. Rita would be staying at the orphanage school while Jebet went on to study.

Although she hated to be away from her mama and sister, Jebet studied hard with the intention of returning to the orphanage to get a good job. She knew that once she had a proper salary to rely on, she could take care of her mama and Rita and they would finally have the freedom they deserved. Her mama would no longer be forced to cook or clean and, instead, would have the financial security to do something that interested her. Rita could then take her turn at school.

Four years later, Jebet received the twenty-four credits she needed to graduate from high school and she returned to the orphanage. The former *mkuu* was leaving, and Jebet gladly accepted the job.

She built a home for her mama and sister on the orphanage land and the three of them worked together to rescue children from the slums and take care of them when they needed it. Many of the children had been left on their own after both parents had died; others were abandoned by parents who couldn't care for them. Whatever their circumstance, Jebet, Rita and Mama Susan worked together to ensure as many children as possible were safe, full and happy.

The years went by, some tougher than others, and Jebet continued to run a successful orphanage that housed many children. She loved her work and was happy to be able to save children in need; it fulfilled her greatly to be able to rescue the kids from the same slums that had devastated her family with its famine and dirty water.

There were never enough beds or medical supplies, but Jebet did what she could, and sourced as many volunteers to help as possible. While the majority of them came and went, a constant contributor was Mama Bu, whom she had met through a mutual friend — Moses — at the market one Saturday in April. Mama Bu loved to surround herself with the laughter and smiles of toddlers and young children. Admittedly, Jebet grew fond of having Mama Bu's company at the orphanage. The two would often spend their afternoons chatting over chai on the covered wooden porch when the majority of the children were in school.

One November, Jebet, Rita and Mama Susan made plans to visit Mama Susan's sister, Maria, and her husband, Frank, who lived about four hours away. Maria and Frank had lived on a farm next door to Jebet's family when they were in Ethiopia, but they had been separated when they all fled to escape the Sahel Drought.

While Jebet's family had ultimately ended up in Ngong, Maria and Frank had built a small home for themselves in a tiny town called Eldoret. Although they greatly missed Susan and her family, they didn't get to see each other often. Jebet, Rita and Mama Susan had obligations to the orphanage and couldn't often leave the children for long periods of time. Maria was unable to travel after she had lost the use of her legs in a farm accident that happened in her mid-thirties. But after sensing Jebet and her family needed a break, three Australian orphanage volunteers graciously offered to stay with the children over the holidays so that Jebet, Rita and Mama Susan could go and visit Maria and Frank in Eldoret.

Jebet and her family arrived at their extended family's home on the night before Christmas Eve. Maria and Frank had decorated the house with curly ribbon. They spent the next few days together eating meat, attending church and singing carols while Frank played harmonica and Maria gazed lovingly at him from her wheelchair.

Two days after Christmas, once the festivities had peaked and everyone was lounging about the house, tired and happy, the family watched the results of the presidential election on television. President Mwai Kibaki was declared the winner and trouble had started to brew as soon as the results were revealed. The family looked on, frantic and dismayed, as supporters of Kibaki's opponent, Raila Odinga of the Orange Democratic Movement, took to the streets, screaming accusations of electoral manipulation. The protests predominantly took place in Odinga's homeland of Nyanza Province. A few popped up in the slums of Nairobi, but remained, for the most part, non-violent, and demonstrated solely by voice.

As the hours and days ticked forward, the police ended up firing their guns in attempts to stop the protesting and demonstrators were shot in clear view of TV cameras. Along with the rest of the nation, Jebet and her family watched the police shootings over and over, knowing that demonstrators were on the path to rebellion and violence. In one form or another, they would take over.

In quick time, the protests grew more and more heated, and the family watched, horrified, as they became particularly aggressive and, ultimately, turned into targeted ethnic violence. As the protests heightened, fear bubbled up inside Maria and Frank's home. The most vulnerable group was the Kikuyu people — the community where President Kibaki was from. The Eldoret area was filled with its members. Not knowing where else to turn, Maria and Frank sought refuge by taking the entire family back to the church where they had been days before to celebrate Christ's birth.

For the most part, the church remained dark, quiet and still as the Eldoret people waited for the violent protests to stop. As time passed, hundreds of people trickled through the church's doors, each afraid of what might happen; they all wanted to be in the safest place they knew. The people brought with them a few comforts of home, as well as small amounts of food, which ended up being shared throughout the group.

With tears of fear streaming down trembling chins, the Eldoret people joined hands and prayed silently together — their words were quiet, but their motions were strong, focused and emphatic. Toddlers sat curled in their mothers' arms, unaware of details but knowing something bad was going on; crying babies were shushed over and over, their mamas trying to get them to be quiet in fear of being heard and identified.

Maria, stuck in her wheelchair, was forced to sit in one place, frightened as she was, as she couldn't get around the many mattresses that had been set up as beds, while Frank paced throughout the church, wanting to do more but unable to help.

Out of sheer exhaustion, Jebet had fallen into a light sleep on a section of the mattress puzzle that had been pushed together in the centre of the church, only to quickly awaken to a new buzz of emotion. The church people were huddled in groups, banded together by fear and whispering in the dark. Then, listening.

From far away, Jebet could hear murmured chants repeated over and over in unison, followed by songs sung by an impromptu choir. As she listened, the chants and songs got closer. As they drew even nearer, Jebet recognized what she thought were youthful voices. The sound was later identified as two hundred teenagers and young adults chanting war songs as they closed in on the church. When they were close enough to identify words, Jebet heard their voices ringing out in the still air, maliciously accusing the church campers of contributing to political corruption and voting for President Kibaki. The boys surrounded the church, fighting off the citizens standing guard at its door, and making roadblocks to ensure no help could get through to the compound.

Some of the boys carried bows and arrows while others carried cans of gasoline, which they dumped in a double circle surrounding the church. When the match was struck, the blaze happened quickly, and pain within the church emerged as rapidly as the ferocious flames travelled.

Barbaric chaos erupted as the Eldoret people fought for their lives and tried to escape the inferno. People scratched their way over others as they tried to make it to the windows, where they knew they could breathe again. Those who had been sitting near the front of the church didn't have a chance and the smell of their burned flesh made Jebet retch as she searched frantically for her family. Her eyes scanned pandemonium and she found Frank trying desperately to carry Maria over his shoulders. Having been confined to a wheelchair for so many years, her weight had surpassed his over the years, and his muscles fell limp underneath her. Rita and Mama Susan tried to help, each taking one of Maria's arms and dragging her over the items that had been left behind by people escaping through windows.

The fire licked its way through the mattresses at increased speed. The wildness and ferocity of the flames mounted.

The three women and Frank attempted to lift Maria through the window. The flames were quickly closing in, and the women's strength lost steam. Frank refused to leave his wife, and yelled at Mama Susan, Jebet and Rita to free themselves from the church. He turned back to his wife.

Frank held Maria close, trying to protect her from the heat. He sang loudly over the scorching fire that ultimately silenced their bodies and voices.

With her own burning skin no longer giving her a choice, Jebet hauled herself through the window, clumsily falling six feet to the dirty, hard ground outside. She crawled away on all fours, coughing and heaving, gasping for clean air and praying that her mama and sister were right behind her.

Jebet turned to search the crowds, desperate to find her sister and mama but unable to do so. Horrified, she watched as one of the activists grabbed a hold of a mother and baby who had managed to escape the church and were scurrying away from the blaze. The mother screamed for help as the young boy's arms wrapped around her, fighting the mother for her child. The demonstrator won. He seized the baby from the mother's arms, and threw the child through the open window, back into the welcoming flames.

Not knowing what else to do, Jebet lobbed herself into a nearby ditch; she pretended to be dead. A demonstrator carrying a bow around his shoulder, with three arrows in his hands, saw her lying on the ground, and kicked her hard with his right boot. Somehow, Jebet managed to stifle her cry, and when the second and third blow hit her ribs, she thought her forced silence would no longer be required. She knew she would soon die. But like a prayer being answered, the boy suddenly seemed satisfied with the limp body in front of him, and moved on to find his next victim.

Jebet lay in the ditch, her nose smashed into red clay dirt as she inhaled its contents. The church continued to burn, creating heavy clouds of smoke that choked up both the demonstrators and the church campers who had managed to escape.

When Jebet felt certain the protestors were no longer around her, she jumped up and hurried to find her family. Running as fast as her limp legs would carry her, she finally saw her mother and Rita clinging to one another, a circle of weaponed boys pacing around them, taunting them with their force. The boys took turns delivering kicks with their boots, graciously allowing each member a turn.

The punches came next, until both the mother and her child were no longer able to stand. Mama Susan was the first to crumple to her knees. She was quickly followed by a defeated Rita.

Jebet stayed frozen in fear as she watched her mother and sister beg for their lives, clasping hands together in a prayer position as the boys continued to deliver blows to their heads. It wasn't long before they collapsed. As Jebet watched in horror, Mama Susan and Rita lay heaped together on the ground, hugging one another as the teenagers delivered the final blows that killed them both, and the life Jebet once knew.

## 19

I was silent, trying to absorb all that Mama Bu had told me. I was horrified to hear the tragic story she had exposed and deeply saddened
to learn about everything Jebet had been through. The tragedies Jebet
had faced and the multiple losses she had personally suffered were too
numerous and devastating to even imagine.

"When did this all happen?" I asked quietly. I looked down at my
hands. Bit my lip to try to void my eyes of tears.

"Almost exactly a year ago, Nicky," Mama Bu responded, patting
my knee and shaking her head. "As you can imagine, it has been a very
rough year for Jebet. She has not been the same since she returned

from Eldoret. She has turned into an entirely different person. The only way I can put it is that she was broken when she returned. Her eyes were different. Her mood. Everything she said and did. She was just . . . different. It was like one person left for Eldoret and another person returned to Ngong."

"Like something in her snapped?" I asked.

"Yes, *rafiki*. Exactly like that."

The tears I had been fighting fell. "I had an uncle who went through a massive tragedy and he responded in a very similar way. He lost his wife — my mother's sister — in a car accident and he was never the same person again. Ultimately he was diagnosed with mental illness. He has been on medication ever since, but, even with the meds, he's not the same guy I remember from when I was younger. It's like he died when my aunt died."

"It is really sad. It is so difficult to watch someone you care about go through something so tragic and lose so much that their soul becomes smothered. Like the fire inside them is put out. And no matter what they do, or what anyone else does, they simply cannot seem to find themselves again."

I nodded, wiping a tear from my cheek. "So what do we do now, Mama Bu?" I asked. "Jebet's story is absolutely awful, but we can't let her continue hurting the children."

"You are right. I will come with you tomorrow when you go in to teach at the school," Mama Bu responded. She rubbed her chin. "I am not quite sure what I will say to Jebet, or what should happen now, but we have got to stop her from hurting those children. I have always known the post-election violence, and all that Jebet went through there, had changed her, but this is too much. It is understandable if she is no longer the loving woman she once was with those children, but all of this? It is too much. It is not right." Mama Bu closed her eyes.

"I will figure something out by tomorrow. I have to sleep on it tonight and the answer will come."

"Well, I'm glad to have you on my side with this. I've missed you."

"I wish I could have been here this week, Nicky. It was just not possible."

"I know."

"How have things been, other than what you've told me? I know there has been a lot that has happened, but how have you enjoyed your stay in Kenya otherwise?"

I shrugged. I thought about the best way to answer her question. "Well, I adore the kids, as I think you know. They are all so special. Adorable, really. And so full of innocence."

Mama Bu nodded. "Yes, they really are. Very special, indeed."

"And I've loved staying here. You and Petar and Kiano — you've really welcomed me into your home. I will forever be grateful for that."

More nodding. "We are happy to make you feel at home. I hope you will continue to feel that way."

I paused, then, unsure of what else to say.

"Anything more? Good or bad, *rafiki*?"

"I don't know. It's harder, I guess. Harder than what I was thinking it would be like."

"What were you expecting?"

"I guess . . . I don't really know. I thought it would be difficult, particularly seeing the kids at the orphanage. But you know what? That's been the easy part. They are so full of life and energy. They are so happy, yet they have nothing. It's amazing, really. Amazing to watch."

"So what is bothering you so?"

"The things I wasn't prepared for, I guess. The garbage smoke. It's everywhere. And I'm constantly sick because of it. I think it might be my allergies, but I can't stop coughing or sneezing. I've always been really sensitive."

"You also might have a cold. The children at the orphanage? They are always sick. Makes it easy to pick up their bugs until you are immune."

I nodded, realizing she was right.

I continued, "I also didn't realize there would be so much violence. I've always known that people from Africa have really suffered because of external and environmental factors — drought, famine, poverty — but I never suspected there would also be so much suffering from each *other*. It's not okay for people to beat each other to death. It's not okay for orphanage directors to hit children until they bleed . . . or *worse*."

Mama Bu nodded, agreeing. "You are right, *rafiki*."

"So then tell me, Mama Bu, how do you cope with it?"

"I have gotten used to it, I guess. But it still bothers me. And frightens me. I wish I could do something to change it, but it is the way it is here, I am afraid."

"And Jebet?"

"Well, hopefully that is one way we *can* do something to help. We will get Jebet to stop hurting those children. One way or another, we will make sure it happens. Together." Mama Bu put her arm around me, bringing me in for a squeeze. Then she continued, "You know, Nicky, I am a really good listener. If there something else you want to talk about, I would love to listen."

She paused, watching my face.

"You do not seem right at night, tossing and turning in your bed. Kiano and Petar sleep right through everything, but I have *mama* ears. I hear your tears. I see your pain. What is the matter, dolly? Do you want to talk about it with Mama Bu?"

I looked at the woman I had grown so fond of, wondering how she could know all the pain I had kept inside since arriving in Kenya. With all of her wisdom and warmth, she was very special, and I suddenly couldn't keep the story inside any longer.

Like lava erupting from a volcano, my words poured out. Without conscious thought of what I was even saying, the story of Eric and the loss of our daughter came bursting out.

I had tried to bury my feelings by escaping to a new life, but even *that* couldn't silence me. Just as I had done immediately after we lost Ella, I had an innate need to talk about her and all that Eric and I had been through.

Through it all, Mama Bu sat patiently, absorbing every word that I said while she listened. She nodded her head in sympathy throughout my story and I could tell by her warm eyes that her own heart was clenched with pain as she learned what had really happened to me.

As I continued the story, Mama Bu moved closer. When I described Ella to her, she squeezed my knee and handed me the tea cloth she had resting on her shoulder. I wiped away my tears, and passed it back when she shed her own.

"Eric and I tried to make it work, but somehow we never found our way. I still love him with all of my heart, but I feel as though he left me when Ella died. No matter how hard I tried, and no matter what I did, I just couldn't seem to bring him back to me. He's gone. Like Ella." I sobbed into Mama Bu's arms, which she opened fully to me.

"*Rafiki*, losing a child affects *mamas* and *babas* in different ways. It happens far too often here as well, and I have seen many marriages fall apart after a couple goes through something so devastating. We all know that men and women are completely different. It is only natural that you and Eric responded in your own way."

I sniffled, then blew my nose into the tea cloth.

"In marriage, *rafiki*, two become one by turning to each other. In grief though, particularly with the loss of a child, the *mama* and *baba* often turn away from each other, and become even more alone. It should never, ever happen, but sometimes, like all things in life, it does."

"But why didn't Eric want to protect me and take care of me the way he should? The way he always has? Why did it feel like he didn't love me?"

"I do not know, child. Maybe the grief was too much for him to be able to cope with. Maybe it took everything in him to just exist. You both went through the absolute hardest kind of sadness — the kind that reaches down to the bottom of your soul. But it hit you in different ways. And you reacted in different ways."

"He pretended like Ella just didn't exist. He erased her from his mind. Do you know he went back to *work*? Two *days* after she died?"

"I suspect Eric was trying to flee his pain. Men . . . they go through grief like they are in a cocoon . . . they wrap themselves in it as they try to deal with the suffering. They want no part of the world that is making them feel so sad. Unfortunately, this all happens at the exact same time the *mama* desperately needs her husband for her support. I am so very sorry to hear what happened to you and Eric, but unfortunately it is not surprising."

As I listened to Mama Bu's explanation, it dawned on me that I had done the same thing as Eric. Ultimately, when things got *really* bad and our marriage fell apart, I ran. I fled my pain, and the only world I knew. I needed to get away from everything, but instead of burying myself in work, like Eric did, I went to Africa.

I sniffled into the tea cloth, now drenched in our shared tears. After such a long time facing internal grief, feelings of relief pulsed through my heart as I listened to Mama Bu. She was kind and thoughtful — and so in tune with what Eric and I had been through.

"You know these men, Nicky, they talk only for practical reasons.

Even in everyday life, they only want to talk about something so they can come to a solution, and then just move on. But us women? We want to talk about all that happened to us . . . and usually over and over until we have over-evaluated and over-analyzed every last detail."

"Yes," I agreed, laughing. "Eric used to always accuse me of 'analysis paralysis.' He said I could talk about any detail until I forgot what I was talking about. But Eric? He never wanted to talk about *anything*. Sometimes, he wouldn't even want to tell me about how his day at work was."

"Hmmph. Kiano too! And he always approaches any situation with his head. Our men, they think on *facts* and seem to talk *only* to find a solution." Mama Bu's voice turned gentle. "But with the loss of a child, there is not a solution. So they do not talk. They just try to avoid the situation."

I nodded, remembering, as though it had just happened yesterday.

"And this reaction of theirs does not mix with the fact that women . . . well, we just want to talk about *everything* that has happened. Finding a solution is not why we talk . . . we just want to know that someone is listening. And usually we want that person to be our husband. We approach loss — especially big loss — with our hearts. We need to discuss. We need to ponder. *Babas* . . . they need to move on."

"Like Eric did."

"Yes, like Eric did."

"I guess I understand what you are saying. But why couldn't he heal? Why couldn't he take the time to be in his damn cocoon and then come back to me?"

"Everyone's time is different, Nicky. Maybe he still will."

"No. It's really over. *We're* over. We're separated now, Eric and I. There's no turning back. Too much has changed. We've gone through too much."

"Maybe you are right. Maybe."

"So how do *I* get through this? How do I stop hurting?" I asked Mama Bu, craving more words from her. Each one seemed to be lifting the teeniest, tiniest piece of the world off my shoulders.

"I do not know that you ever will. But I can promise you that it *will* get easier," Mama Bu replied, lifting my chin. "But you need to know that for you, *rafiki*, your way of dealing with Ella's death was the right way. For *you*. Whatever you did, and whatever you need to do now, well, that is okay too. You have got to cope *your* way. Dealing with something this big takes you one step from survival and you have got to do what you can to not shut down. And my belief is that ignoring something big like this that happened — by shutting the door in its face — well, it just ends up darkening each day you have got to live. But by *talking* about it, and living *through* it, will help you to step out of death's nasty shadow."

"I know. I agree. And I'm trying! Really, I am. But I just miss Ella so much — and I only knew her for less than a day," I cried.

"No, child, you knew her for a lifetime. And you knew her well for the nine months that you carried her. The nine months that God gives to us is a gift to a *mama* and her child. God brought you together in the most intimate form. You felt her kicks, her movements, her presence. You felt *her*. And you loved her. You will always love Ella." Mama Bu squeezed her cheeks with the palms of her hands. "Bless your soul, child, you will never lose her, no matter how much you talk or do not talk about her. We do not lose the people we love, even to death. The presence you felt for nine months — and the glorious day she was here on earth — well, those moments will continue to participate in every action you take and every thought you make for the rest of your *life*. Ella has left a mark on your soul and there is *no one* and *nothing* that can take that from you."

I smiled through tears at my host mother, thankful to be sitting with her in that moment. She seemed to have a gift for making me feel better. A way of encouraging me to think beyond only my view. Her words gave me perspective, particularly coming from someone who hadn't gone through it directly with me, but who had experienced more than her fair share of tough times and grief. "Thanks, Mama Bu. You've made me feel so much better."

"Nothing really that I did, Nicky. I swear to you, you do not feel better because of me. You feel better because of the chai." Mama Bu winked at me. "As the expression goes around here, 'There is nothing that a big, steaming cup of chai can't make better.' At least, a little bit better."

"Well, then, no wonder I feel like my heart is starting to heal, even if just a little bit. I've had more tea in my time here than all the tea I've had in my life!"

"Well, maybe that is the solution with Jebet too? I will just go and talk to her honestly, over some good chai that I will bring by. She is probably hurting, just as much as you. The girl has got to let it out! I never wanted to press her, because she seemed so resistant to talking about the post-election attacks. But it is now way past her wanting to talk. She has got to get better, and if she does not, those children need someone who will take better care of them."

"Are you and Jebet close?"

"We used to be. I spent so much time there that we had developed a chummy friendship. But like I said, she is different now. She is different without her *mama* and sister, Rita. Not many people know about what happened, because Jebet blocked everyone out when she got back. And she lied about what happened. As far as most people know around here, her *mama* and sister stayed with her aunt to take care of her. Jebet did not want to talk about it or receive any sympathy or have to deal with it at all. She just wanted to ignore it and make it go away."

"Kind of like Eric did. . . ." I murmured, thinking of all Mama Bu and I had just talked about.

"She certainly blocks people out. And her feelings too. It is probably one of the reasons she has never married. My guess is that she lies to protect her heart from *everything*. She does not want anyone to know just how little she has — no father, no husband, no children — and then the only family she had left was taken as well." Mama Bu shook her head, sorrow filling her warm, brown eyes.

"Why is it that you know her story?" I asked, not surprised, but intrigued to know why Mama Bu knew the truth when no one else did.

"I picked up on some things when we spent time on the orphanage porch swing, having our chai. A few things were not adding up and I asked her about it. Jebet collapsed into tears and there was no way out after that. She swore me to secrecy, and so far I have not told anyone. Not even Kiano. But that was before I knew she was *really* hurting the kids at Kidaai. If Jebet cannot cope with her loss, she must get out of that orphanage. And we will figure that plan out together."

I nodded my head. I was distraught by what had happened to Jebet and her family, but couldn't allow her personal pain to put the children in jeopardy.

"But *rafiki*, I trust that you will not tell anyone about what happened to Jebet in Eldoret. No matter what she has done, she deserves for her story to be kept in confidence."

I promised, knowing that I could never send any more hurt Jebet's way by letting her secret escape. She had been through too much already and deserved the respect of deciding who should or should not know of the enormous tragedy that had taken place on that deadly day in Eldoret.

Later that afternoon, after we finished cleaning the kitchen, it was time to do the laundry. I hadn't done it since arriving in Kenya.

"My guess is that you are wearing some pretty dirty clothes, *rafiki*?" I blushed, given that my clothes were, admittedly, all filthy. I had tried to keep them as clean as I could, but I didn't want to waste water and I wasn't sure how I should be washing my clothes. Mama Bu hadn't been there and I doubted that Kiano and Petar had ever done a load of laundry in their lives.

"Here, I will show you how we do it," Mama Bu said, grabbing laundry from her bedroom. Then she grabbed Petar's. "Go on, now. Get what you want to wash."

I hurried to my room, filled my arms with dirty clothes and returned to the living room.

"We have got to fill the two buckets out back. It is okay to use the water for this. We wash our clothes every week too, you know. We just do not have those fancy machines you have back home. It is all in our arm muscle. With a little bit of soap."

I carried my clothes to the backyard. It had turned into a hot and steamy day and my face was glowing with sweat before I even started my washing workout.

Mama Bu showed me how to fill both tubs with cold water, placing soap in one and leaving the other for rinsing. Since there was no hot water that could be used, Mama Bu explained that we would need to be even more "spirited with scrubbing" to ensure the germs and stains came out.

We dumped as many clothes as would fit into the soap bucket, and rubbed them vigorously against each other to get the dirt out.

I scrubbed and scrubbed. Scrubbed harder. And harder. Then . . .

"Not like that, silly. You've got to put soap on the clothes and rub the corners of the shirt together, over the stain," Eric teased. He took my shirt from me to demonstrate.

We had just moved into our first apartment together, which was "simply charming," as Eric's mother had said. So charming, in fact, that it didn't have a washer — or a dryer.

We had planned on doing our laundry that Sunday afternoon, but had gotten distracted christening the bedroom . . . and then the living room . . . and, finally, the shower.

We arrived at the Laundromat half an hour after it closed. With nowhere to do our laundry, and in need of clothes for work the next morning, Eric and I were using our bathtub.

"There, Nic. That coffee stain you spilled on your shirt this morning? Completely gone." He handed me my shirt and gave me a delicate kiss on the tip of my nose. . . .

"Nicky? I think that one is clean," Mama Bu said, pointing to the shirt I had overwashed.

"What? Oh, thanks. I guess I got lost in thought for a minute. . . ."

We finished the laundry, and I stood to full height, stretching my back. I was soaked, both from the bucket splashes and the sweat that has resulted from how hard I had scrubbed. I stretched further, then fell back to the ground, exhausted, lying on the dirt.

"Tough work, *rafiki*?" Mama Bu asked, teasing me about avoiding hard laundry work for my whole life. She splashed droplets of water from her hands onto my face. Despite being dirty, the cool water was refreshing and I resisted the temptation to jump into the bucket. I sat up.

"It is definitely that. I never knew my washing machine had to work so hard!" I retorted, splashing her back.

Before I knew it, Mama Bu and I were in an all-out water fight. We ended up in heaps on the ground, dripping wet and laughing uncontrollably.

She winked at me, then, almost as if she knew the water fight and the gut-aching laughter that resulted were exactly what I needed.

## 20

When Mama Bu and I got to the orphanage the next morning, Johanna told us that Jebet was still sleeping. I could see the surprise register on Mama Bu's face and she murmured to me that Jebet had typically been an early riser, getting up at the crack of dawn to brush the kids' teeth and prepare their breakfast with Mama Susan and Rita.

"No, no . . . she no done that for long as I been here. She sleep to end of morning. Sometimes lunch," Johanna said, shaking her head. "She no help me feed kids. Only by myself."

"Well, that is it, then. There will be no more of it. That woman has an orphanage to run," Mama Bu retorted. I watched her disappear up the steps, a knot forming in my stomach, before I turned and made my way into the school room to start preparing for that day's lesson.

Five minutes before I was about to ring the bell, Jebet stormed into the classroom. "You causing trouble 'round here, girly?"

"N-no, Jebet. I just want to make sure the children are alright. And safe."

"Bu know 'bout what happened last week with Gracie. I wonder how *that* happened?!" Jebet screamed at me. Her hair was disheveled and frizzy, and it looked like she was wearing the same muumuu that she had slept in. I could see her fat belly jiggling under the dress as she screamed.

Mama Bu flew into the classroom directly behind the orphanage director. "Jebet, I told you, I do not know exactly what has been going on around here, but I wanted to make sure you are okay. It is just me, your friend, wanting to know that all is right with you. Now, come, we will sit on the porch and you can wake up with some of my famous chai."

They left, but my hands were still shaking from fear, and I needed to get out of the classroom to clear my head. I found Johanna in the kitchen, just about to serve each child their breakfast. She had lined the plates in multiple rows of five, and had just started scooping some unknown form of yellowish slop onto each plate.

The older children came to retrieve the plates from the kitchen, and took them to the hungry bellies waiting in the common room. The children slurped up the slop in a matter of minutes, still looking hungry, and I asked Johanna about seconds.

"No, no . . . there not enough for more than one per child. That's it."

"What about you? Have you eaten? You need to make sure you get something as well." Johanna seemed to be even skinnier than the last time I saw her, and I was suddenly concerned.

"Me? No, I not so good these days," Johanna said, looking a little green. "Can't keep nothing down. Try to eat to feed my l'il one, but most times, well, I just start puking my stomach out." Johanna patted her belly.

"Wait . . . you're *pregnant*?" I asked, unable to hide my surprise. I had had no idea, and certainly hadn't suspected anything given how tiny Johanna was. She wasn't even showing.

"Yes ma'am. More than halfway through."

"Does Jebet know?" I asked, suddenly worried that Jebet would kick Johanna out.

"Yes . . . she why I got work in the first place. Jebet be mean to those chil'n, but she took care of me when I got nowhere to go. I got no family to turn to, and no husband. And my friends go away. I lost my job when my bump came and I told my boss I pregnant. Jebet took me in, and now I got food and safety and water and a place to sleep."

"But . . . you're not even showing. How did your previous employer know you were pregnant?"

"I lost weight since then," Johanna said quickly. "It was bad time. Plus now I in looser shirt and pant so harder to tell."

The children started coming into the kitchen, carrying their plates and placing them in the sink. They greeted me with chirpy, singsong voices and I could tell they were genuinely happy to see me. Gracie ran to me, hugging my legs and pulling at my arms.

"*Mwalimu* Nicky, we got surprise for you," a few of them cried out at the same time. "We sing you song. We practise a lot." Ten of the children, all of them Maasai, pulled at my arms and shirt to drag me into the common room, before quickly lining up in a row.

Together, the children started singing a song in their tribal language, Maa. They jointly danced and kept the beat of the music by fluidly bending their knees in sync before pushing their little bums out behind them and bending their waists forward over and over and over throughout the song. The children who weren't singing with them watched from the sidelines, laughing and clapping along.

"*Oh! Oh oh oh oh oh oh! Yo quiero vivir como un Maasai! Yo quiero vivir como un Maasai! Oh! Oh oh oh oh oh!*"

"How wonderful! That was amazing!" I exclaimed when they were finished. I suddenly felt more a part of the Maasai culture.

"It Maasai song for you," John called out, clapping his hands. It was obvious how proud he was of himself and his songmates. "We happy you here. Wanted to do nice thing."

My heart swelled and I wrapped the little boy in my arms, waving the others to come in and join us. One by one, they piled on top of John and me, until we were all giggling uncontrollably. Every one of the children had a wide smile on his or her face, and it hit me with mixed emotions how a little love — just a *very* little — could give them so much.

"I love your hair," Esther said, gently combing through it with her fingers. I knew her hands were filthy and probably crusty with snot, but I didn't care. I had long ago accepted my time in Africa wasn't going to be daisy-fresh.

When I noticed Gracie shyly hanging back from the crowd I motioned her over. I hadn't stopped thinking of her since the previous week, and I was relieved to be spending more time with her. She snuggled into my cross-legged lap, and opened her heart up to receive the love I had to give. Thankfully, she seemed to be doing well.

"Are you okay?" I asked her quietly.

She said nothing, but nodded and smiled. I took it as a good sign.

"You come outside with us?" Ita asked, his inquisitive face hopeful and innocent.

"I'd love to. Why don't we go out there and start the day by playing in the field. I'm sure we can think of lots of fun gym games to play." I made the quick decision to switch gears from my previous lesson plans. It was a beautiful day, and it would be good to show the children some new organized games.

Once in the field, I could see Jebet and Mama Bu sitting on the porch; it was clear they were having a heated discussion. Jebet was animated, throwing her hands in the air, and Mama Bu kept shaking her head. Every once in a while, Mama Bu would bury her head in her hands. Their voices were raised, but both the distance and the language barrier prevented me from understanding what they were saying.

I introduced the kids to a game called Doggy Where's Your Bone — a favourite childhood game of mine where a blindfolded child sits in the middle of a circle and places the "bone" (in this case, a stick) behind her back until one of the other students quietly sneaks up and takes the bone without her hearing them; the successful bone stealer then takes their turn in the middle of the circle.

As I watched Nadia try to successfully rescue the bone in an attempt to steal the coveted position of "doggy," Mama Bu came up behind me and gently put her hand on my shoulder. "Unfortunately we have to go, Nicky," she said sadly. "Jebet has asked that we both leave."

"But I just got here! And I haven't begun to teach the children *anything*," I cried, disappointed to hear the news that I, once again, would need to leave the kids. "She kicked me out for the remainder of last week, and I went crazy not being here. I'm so happy to be back! Do you think she'll talk to me? I'd like to try to convince her to let me stay."

"She needs to cool off, Nicky. She is more upset and disturbed by my questions than I anticipated, and she is mad that I 'stuck my nose in it all,' as she so clearly just said to me. Do not worry, I know she will not want you to stay away forever. To be honest, I think she will want you to come back soon because she will not want to deal with taking care of the children all day, every day."

"I hope you're right."

"Jebet's not well, I am sorry to say. My guess is that if you give it a day or two, and then come back, she will say nothing when you return. The teachers' strike is still going on, so Hasina will not be here and Jebet has no one else to mind the children all day."

I watched the children play their new game. My heart crumbled. I didn't want to disappoint them — or myself — and was so delighted to be back with them. Plus, I was worried about what Jebet might do now that she was in her snit.

Mama Bu gently pushed me forward. Begrudgingly, I tried to explain to the children that I needed to leave for the day.

"I'll be back tomorrow," I said. Esther quickly translated for me.

"*No!*" the children cried in unison.

"*Mwalimu* Nicky . . . *tafadhali ngoja*," Ita said. Teacher Nicky . . . please stay.

"We need you!" John piped up. "Please, don't go!"

"Please, *don't go!*" Sadika yelled at me. She stomped her feet and angrily threw the stick she had been holding into the empty field. It reminded me of the two-year-old temper tantrums I had so frequently witnessed with Eric's nieces and nephews.

I looked at Mama Bu, quietly asking her if there was any way we could find a way to stay. When she shook her head, her eyes filled with sadness and regret, I trusted that there was no way around leaving for the day.

"I'll be back as soon as I can. I promise." I blinked back my tears and told the children to watch out for one another. "You take care of each other, do you hear me? And if you need anything at all, go and find Johanna. She'll help you."

I looked at Mama Bu. "Can you give me five minutes?" She nodded yes.

I quickly made my way to the back kitchen door to find Johanna.

"Time for dishes now," Johanna said nervously, nodding at the pile she was tackling. She seemed skittish and a bit panicked. "Don't wanna upset Jebet or . . . I lose job."

"Here, I'll help you. I've got a few minutes to spare, and you shouldn't be on your feet for so long!" I grabbed a tea towel and started drying the dishes that Johanna had washed.

"What happen with Bu and Jebet?" Johanna asked quietly.

"I think Mama Bu is worried about Jebet, just like we all are. Something isn't right, and we want to help her." I pressed gently, not wanting Johanna to shut me out. "Johanna, I was *really* upset at what I saw happen to Gracie last week. You mentioned that day that you see Jebet use her stick on the children regularly. Can you tell me more about that?"

"Me no say. I get kicked out. Bu take care of everythin' now that she here. It okay."

"That's true, Johanna, but for today Mama Bu and I are going to have to leave. I'll be back tomorrow though — bright and early. Jebet isn't happy right now and has told both Mama Bu and I that we need to go home. I think she is upset or embarrassed that we know about what happened with Gracie." I took a deep breath and continued. "I won't be here, Johanna, so I need to know that you'll watch out for the children. And that you'll protect them and keep them safe. Can you do that, Johanna?"

"I try, but Jebet sometimes real mean. Especially when she mad. Is she really mad? I scared for what happen." Johanna looked around her for a chair. I could tell she needed to sit down.

"Has Jebet always been like that, Johanna?"

"Ever since I come to work, but that only couple months ago now. But the older chil'n tell me she not been like that b'fore. She just like that now."

"What does she do?"

"She hurt 'em. Lots of 'em. With her stick, or foot — sometimes lots of kicks. She punch 'em, too. Jebet get real angry sometimes."

I cringed. Hearing the words out loud turned them into more of a reality. I started to ask Johanna for examples, but she cut me off mid-sentence. "I say no more, Nicky. I wanna help, but I scared. You don't need know nothing except that them chil'n scared of Jebet. Real scared. Just watch 'em and you'll know how bad it is. I no wanna say. Don't wanna get Jebet mad, or she might hurt the chil'n — or me."

"Does she hit you too?" I asked Johanna. I hadn't even thought of that as a possibility.

"Not real bad, but she push. And sometimes she pinch real hard. But I can take pinches, as long as I gotta place to stay and food to eat. I be okay." Johanna's gaze revealed both truth and sadness. She shifted her eyes downwards.

"Do you have a cell phone?" I asked Johanna. My fear for Jebet and what she might do was escalating by the minute.

"No, but Jebet do. She leave it in the kitchen drawer mostly so I know where it is. I can't use it though. She might get mad."

"Well, as long as you have an emergency phone that you can use if you need to, that makes me feel a bit better. If anything happens at all, please call me immediately. Here is my cell phone number. I'll leave it on all day — morning, noon and night," I said. I wrote my cell phone number down on a piece of paper and made her promise to call if she needed *any* help. When Johanna finally agreed, I slipped out the back door before an angry Jebet could find me in her kitchen.

## 21

After our mandatory evacuation at the orphanage, I told Mama Bu I would see her back at the house. I wanted to use my free afternoon responding to a few friends' emails that I had been avoiding. I had always intended to respond properly, but it seemed that every previous minute I had spent in Kenya was with either my host family or the children at the orphanage.

I paid my fee and sat down at the only open computer left in the small room. I waited through the click-click-click of the slowly creeping internet; I was now used to its speed, but no more patient with its sluggishness.

When Yahoo! finally flipped from that day's headlines to my inbox, the third email nearly flattened my lungs.

*Eric.*

I hadn't spoken to him in 127 days — not that I was counting.

The subject line was a casual and breezy "Hi." I paused before opening the email. A big part of me was desperate to soak up every word he wrote — the other part of me nervous, and not really sure I wanted to communicate with him at all.

Read or delete? Read or *delete*?

I promised myself that I would count to ten before making a decision. I started counting: one . . . two . . . three . . .

Forget it, I couldn't make it to ten.

I clicked the email open.

> Nicky,
> I don't know what to say, except that I miss you.
> I think of you every minute of every day.
> How are you?
> Love, Eric

I read the email fourteen times before his words sank in. Then, following a solid minute during which I stared blankly at the screen and contemplated what to write, I began my reply.

And then I deleted it.

> ~~Hi Eric — I'm great! I'm in Africa and it is fantastic — I am loving my time here!~~

I started again, and hit the backspace key once more.

~~Eric — I miss you too. So very, very much!
I'm miserable and cry myself to sleep every
night without you. Even my host mother
knows how upset I constantly am — she
heard me crying at night, which I'm pretty
embarrassed about. What happened to us?~~

Again.

~~Hello, Eric. Nice to hear from you. It has
been a while~~

Until — finally,

Hi Eric,

Thanks for your email — it was really nice to
hear from you. I miss you too and think of
you often. A lot, actually.

Not sure if you heard or not, but I am in
Africa, volunteering in the classroom at an
orphanage. I needed the break. Needed to
clear my head. It has been challenging, but
rewarding. There are so many people (particularly the children who I am working with)
who need so much, and I really struggle with
it since I only have so much to give. But the
kids are adorable and full of life, energy and
happiness — despite having next to nothing.
A wise person once told me that they would

give me far more than I could ever give
them, and I already believe this to be true.
How are you doing? I would love to
know everything.

Love,
Nic xoxo

I took a big breath, reread the email one final time, and hit send. I knew I wouldn't be emailing my friends back that day, as originally planned. I was too distracted and practically chewing my nails to nubs.

I paused to let the emotions sink in. For the first time in as long as I could remember, my spirit was breathing again. And my soul felt comfort; it was like being under an oversized quilt with a steaming mug of hot chocolate on a snowy, Saturday morning. *With* Eric.

And then there were other feelings of recognition.

Trickles of excitement.

Hints of bliss.

The flashback feelings took me to a previous evening many moons before, when Eric finally got the nerve to ask me if I'd like to join him for a beer after one of our lifeguarding shifts. The same butterflies resurfaced. The buzz in my brain was reborn. And it was all from a simple email, no more than a few lines long.

I tried to push the memories from my mind. The feelings from my heart. I knew I would be headed into dangerous ground if I couldn't clear them.

Just as I was about force myself to sign out, my inbox notification showed a new message was waiting. Apprehensively, I checked.

More Eric.

Hi Nic,

So great to hear from you! Thanks for
emailing me back — I wasn't sure if you
would. I was just about to hit the gym for
an early morning workout when I saw your
email — and I wanted to write you back
right away.

I loved reading about how you are
doing. I had heard through the grapevine
that you were in Africa, but it was nice to
hear the details from you. Congratulations,
by the way — it sounds very exciting, and
I'm happy for you. It's great to know you are
making such a difference over there — not
that I'm surprised at all. You're one of the
good ones, Nic. Always have been, always
will be. You have a way with people and I
have no doubt you are touching everyone
you meet over there with your generosity,
spirit and kindness.

Things are okay with me. We're pretty
busy at work. Too many cases if you ask
me, and we're all going crazy. I'm working
longer hours than ever before, but I guess
that's a good thing. . . . It is pretty tough to
go home to an empty apartment at the end
of the day. I'm considering getting a dog.
Just a small one. Maybe a wiener dog, or a
wrinkly pug. I've always wanted one, as you

know. I think I'd call him Griffin, after Family
Guy. I'd need to get a dog walker, but they
are all the rage in the city so it would be
pretty easy, I'm sure. We'll see.

Love,
Eric

P.S. How is your family?

I couldn't hit reply fast enough. I craved his words and needed to
hear more.

Eric —

A puppy?! Wow. That would be a big
change for you. I know how much you've
always wanted a dog though, so I'm not surprised to hear you are considering getting
one. My vote is for a wiener dog — they are
so adorable! A former colleague of mine
had one and she said they are the most lov-
able, cuddly dogs. Apparently they are bur-
rowers . . . so they sleep under your covers
at your feet. (That is, if you decide to let him
or her sleep in your bed — although I think I
already know the answer to that one!)
Thank you for your kind words — they
were really encouraging and nice to hear.
I'm going through a rough patch here right

now, and I'm not quite sure what to do.
To be honest, it felt a bit serendipitous
to get your email today . . . all I've been
thinking of lately is how much I wanted to
be working through this problem with you,
to talk to you about it and get your advice.
If you're willing, I'd still love to hear your
perspective. It has always made me feel so
much better. No one seems to have clearer
judgement than you when it comes to these
things.

Love,
Nic

P.S. My family is great. Things are the same
as always for my parents, and my sister is
now in Vietnam . . . always the world traveller! How is your family?

A couple of minutes later, his response came,

Nic — I would love to help you in any way
I can. More than happy to listen to what's
going on and to help you figure out what to
do. I'm at work, but able to chat. Can you
log in to MSN Messenger?

After our agreement of no communication, I had deleted Eric's
name from my MSN list — and thought it would never reappear. But

with his invite, I sent the cursor flying to the "Add a Contact" key and started typing his email address from memory.

Then, like a jolt from nowhere, I couldn't get up from the computer fast enough. The chair I was sitting on flipped behind me as I stood up abruptly.

My heart had sung when I got the first email from Eric, and I had temporarily gotten caught up in it. I even asked him for his advice! But chatting with him so casually now sent fear through my veins.

I had flown thousands of miles around the globe to a world that couldn't be more opposite from the one Eric and I lived in — and I had, in an instant, reverted right back into the simple and comfortable conversation of our past. We couldn't go down that road again. I wouldn't let it happen.

I flew out the internet café door, barely escaping a smackdown with a speeding *matatu*. The driver screamed at me, hanging out the window. "*Chunga! Chunga!*" he screeched. Watch out! Watch out! The driver's arm hung out the window, giving me the finger as he blew by me, leaving a trace of dusty red dirt on my sneakers.

———

"Where have you been for so long, *rafiki*?" Mama Bu asked when I returned to the house. She had just finished scrubbing the floors, which were still a bit wet, and had moved on to dusting the tables. I grabbed a second cloth from the kitchen and began to help her.

"I was emailing a bit and then I took a walk through the market. I thought it might clear my head and make me feel better. No dice, unfortunately."

"No dice?"

"Sorry, I forget about expressions. We use it back home to mean there is no chance or possibility of it happening. My head is still a muddy mess of thoughts!"

"Poor thing, I wish you found your dice. What is on your mind?"

"This whole thing with Jebet is really getting to me. I'm desperate to help the kids and so scared for them. What if one of them gets really hurt? A big part of me thinks I should just go back to the orphanage, even though Jebet kicked me out."

"I know it is different here, Nicky. And I do not like what is going on there any more than you do. But you have to know what you can change here and what you cannot. It is different here than in your Western world. What Jebet did to Gracie is not right, but it happens here all the time. I am not saying we should not keep watch over the children at Kidaai, but fixing all of the problems we have got here in Kenya . . . well, it would be easier to boil the ocean."

"So what do you think we should do?"

"We wait, *rafiki*. We wait."

Mama Bu turned from me then, quietly humming a song I recognized from church. She stopped suddenly. "You have got to trust in God. He knows what is best. He will take care of you, no matter what. He knows. He always knows, and He will guide you to the right spot."

"I heard from Eric," I said gently, anxious to speak to someone about what had happened. I wanted to know Mama Bu's thoughts on it all. "He emailed me and we bounced a few messages back and forth. Pretty casual . . . nothing complicated."

"And how are you feeling about that, dolly?"

"I don't know, to be honest. At first I was excited and so happy to hear from him. I really miss him, you know? It felt like old times . . . before . . . well, just before. But I'm not sure it's a good idea to go there."

"Remember what I told you before, Nicky. There is not a right or a wrong answer. You will know what to do. And whatever you do will be the right decision. Want to know how you will know that it was the right decision? Because you made it."

Mama Bu started humming again, but my thoughts ran rampant against her tune, flipping between the kids at the orphanage and Eric. We continued working, side by side, dusting furniture, washing walls, fluffing couches.

—

That night, I lay in bed, frantic for sleep and hopeful I wouldn't cry out once I found it. The hard bed seemed to be even more uncomfortable than other nights and my right side was numb from lying on the hard surface.

I tried to ignore my thoughts of Eric, struggling to stop my mind from reeling through our earlier email conversations — yet every word played out in my mind, over and over and over.

I wanted to ignore Eric. Yet I couldn't. I wished I wasn't so happy that he had reached out. I had no choice but to force myself to ignore him and, hopefully, start to stifle my feelings for him. I would block him from my email. Permanently remove his name from anything that would allow him to communicate with me. We were over. Finished. And I needed to move on, or I would never find happiness again. It really was as simple as that.

I waited for sleep to take over. Wanted it to find me. When it didn't, I listened to the sounds of Africa that I finally found calming.

Muted bongo drums beat in the distance.

A dog barked twice, then fell silent.

Wind whispered its way through the leaves of the mango trees.

And, then — finally — the almost silent splatter of raindrops against roof.

## 22

The next morning, Johanna tapped lightly at the front door. She came with a message from Jebet, who requested that I return to the orphanage to continue teaching the children.

Nothing was said about the day before, only that she needed someone to mind the children during the day and she wanted me to do it. I refrained from commenting on the description of "minding" the children; although it required forcibly biting my tongue, I didn't want to say anything that might lead to Jebet reneging.

I quickly dressed and walked with Johanna to the orphanage. She was tired, her steps sluggish and slow. She tried to keep up with me and I felt sorry for her. I slowed to match her pace, but didn't voice my concerns about how much she lagged.

"Why did you walk all this way, Johanna? I gave you my cell phone number, why didn't you just call me?"

"Jebet, she tell me to come get you. She not know I have your number, and if I called you, she might take my phone away. Or ask me why you gave me your number. So I just come get you."

"Why did she change her mind?"

"I dunno. But Hasina come by yesterday afternoon and I overhear her talking to Jebet. The teacher strike almost over, but Hasina tell Jebet she no want to go back to orphanage. She found new job, paying more money."

And just like that, Jebet's quick change in attitude was clear. She had no one to teach the kids — or *mind them* as she referred to it — and needed me back at the orphanage to get them out of her hair. I started to ask Johanna more about it, but I could tell she was having a tough time talking as we walked; her voice was raspy and her lungs puffed as she tried to keep up.

Instead, I slowed even more, and let silence take over. I turned my attention to the newfound surroundings around us. The rain that had showered the land throughout the night had covered the outside world with a sheen that resembled slick varnish. Gone were the dust clouds that I had grown so used to; the allergies I had been battling disappeared as though I had taken a heavy dose of antihistamine. The red dirt had deepened in hue, turning to a rich russet, and the air surrounding us held a crisper clarity that felt good to breathe.

We kept walking, my thoughts suddenly on the rainmaker, Wambua. I wondered how he would be celebrating.

Once in the classroom, I was relieved to see the learning stations still set up in the places I had left them. I had been worried that Jebet would take her anger out on the classroom and had been certain I would be returning to upside-down desks.

I retrieved the bell from the teacher desk. I rang it loudly and the children came running. They each hugged me on their way in, taking their seats and facing the front of the room in a style that reminded me of troops taking their posts.

We spent a quiet morning working through math puzzles and English lessons. Bursts of pride pumped through my veins as, one by one, different children absorbed bite-sized pieces of knowledge. I could see their confidence growing with each new thing they learned and I relished the fact that the only face showing more delight than mine was that of the student who had accomplished the task.

Once the children were buried in their activities, I panned the room for any sign of abuse: scrapes, bruises, scars. A child acting isolated and inward. Hurt of any kind.

Thankfully, nothing stuck out.

⁓

A few days later, I called my parents. It had been almost a week since I had spoken to them and I needed to hear their voices — just as I knew they needed to hear mine. It was tough for them, having both Maggie and me gone, and I had promised I would call home as much as I could.

"Mom? It's me! Can you hear me?" I asked, excited to hear her pick up the phone. It was just before eight o'clock in the morning and I had purposely called then as I knew they would likely be at home, drinking their coffee and reading the newspaper.

"Oh, yes, sweetie! I can hear you perfectly. It's so clear it's almost like you are in the same city."

"Nicky? How are you?" my dad asked, once again on the other extension.

"I'm fine. And so glad to be talking to you! I have so much to fill you in on. So much has happened since I last emailed you."

"So fill us in, Nic. How is being a teacher in Africa?" my mother asked. I had sent my close friends and family a detailed email letting them know about the teachers' strike and that I would be taking over the classroom, but they weren't aware of everything else that had gone on. I had thought about emailing just my parents about it but, even then, it somehow didn't feel right to simply email them the tale of the hardships I had learned about and faced.

I was careful to speak of Jebet's story only in vague details. A promise was a promise, after all, and I had given my word to Mama Bu. I told my parents that, despite Jebet's abuse and neglect towards the children, the situation was complicated given Jebet's own recent tragedies, which had changed her, making her jaded and hateful of the world.

"Still, she sounds dangerous. I don't know about this, Nicky," my mom answered. "I think you're right to trust your gut and find a way to get her out of there."

"Mama Bu and I are working on it, Mom. It's just going to take some time. Things don't work here the same way they do back home."

"Speaking of home, Nic, there's something I need to tell you. Eric called. Two nights ago. And he didn't sound like he was doing very well. We hadn't talked to him since you guys sold the house and he seemed almost apologetic for calling, but he said that he really needed to speak with us. That he needs to talk."

I paused, listening to a faint crackle in the phone line starting to set in.

"Nicky? Are you still there?"

"I'm here."

"What do you think about that? I told him I needed to speak to you first and make sure it was okay. If you prefer that we don't see him, we won't. You are our daughter, and you come first. Whatever you feel, or want us to do, is okay and we'll respect that."

"Well, I'm not sure. . . . I wasn't expecting you to say that."

"I know. And I almost didn't, Nic. And I wouldn't have, except that I've never seen that side of Eric before. He's really broken, Nicky. He ended up begging me for our help, something about trying everything else and not knowing where else to turn."

"Er . . . well . . . it's okay, I guess. You can get together with him. I know you were a big part of each other's lives, for a long time . . . and this has been hard on everyone." I gulped, listening to the words coming out of my mouth, but not sure I wanted to be saying them. I was torn — a big part of me wanted to tell my parents to hang up on Eric for good and remove him from their lives, just as I had chosen to do. But another part of me silently wept to hear of Eric's sadness and difficulty moving forward — and if my parents could help him heal, then I felt they should. (Plus, even though I was trying not to admit it to myself, a big part of me wanted to know exactly how Eric was doing, what he was thinking and feeling, and I hoped my parents would share at least some of it with me.)

"Okay, honey, as long as you're sure?" my dad asked.

"No. Really. It's okay. I would tell you. I'm okay if you see Eric. Truly. But I should probably go now. This call is costing a lot and I don't make much of a salary these days!"

"Okay, honey. We love you! Stay safe, and email us soon. We wait every day for another update."

"Will do. I love you guys too. Bye."

I blinked back tears, thinking of my parents — and Eric — thousands of miles away.

## 23

As the days crept forward, the children and I settled into a consistent schedule. We had lessons and activities for the majority of the day, and then spent the second half of our afternoons outside in the field, playing games that reinforced the lessons we had reviewed that morning.

Jebet always kept her distance, although I knew she lurked about. I would see her watching from her bedroom window, thinking the sheer curtain was hiding her stare. Frequently, I could overhear her barking at Johanna; Jebet's words were always clipped and forceful — and easy to hear from far away.

As my number of days in Africa increased, so did my bond with the children at Kidaai; the strength of my connection and innate need to protect them, teach them, guide them and love them surprised me. My attachment to the kids was so strong it was subtly lined in fear. I wondered what would happen when I needed to go home, knowing that it was only a matter of time until I would no longer be able to spend my days with them.

At the end of each week, I was disappointed to greet the long and empty weekend that lay ahead of me. Although Sundays were reserved for church and family time, I began going to the orphanage on Saturdays to hang out with the kids in the common room or play with them outside. I never imposed lessons on Saturdays; we simply spent the time playing together and having fun. I wanted them to be kids. I knew they hadn't had a lot of that — not with all of the chores Jebet made them do.

Each day when I had to leave the children to make it home to Mama Bu and Kiano's before dark, my heart would break a little more. I would miss them, yes, but more than that, it was the fear that something would happen when I was gone.

There hadn't seemed to be any more beatings, but — even when she was keeping her stick to herself — I didn't like the way Jebet treated the children. A ten-year-old chopping firewood for hours, constantly falling behind and desperate to replenish the dwindling stacks that were needed to make a fire for the *jiko*. An eight-year-old forced to get water, which I knew from firsthand experience was even heavier than his own body. A four-year-old forced to clean her sheets if she accidentally wet the bed, lowering her head in embarrassment and shame as she suffered the ridicule that came from her two bedmates.

I craved being with the children in the way I suspected a crack addict needs drugs. I couldn't get enough of them and never tired of teaching them — which was a new phenomenon for me given that in my earlier teaching experiences so many of my previous students had nearly driven me to drink at the end of the day.

I changed all of my previous plans I had to tour Africa; while thinking I would treat myself to a safari to see lions up close, I couldn't seem to tear myself away from the children for long enough to go — and knew there was no way I could spend money on a safari when I could use it to help the kids.

Johanna and I grew closer and I trusted the bond to keep the children safe in my absence. I knew Johanna would call me if I was needed at the orphanage.

"I glad you here, Nicky. It nice havin' you, and you make the chil'n laugh like I never heard," she told me one afternoon after school was over. I was helping her make that night's dinner, and was planning to stay as late as I could to do the work. "You got a gift, Nicky. These chil'n love you."

And I cared about them as much. Nothing gave me greater joy than to listen to the laughter bubble up in their throats. I felt happiness attach itself to me as I watched them play in the field, their glowing faces turned upwards and smiling as they twirled in the sunlight. Their bliss was contagious, and it filled me with hope; they were joyful and full of spirited highs — despite being barefoot, dressed in rags and still hungry from the insignificant breakfast they had eaten that morning. The children had next to nothing, yet they were filled with a richness that money couldn't buy. It was both lovely and sad to watch.

The language barrier continued to be a challenge, but we communicated mostly through love. The kids responded to attention in a way I had never seen before. All they wanted was to be held. To be given affection. Hugs. Security. Protection. And I was addicted to giving them as much as I could.

As Johanna's belly grew, proving her pregnancy to the world, she became increasingly tired and weak. She struggled to make her way through the day, taking care of the children, then tending to the daily duties of cooking, cleaning and tidying.

Somewhere in the beginning of her twenty-third week, her face went ashen. And it stayed that way as she forced herself to soldier through the motions that were required for her job security.

I tried to help as much as I could, although I was often met with her superhuman resistance. She agreed to let me help her only when Jebet was out; even then, she would let me wash only the large piles of dishes or clean up after the children. In turn, I would mandate that she put her feet up and rest. Johanna always resisted, even when Jebet was nowhere to be found, but I could see relief fill her eyes as she took her needed break.

One Tuesday morning, I arrived at the orphanage to start that day's lessons. When I got there, I found Johanna huddled over two of the children — Kevin, a seven-year-old boy who had lost both of his parents to AIDS by the time he was five, and Rhoda, a nine-year-old girl who had just arrived at the orphanage about a week before.

They were both lying side by side, on their backs. Rhoda was moaning in pain and clutching at her leg, while Kevin was curled up in a ball, his eyes glassy and distant. Some of the other children huddled close, their faces grim and concerned.

"What happened?" I asked, taking Rhoda's hand. I rested my other hand on Kevin's back. Neither of them spoke very much English, so I stroked their cheeks and rubbed their backs to let them know I was there, that I would take care of them.

"We not know, Nicky. Kevin woke up this mornin' in real pain, and Rhoda not been right since she got here. And then I found this . . ." Johanna lifted Rhoda's pant leg to reveal an open gash that was oozing pus.

"Jebet gone — she left this mornin'," Johanna continued, "I don't know what to do. I told Jebet that both kids seem real sick and need hospital, but Jebet say she got no money to get 'em treated. Then she left."

"Did Jebet see Rhoda's leg?"

"Yes. She said Rhoda came to orphanage with her cut already there . . . so it not her fault. And Jebet say it look gross like that for a while, but we got nothin' to fix her up . . . so we can't do nothin' 'bout it. But the reason we don't got nothing is 'cause she sold every bit of medicine and bandage that get given to us as donations. That's why. And it make me real mad . . . 'specially now! But I not say that to her. I scared of what she do."

Without saying another word to Johanna, I grabbed my cell phone from my backpack. "Mama Bu? I need your help. I don't have time to explain right now. Just, please, can you come quick and help us? Two of the children are really sick and Jebet is not here. Please come, Mama Bu — and be quick." Mama Bu hadn't been back to the orphanage since she had confronted Jebet on the porch, and I knew she'd be thinking about what altercations might occur when she arrived.

Mama Bu arrived as quickly as her legs could carry her. We agreed that Johanna would stay with the kids while Mama Bu and I took Rhoda and Kevin to the hospital. Some of the younger children who were particularly close to Kevin were crying in the corner. Others seemed oblivious to what was going on and played on their own; saddened by the thought, I wondered if it was because they had seen so much pain in their lives that they were unaffected by what was going on.

Neither of the children could walk well. We helped them as best we could, but it was impossible for Mama Bu and I to carry them the entire way. We took turns trying, but short of collapsing underneath the weight of the kids, we were forced to put them down.

I hated being forced to encourage them to walk, but we had limited time to get them to the hospital. Kevin's eyes were growing increasingly glazed over, as though he wasn't present in the moment. And Rhoda had developed a fever that was so high it scared me.

We wrapped our arms around them, letting them use our bodies as crutches, and Mama Bu told them in Swahili to use us as support. To put as little weight as possible on their legs.

Rhoda was grunting and grimacing, sweat forming beads on her forehead as she struggled to put one leg in front of the other. At one point, I feared she would faint.

Kevin stayed silent, but his limp body seemed fragile. It was as though he would be willing to give up at any step.

My insides cranked with fear, I was suddenly teleported back to the hospital room at Mount Sinai. Despite the differences in situations, the feelings exploding through my veins were too familiar to what I had gone through over a year before, and my panic was close to unbearable.

I could hear Mama Bu praying out loud as we walked and joined her with my own pleas for health. I begged internally, hopeful that Mama Bu's messages would reach the God she swore would always guide us to the right spot.

When we got to the hospital, I emptied my wallet, giving the nurses everything I had so that Kevin and Rhoda could get the care they needed. We were placed in a crammed hospital room. Rhoda continued to groan in pain as she lay on the dirty bed she had been given. Kevin stayed silent.

When a nurse finally arrived, she took one look at Rhoda's wound and called in two other nurses to help her. Rhoda's infection had swelled to a state where she could no longer bend her knee, and the nurses surrounded her and began to push on her knee to get the pus out.

They took turns, two holding her to the bed, pinning both her arms and legs, while the third pushed directly on her gash to free her of the yellowish discharge that seeped from her five-inch cut. Despite her screams, they held her down. She begged them to stop, drooling from so much pain. I had to hold myself back from forcing the nurses to leave her alone.

My face blazed with anger towards Jebet. If she hadn't sold the medical supplies that had been donated by previous volunteers, if she had just *cared* for Rhoda in the first place, this wouldn't have happened. I cursed myself for not realizing Rhoda had had a cut on her leg, thinking I should have paid closer attention. I racked my brain to think of any signs of her limping or hurting in any way. I came up empty.

"Don't they have anesthetic? Or anything that would help her?" I asked Mama Bu.

Shaking her head, Mama Bu explained that hospitals don't use painkillers in Kenya. She whispered, "We do not have any type of pain medicine for the children. Nothing is used here. No painkillers of any kind."

Rhoda's cries grew louder and more intense, and I held Kevin closer, knowing that his fear was mounting. I wanted to take him from the room, to shield him from Rhoda's agony, but was instructed to stop.

"The beds are all full, some two and three to a bed, and there is nowhere for you to go," the pudgy nurse said as she pinned Rhoda's arms on either side of her. "Sit and stay. You and the boy are fine here. You leave, and you risk getting no treatment."

One side rock, other side hard place. I had no solution.

Kevin faded in and out of consciousness. I held him close, desperate to free him of Rhoda's wails. I hugged him tighter, whispering in his ear and hoping he would hear my voice over Rhoda's cries.

When they finished cleaning out Rhoda's gash, they gave her a tetanus shot. She whimpered into Mama Bu's arms, who was leaning over the bed and hugging her tight.

One of the nurses left. The other two stayed and prepared Kevin's needles. After deeming that he had an infection in his ankle — but not from a wound, like Rhoda — they gave him a tetanus shot as well, followed by a second needle in his hip to bring down the infection. Then, they took out a scalpel — and *cut* his ankle open to drain the infection. Kevin screamed less than Rhoda did, but the pain in his eyes somehow seemed worse. He barely blinked through the whole ordeal.

Once the nurses were finished, we were pushed out of the hospital. The kids weren't ready to leave, but the nurses told us it didn't matter — people were waiting and they needed the beds.

"These two children will need to recover in their own beds," the slim nurse said. "Now, take them home."

I couldn't bring myself to tell her that Kevin and Rhoda didn't *have* a real home. Or that each of the beds she spoke of would be shared with two other children.

24

On our walk home, Mama Bu and I took the kids to a store. I told both of them they could get whatever they wanted. Kevin requested juice, and Rhoda chocolate. Nothing more, they said, and I could tell they didn't want to be greedy. It just made me want to give them more, so I ignored them. I bought them both juice and chocolate, along with some nuts, and I knew they were happy.

When we arrived at Kidaai, we took the two children to their beds and tried to make them as comfortable as possible. They were still far from better and the medicine they had been given at the hospital was starting to kick in, making them drowsy. All I wanted them to do was sleep so they could get better faster.

I tucked both kids into their lower bunks and sang to them until they fell asleep. Despite the warmth outside, the orphanage was drafty. Both children shivered, clinging to the only sheets that I could find.

I kept the medicine we had purchased at the local chemist tucked in my backpack. I didn't trust Jebet to give it to them; I planned to stay until later that afternoon so I could give Kevin and Rhoda their next dose. If I left the medicine at the orphanage, it would be sold by dinner.

Jebet hadn't returned and Johanna was busy completing the list of tasks Jebet had left for her, anxious to have them done by the time the orphanage director returned. The kids had been left to care for themselves all morning.

I joined Mama Bu and some of the kids in the common room and we played a few of the tattered board games that had been left by previous volunteers. I knew the only reason Jebet hadn't sold them was because she could get nothing for them; the board games were all completely falling apart and many of the pieces were missing.

So, the only games we could play with the broken and missing pieces were ones that we made up rules for. They definitely weren't very fun by North American standards but, not surprisingly, the kids of Kidaai seemed to love them, clapping their hands and asking to play again.

An hour later, I took all of the children outside and Mama Bu helped Johanna make dinner. We played all of the kids' favourite games, including Duck Duck Goose and Red Rover.

From a distance, I saw Jebet trudging towards the orphanage. I felt every muscle in my body clench. I ran inside to warn Johanna and Mama Bu that Jebet had returned.

When Jebet walked into the kitchen, the explosion of Swahili was too much for me to fully absorb. Johanna slinked to the back of the kitchen, keeping to herself and chopping carrots, but Mama Bu and Jebet went nose to nose, battling about how Jebet had sold the children's medicine and first-aid supplies and put the children's lives at risk. I could follow only a handful of Jebet and Mama Bu's heated words, but their volume and hand gestures would have told a two-year-old how upset each of them was.

Jebet seethed. Mama Bu hissed. Jebet scowled, and Mama Bu raged. Then, Jebet spit at our feet, followed by Mama Bu storming out of the kitchen and slamming the door behind her.

The orphanage director turned and barrelled straight at me; she threatened me with a motion that implied slitting my throat, and it was then that I knew, without a doubt, that Jebet was crazy.

—

Before leaving for the day I sneaked upstairs to give Kevin and Rhoda their next dose of medicine. They were both still groggy from the medication the hospital had given them and they needed help sitting up. Like little birds waiting for the worm, they opened their mouths and swallowed what I gave them. Kevin was still battling a fever, so I removed his blanket to let the heat escape.

When I went downstairs, Mama Bu was just finishing serving the children their dinner. "Come on, Nicky. We must go. The dark is coming."

With the sun threatening to be gone entirely by seven o'clock, we sprinted home as fast as we could, and were just sitting down to dinner when my cell phone rang. "Nicky? It Johanna. Kevin taken turn for worse. He bad. Real bad. Got a bad fever. Much, much worse than today. You come back? You help him?"

My heart sank. I needed to help, but knew what Mama Bu and Kiano were going to say about walking back to the orphanage in the dark.

"Can you put cold cloths on him? Try to break the fever?" I asked Johanna, hopeful that I could help over the phone.

"It no working. Tried that for last hour. He real, real bad, Nicky."

"Where is Jebet?"

"In her room. She gave me phone to call, but then went back to her room. She watching TV in her room," Johanna said. I scoffed out loud, not surprised to hear that Jebet had a TV in her room but the kids didn't have medicine.

"Okay, Johanna. Give me fifteen minutes and I'll be there," I said. I ended the call, and turned to find Mama Bu, Kiano and Petar all staring at me.

"You are not going anywhere," Kiano said, shaking his head.

"But Kevin is *really* sick and they can't help him. Johanna doesn't know what to do and Jebet isn't helping. Kevin needs us and I'm really worried about him. He seemed hot when I left, but now Johanna says his fever is worse. I don't really think we have a choice."

My host father shook his head and crossed his arms. He looked pretty set in his ways. "You are not going anywhere, Nicky. It is my job to protect *you* and I say you need to stay here, so that you can stay safe."

Mama Bu gave me a look, telling me she understood. I knew she would fix it.

"Kiano," she started, gently putting her arm on his back. "I know this is not good. But that little boy needs us. He has got no one. I know going to the orphanage has risks, but leaving that little boy all night by himself with that fever . . . well, I think that is a bigger risk. We cannot do it," Mama Bu pleaded. I watched as Kiano started to soften, his arms slowly coming uncrossed.

"You are not going anywhere without me," Kiano said, grabbing his sweater. "And you best get ready to run fast, because we are headed into danger."

Mama Bu and I nodded in silence, fully aware of what we were about to walk into. All of the nighttime crime stories that I had heard since arriving in Africa filled my mind. I shuddered, fear ripping its way down my spine, yet I knew I had no choice but to ignore it. We needed to move forward, one foot after the other across the violent land of Kenya, so that we could try to help Kevin.

We collected our things and told Petar to stay close to his cell phone; he needed to send the night guard if we needed him. Even if he got a single ring from one of our phones, Petar was to take the shillings Kiano had stashed behind the bathroom pipe to pay the guard and send him in the direction of the orphanage.

The three of us sprinted to the orphanage as fast as we could. I was out of breath and hurting when we got there, but happy that we had made it safely.

Kiano waited on the couch in the common room while Mama Bu and I rushed to Kevin's side. He was curled up in the same bed I had left him in, both sweating and shivering, and cowered in a fetal position. Tears streamed down his cheeks and he begged for his *mama*.

We didn't have a thermometer, but I guessed his temperature near 104 degrees. I lifted the sheet off Kevin and gasped at the size his foot had swollen to. It was puffy and pink and taut to the touch. White pus dribbled from the place the nurses had cut him open earlier that day and I knew the infection had become very serious.

Without needing to talk it over, Mama Bu and I instantly came to the same conclusion — we needed to get Kevin to the hospital immediately, and no one — not even Kiano — would stop us. We gently lifted the fragile boy up to prepare him to go.

Standing across from each other, Mama Bu and I locked arms and

Ita helped to lift Kevin into our human seat, guiding his arms around our necks for support. We shimmied together down the stairs, our movements in sync, until we reached Kiano in the common room. He knew instantly what we were doing and was smart enough to not protest but simply help. Kiano took Kevin easily into his arms, like a father cradling a newborn baby, and we continued to the hospital as fast as we could go.

Jebet had stayed in her room the entire time, either stupidly ignorant to what was going on or selfishly pretending not to know. Either way, we didn't need her butting in. I was happy she had stayed where she was.

At the hospital, a new nurse we hadn't seen before abruptly took over. Taking one look at Kevin's ankle, she recut it and injected iodine to get the infection out. The pus drained once again.

I could see the pain in Kevin's eyes and he was pushed into pure panic. He grabbed onto my neck with a grip that was so tight I thought death was knocking. "*Mimi tu taka mamangu . . . mimi tu taka mamangu*," he cried to me. I just want my mommy.

My heart broke as I thought of the kind and affectionate mother who had been taken from Kevin two years earlier by the AIDS virus. Mama Bu had told me all about her one evening, speaking tenderly about what a sweet and loving *mama* she had been to her only child, always doting on Kevin and making sure he was well taken care of. It should have been *her* helping Kevin through his pain, not me. But an unsympathetic virus had taken her far too early. It wasn't fair.

With lots of consoling, hugging and kissing his forehead and cheeks, Mama Bu and I were finally able to get Kevin to start to calm down and begin breathing normally again. The nurse bandaged his foot, which was already less swollen.

"There is *no* way I am leaving this child with Jebet tonight," Mama

Bu said, when we were once again kicked out of the hospital bed Kevin had been occupying. "We will take him home with us tonight so we can keep an eye on him and make sure he is okay."

The trip home took longer than we were planning, with Kiano carrying Kevin through the dark the majority of the way. Kiano moved swiftly, but was cautious to keep Kevin comfortable and not hurt him further.

Five minutes from home, we neared a gang of six men standing on the side of the road. I almost didn't see them — they were dressed from head to toe in black — but I sensed we were approaching danger when Mama Bu grabbed my hand and squeezed it tight.

Kiano crossed the road to the other side, opposite of where the gang was standing. Mama Bu and I directly followed suit, looking down and refusing to meet the gaze of any one of the gang members.

"We are not causing any trouble," Kiano said in confident Swahili. "We have a very sick child and are returning from the hospital. We have no money and nothing to give. Please, let us pass."

The gang eyed us up and down and I sensed they were assessing Kiano's story for truth. They cared mostly about the money and whether or not he was being honest about it. I stuck my hand in my coat pocket and felt the extra shillings I had brought with me, in case we needed them. My mind raced, struggling with whether or not I should hand it over. I had no idea what the men would do if they found it without me willingly handing it over — but, worse, I didn't know how the gang would react if I confessed to having money after Kiano told them we had nothing to give.

The tallest of the men took a step forward. Then, a second man. Finally, a third. They began to surround us. Mama Bu squeezed my hand harder and I closed my eyes and wished for it all to be a nightmare.

"Please, we have nothing to give you. We have done nothing but help a sick child. Look into my eyes and know that I am speaking the truth," Kiano begged, adjusting Kevin's limp body in his arms. Miraculously, he stayed asleep.

With one fist closed around the shillings, I had my other on the cell phone in my pocket — and was about to hit send — when Kiano looked at me. He slightly shook his head. I knew instantly he was telling me to wait on calling Petar.

The men encircled, their drifting gazes moving up and down our bodies. The first man stepped forward and scoffed, in English, "Fine. Go home. We don't need trouble tonight anyway."

I let out breath I didn't know I had been holding and scurried behind Kiano and Mama Bu to race home. We reached the house breathless and filled with relief.

Mama Bu quickly opened the door and ushered Kiano to the biggest couch. He gently laid the little boy down. The medicine he had been given at the hospital had knocked him out completely.

"I'll sleep on the other couch," I said quickly, wanting to make sure Kevin was okay. "You know, in case he wakes up and needs someone."

"You can if you would like, Nicky," Mama Bu said gently, "But I do not think it will matter. Kevin's pretty sleepy from the anti-infection medication he is taking. He will not wake up before morning."

"Well, if it's all the same, I'd like to sleep out here. Just in case. I have to give Kevin his meds at 2 A.M. anyway."

"Up to you, *rafiki*. I will be in my room in case you need me. Just holler and I will come."

"Good night, Mama Bu. Thanks for all of your help today, and for coming with me to the orphanage and the hospital. I would have been pretty scared without you and Kiano there." I smiled appreciatively at my host mother.

"You would have been dead, that is what you would have been.

Tonight was an exception, because of Kevin, and how sick he is. But we cannot go out after dark — *ever* again. We had a close call tonight. To be honest, I did not know which way it was going to go, and all I could think of was poor Lucy and Chege. We were very, *very* lucky."

I nodded my head, agreeing. I wanted to be out after dark in Africa about as much as Mama Bu did.

I set my cell phone alarm to go off at 2 A.M., and settled into the uncomfortable couch I had taken opposite of Kevin. I could hear the little boy breathing evenly and I took comfort in his ease. I tried to find my own sleep but lost the battle with insomnia. I lay wide-eyed on the couch, staring into the darkness, trying to erase the recent memories of the day and fighting the urge to talk to the one person I knew would make me feel better.

Eric.

Since the day we had emailed back and forth, I hadn't communicated with him. He had sent me emails almost every day since then, and I had read all of them but hadn't replied. They were all light and low-key, and I knew Eric couldn't bring up what we had been through — he actually didn't have it in him to discuss it. And that continued cavalier attitude irritated me; it was exactly what had driven a wedge the size of the Grand Canyon between us before I left for Africa.

Then he sent a few more emails, asking more directly if we could talk. When I still didn't respond, he sent shorter, more clear emails, saying that he had something to tell me and really wanted to talk. He had even left me a few voice mails on my cell phone; I could only guess it was Maggie who gave him my number — or maybe even my parents, if they had actually gotten together. My momentary lapse in wanting to know the details of their conversation had been forcibly pushed behind me and I had never asked my parents about it, nor had they offered to discuss it.

But I couldn't bring myself to talk to Eric. I considered it, and the temptation to talk to him was intense, but the fear of pain was stronger. I couldn't get hurt again. We no longer worked and talking to Eric would just make it harder. So I simply responded by not responding. I wasn't going to trace my steps back down a path I had fought so hard to exit. And that was that.

## 25

Just before 5 A.M. the next day, I heard buzzing. Continued buzzing that wouldn't stop. Confused, I turned over on the couch; sleep had finally found me and I wasn't ready to give it up.

The buzzing persisted and I was finally coherent enough to realize it was my cell phone.

"Nicky? It real bad here. Jebet real drunk, and she waking up all the children to start chores, even though rise time ain't for a long bit. She yellin' and screamin' and swearin' at the kids."

I could barely hear Johanna's whispers. "Jebet bin' real mean. The kids all cryin' and askin' for you. And she hittin' some of 'em real bad

— 'specially the ones who won't stop cryin'. Ita bleeding from his lip, and she just kicked Esther down the stairs, when she don't move fast enough 'cause she crying too hard."

"Oh, shit. Oh no!"

"And Gracie just peed her pants again 'cause she so scared. I worried about what Jebet do to her, but I got her changed and into new clothes 'fore Jebet saw. I think she too drunk to know Gracie did it anyway. I hid Gracie's wet clothes behind a bed. Hopefully Jebet not find them."

"That's good, Johanna. We can clean them later."

"Jebet keep saying she mad that she can't keep her orphans in check. Say she goin' prove that she got control of the kids."

"Are Ita and Esther okay?"

"They seem good. Esther limpin', but helpin' with the chores. Ita's cut startin' to stop bleeding, I think."

"Were any other children hurt?"

"Nuh-uh. No."

"Okay, good. Johanna, where are you now?"

"I in the pantry, hiding with Gracie." Johanna stopped talking and I could hear the whimpers coming from the little girl beside her.

"Does Jebet know you called me?"

"No, Nicky. I in real trouble if she find out."

"And where is Jebet now?"

"She passed out on her bed. Layin' face down in clothes. She real drunk."

"If Jebet's that drunk, she won't bug you now. I think it will be safe for you to leave the pantry. Can you make sure Ita and Esther are really okay? The sun will rise any minute, and I will run there as fast as I can once it does. I'll make up a reason for why I am there so early. Jebet won't know you called me."

"Okay."

"And Johanna? How is Rhoda?"

"She seem to be okay. She hobblin' 'round here, but her fever gone."

"Good. You go watch over the kids, and I'll be there as soon as I can. Tell them to stop cleaning and working — they can play or rest or go back to bed."

We said goodbye. I lightly tapped on Mama Bu's door. She greeted me quickly in a floor-length mint-coloured nightgown. It was the first time I had seen her in anything other than her clothes.

I filled her in on what was going on. She quickly dressed and we waited anxiously for the sun to rise. After the previous night's close call, I knew not to push it for the sake of ten minutes.

Mama Bu changed the dressing on Kevin's leg and I gave him a dose of medicine. Kevin was less groggy than he had been the night before, but quickly turned over and went back to sleep as soon as we finished taking care of him. I had no doubt the safety he felt — for the first time in a long time — was helping to lull him into the deep slumber.

When dawn hit, Mama Bu and I ran to the orphanage, sprinting like we were competing for gold in the hundred-metre dash. When we got there, sleepy children were everywhere, scrubbing floors, fluffing couches and dusting furniture. It looked like something out of the movie *Annie*, and I knew our own version of Miss Hannigan was passed out drunk upstairs. It was a hard knock life, indeed.

"Johanna? I thought the kids were going to stop working?"

"I try. But they scared that Jebet come back downstairs. Don't want to get hit again."

I called all of the children together and told them they could stop the chores they were doing. I declared it to be a games morning and said they could play board games in the common room or go outside and play. If any of them were tired, they could go back to bed.

While the children ran in every direction, Mama Bu inspected the kids who had been hurt. Ita's lip had stopped bleeding but had started to puff up like a pink marshmallow. Mama Bu asked Johanna to bring her a cloth as cold as she could make it. She gently held it to Ita's mouth.

I asked Ita if he had been hurt anywhere else and he pointed to his back. I gently lifted up his shirt and saw two welts forming, the exact shape of the stick Jebet carried around, as though it was her prized possession. I shuddered and looked away, blinking back tears.

Johanna got another cloth and Mama Bu held it to Ita's back, hoping it would make him feel better. But all he wanted to do was bury himself in my lap. I sat on the ground, holding him for as long as he needed me to, softly singing in his ear. When I had made it through all of the nursery songs I knew — twice — I moved to Christmas carols. It didn't matter what songs they were, he just needed to feel love.

Mama Bu asked Esther to walk towards her and watched to see how well she could walk. Esther had twisted her ankle when Jebet pushed her down the stairs, but seemed to be okay, short of a small limp. I suspected she would be better by lunchtime.

After Ita was okay to go and play, I did my rounds, playing with each child to inspect for any signs of injury. Mama Bu went upstairs to check on Jebet, and then we both joined Johanna in the kitchen to make the kids breakfast.

"Jebet is out cold," Mama Bu said. "I suspect she will be like that for hours. Which is a good thing. It will give us time to plan. We need a plan. She has to get out of here."

"What do you think we should do?" I asked her, stirring the *ugali*, a porridgelike, sticky breakfast made from maize flour. Cheap to buy, yes, but the *ugali* offered no nutritional value for the kids.

"I do not know, yet, Nicky. I do not know."

"This might seem a bit obvious, but can we just ask Jebet to go? Point out all that has happened lately and delicately suggest she needs to hand over the director reins to someone else?"

"I tried that already a couple of months ago, after you told me about what happened to Gracie. I told Jebet she cannot do this any longer. I asked her to leave. I even told her that she could live with me. She did not respond well. She got very angry and told me to mind my business. She kept saying she was fine and that no one was going to take the orphanage from her too. That she has lost too much and losing the orphanage would kill her."

"I see. Well, is there someone we could call then? Are there authorities that deal with this kind of thing? Social workers? The police? *Anyone?*"

"It does not work that way, *rafiki*. You know the police are corrupt. All they care about is who will pay them the most. Whoever that is. All Jebet has to do is slip them a few bucks, and they will go away."

"What about social workers? The government?"

Johanna stayed silent and tried to take over my role of stirring the *ugali*. I waved her away. Told her to sit and rest.

Mama Bu continued, "We've got social workers and child officers, but most of them are just as bad. The same thing will happen: people will offer money to keep them quiet and not shut their place down. So the social workers are not used to fixing the problems in orphanages, they are just in search of money. To be honest, I doubt the social workers would do anything at all."

"Surely it can't be *that* bad. Can it?" I asked.

"Our cycle of poverty is bad, *rafiki*. People do what they need to get money and put food on their own tables. It is just the way it is around here."

"Okay, well, does Jebet own this building?"

Mama Bu shook her head. "No, there is a landlord who owns it, but I have no idea who he is or where to find him."

"What about friends? Past volunteers? Anyone who might be able to help us?"

"I have email addresses of some of the past volunteers. I could contact them to see if they know anything. Or have any ideas how to help."

"That would be great, Mama Bu, but I don't think that will be fast enough. We have to get Jebet out of here right away."

"Now I think of it, there a big man who been comin' round here few times lately," Johanna said, interrupting us. "He always ask to see Jebet. Most times she tell me to pretend she not here. She tell me to say she out, when really she just upstairs in her bedroom."

"Do you know his name? Or know who he is?" I asked her. Finally, I felt we were making progress.

Johanna shook her head, discouraged. "Jebet no tell me anything. She keep real quiet about him. Not sure where to get him. Or who he is."

"I think volunteers might be our best option," said Mama Bu. "Maybe they know who the landlord is? I can email the ones that stayed with me and ask Barika to do the same. Two of them stayed with her. And they were the most recent volunteers. I will ask her if she still talks to them and if she knows where they are. Maybe that will help?"

"It's worth a try," I responded, trying to be hopeful, but more than anything, I felt discouraged.

"Perhaps both of you could feed the children breakfast and I will run to Barika's house to see what I can find out? I need to get back to my house anyway to check on Kevin. Petar will be getting up soon and leaving for school, so I will need to figure out what to do with our boy." Mama Bu finished laying out all of the kids' plates. "I will be back as soon as I can. Jebet will not wake up anytime soon, so you will be alright. I will send the kids in for breakfast on my way out."

Moments later, the children came running in the kitchen, now laughing, and picked up their plates of *ugali*. Johanna offered me a plate, but I turned her down, telling her to save it for the kids. Even a little bit went a long way for such hungry children. Johanna offered to do the same, but I quickly scolded her, reminding her that she was pregnant and had her own child to feed. She gratefully took the plate I held out for her and we joined the kids in the common room.

I sat on the couch and watched the kids as they ate. I had Gracie on my lap, hugging her tight as she inhaled the slop. The others finished theirs just as quickly, looking like they were still hungry and wanting more, but knowing there was none to come.

I was about to tell the kids that it was time to start school when I realized it was still only 6:30 A.M. I had arrived at the orphanage so early that I was completely messed up on the time. Instead, we played games.

I was sitting on the floor playing our made-up version of Sorry with Nadia when Johanna pointed over my shoulder. She was looking through the window directly behind my head. "There he is! The man! The big man I was tellin' you and Bu 'bout. He walkin' up the grass. Look, Nicky, *look*!"

I turned and watched as a man about six feet tall walked towards the porch. He was wearing a dark blue suit with a crisp white shirt and red tie. He gently knocked on the door.

"You stay here with the kids. Don't let them follow me," I instructed Johanna, handing her Gracie. "I will go and speak with him. Do you know if he speaks English?"

Johanna nodded yes and I felt a surge of relief. I hurried to the front door and pulled it open, noting the man's obvious surprise when he saw who answered his knock.

"Hello, sir. I'm Nicky." I stepped out onto the porch and firmly closed the door behind me. I didn't want the children to join me — or worse, Jebet. "Do you speak English, sir?"

"I do." The man took my hand and shook it firmly. "And my name is Wekesa."

"It's a pleasure to meet you, Wekesa. I've been volunteering here for the past couple of months, mostly helping in the classroom. You know, since the teachers' strike is keeping the regular teachers out. May I help you with something?"

"I'm looking for Jebet. Is she around?" Wekesa asked, searching my eyes. His own were warm and honest, but there was underlying frustration in his voice.

I explained that Jebet was upstairs lying down, given that she didn't feel very well. I offered to help for a second time.

"Well, I'd really prefer to be speaking with Jebet about this, but you'll have to do, I guess. I can't wait any longer. I'm looking for my rent money. Jebet owes me seven months' worth. I've been patient, really I have, because I feel bad for the kids at this orphanage, but I can't wait any longer. If I don't get my money soon, I'll be getting lawyers involved." The man scratched his chin. "So, Nicky, you sure you can help me? You probably weren't expecting that, were you?"

I sat on the porch chair behind me, feeling a relief so intense it practically knocked me over. For the first time since I had arrived, a door had opened, hinting at hope. I motioned for the man to sit, and assured him that, yes, I could help him.

"I'll talk through all of this with you — and make sure you get your rent money," I said, reassuring the man. "But first, may I offer you a drink? We have some chai."

Wekesa nodded, removing his hat.

I told Wekesa that I would go and get some tea, but suggested we stay outside. "I don't want to wake Jebet when she isn't feeling well." Then I added, "Plus, to be honest, I think we can figure things out faster if she isn't here."

"Sure, sure . . ." Wekesa waved his hand in the air. "I just want my money. As I'm sure you can imagine, I've reached a point that is beyond frustration."

I nodded my sympathies and scooted through the door to get our tea. Johanna joined me in the kitchen and said she would bring it out so the two of us could start speaking right away. When I rejoined Wekesa on the porch, I asked him to start from the beginning. I wanted to know everything so I had the full picture.

At first he seemed reluctant. I could see him briefly mulling over in his head the ethics of telling a volunteer something that should be between Jebet and him. But considering I represented the first possibility he'd had in months of actually getting his money, it didn't take him long to start talking. "For a long time, I got my money — every month, without it ever being late. It's another reason why I've been so lenient with Jebet.

"Seven months ago, the rent money didn't come. I gave Jebet the benefit of the doubt, assuming it was just a bit late, which would be understandable. But it never came. When I asked Jebet about it, she said the orphanage was having tough times. She said the woman who had donated the rent money each month had pulled out and that the orphanage was barely scraping by. Jebet didn't have enough for food or water or electricity, let alone rent money."

Johanna stepped onto the porch, interrupting us. She put the chai directly between us on a little round table that was on its last legs. After she disappeared back into the house, Wekesa continued. "I told Jebet

I could wait, as long as she paid it in full once she got a new donor."
Wekesa pointed to the sugar. Dumped it in his tea. "Month after
month, Jebet begged me for more time. My patience has been wearing
thin for a long time, but lately I've been really pissed off at her — sorry,
pardon my manners and bad language, lady. I don't mean to be rude in
front of you, but I've got no patience anymore, and sometimes it gets
the best of me."

"No problem, Wekesa. I've heard worse." I smiled.

"Anyway, Jebet has been downright ignoring me lately. I've sent
letters, called her phone . . . personally visited as much as I could. I
live in Nairobi, so I don't get here often, but she's been ignoring every
bit of communication I send her. And then, when I make the trip into
Ngong, she's never here. This was going to be my last visit before I
served her papers."

I smiled again and sympathized with Wekesa's frustrations. Then,
I added, "But I have to admit, I'm a bit relieved to hear it all, as well."

"Come again?" Wekesa looked mildly confused and a bit angry to
hear my words.

"Oh, no, no . . . that's not what I meant. Here, I'll explain," I quickly
filled Wekesa on what had been going on and he looked horrified as the
story unfolded. I could tell he was a good man, his eyes full of worry and
concern as I recounted the chronicle of injuries, neglect and abuse.

"It sounds like we've got bigger problems than some missing
rent money," Wekesa said, shaking his head. I refilled his teacup and
passed him the sugar.

"That is true. But I think the missing rent money will end up
helping us. Jebet can't just stop paying you. Surely we can use that
against her."

"But that doesn't help with the abuse, Nicky."

"Sure it does! If Jebet doesn't have a rent donor and has no way to pay, she'll need to find another one. *I* can be that person. I'll donate the rent, but only on the condition that Jebet leaves. Then she can't hurt the kids anymore!" I silently counted the dollars in my bank account. It was going to be tight. Without an income, I didn't know if I would be able to pay the rent. But I knew I'd find the money — someway and somehow. No matter what.

"And if Jebet refuses?"

"She can't stay here if she can't pay you rent, Wekesa."

"No, but what if she finds another donor who is willing to pay, even with her here? And if she goes, who will watch the children? *You*?"

"Yes . . . I'll do it," I responded, a little too quickly and without thinking it through. My words tumbled out before the thought could register. Memories of my father telling me that I had no speed bumps from my brain to my mouth flooded my mind.

"You're going to permanently leave your country? Your *family*? And move here to look after an orphanage. You better think that one through, missy. I'm not so sure it's a good idea."

"I know it would be a huge life change, and I promise to give all of that some more thought. For now, let's concentrate on how we can get Jebet out of here." I reached into my pocket and grabbed my cell phone. "I know someone who can help us. Just give me a minute to call her."

Frantically I dialed Mama Bu's cell phone number and asked that she come back to the orphanage as soon as she could.

"I am on my way, *rafiki*. I am actually very close. We are coming as quickly as we can. And I have Barika with me. And Kevin too."

"How is he?"

"Much better. The medication seems to have finally kicked in for the sweet thing. He is a bit slow on his feet, but fine other than that. And his ankle looks much better. I wanted to bring him back to the orphanage so we could keep an eye on him."

"Okay, good. Get here soon! I'm scared Jebet will wake up and come downstairs. I actually found out a lot while you were gone. Things that will help us. "

"Me too, Nicky! I cannot wait to share. We will be there in two minutes." Moments after Mama Bu hung up, I could see Barika and her barrelling towards us, with little Kevin limping behind. When they reached us, they told Kevin he could join his friends in the common room. I introduced Wekesa and explained what we had discovered.

"Lord have mercy!" Barika said, her cheeks becoming flushed. "I used to be a host mama to a lovely girl named Lesley — she's from Canada too — and she done a lot of good work while she was here. Really rallied the good people and got lots of donations and help for Kidaai, you know? Donations from both the outside, and from here."

"How can she help, Barika?" Mama Bu asked, cutting her off.

"Right, well, I seem to recall the rent money came from someone on the inside. Mombasa, maybe? The donor lives here, I know for certain. I simply can't believe she would just stop giving the rent money. I met her once and she seemed to really care deeply for the kids of Kidaai. And she's wealthy too, so that wouldn't have been a problem."

"Can you find out who she is? Would Lesley know?" I asked Barika.

"Can't see why she wouldn't. Lesley found her — she went out and appealed to the good people, asking for their help. Set up a whole bunch of stuff, my Lesley. She is a grand girl."

"Okay, Barika. You can tell us all about Lesley later. You should try and reach her first," Mama Bu cut in again, trying to bring focus to her chatterbox friend. "Can you call her?"

Barika shook her head and shrugged her shoulders. "I got her number, but I can't call so far on my phone. Last few times we talked been on email."

I grabbed my backpack and handed Barika my phone, explaining that I had included long distance to Canada as part of my plan so I could call my family. I told her she could call whoever she needed to if she thought it would help us.

"Well, I don't got Lesley's number memorized, silly thing. It's at home though. I could go get it?"

"Sure, take my phone and go and call Lesley. See what you can find out." I gently pushed her forward.

As Barika left, Wekesa also rose from his chair, stating that it seemed as though we had everything covered. He gave us his contact details and asked that we call him once we had figured something out.

As he started to leave, I remembered the letters he mentioned sending to Jebet and I called out to him, asking for copies. I had no idea what we could or would do with them, but I thought there was a good chance they might help.

"Of course. I believe there are about twelve separate emails I sent Jebet," Wekesa answered. "And I have all of her responses, as well, with all of her excuses as to why she couldn't pay."

"Perfect," I responded, growing more convinced by the minute that we'd have what we needed to take Jebet down. "Anything more?"

"Cell phone bills . . . with the number of times I called her. That should help too, yes? If we are building a case against her?"

I nodded, excitement growing.

"Great. I'll make copies of everything." Wekesa tipped his hat, and turned, walking away from the orphanage.

With Wekesa and Barika both gone, Mama Bu, Johanna and I sat by ourselves on the porch. All of the kids were in the field, laughing as they always did and playing some of the games I had taught them. I crossed my fingers that the memory of their early morning wake-up call had been forgotten.

Johanna excused herself and said she had to tend to cleaning the windows before Jebet woke up. The last thing Jebet had said to her before passing out in her drunken stupor was that she expected the windows to be squeaky clean and free of "paw prints from the animals who lived there."

When she left, Mama Bu poured me another cup of chai and asked how I was doing. I sighed.

"I'm okay, I guess. I'm sad and frustrated about all that has been going on here in the last little while, but hopeful we can figure something out to get Jebet out of here. The whole situation is just so heartbreaking."

Mama Bu nodded her head, closing her eyes as she sipped through the steam of her tea. "I do not like what Jebet has been doing to the children either, *rafiki*." Then, as if she was murmuring just to herself, Mama Bu continued, "And it is also so hard to see a friend change so much. To be so different. And to impact her life, and others, with violence and drinking."

I sipped at my own tea, lost in thought about how complex and difficult the entire situation was. "I know, Mama Bu. I can't imagine how hard it would be to see a friend of yours go through so much tragedy, and then become such a different person. I sympathize with Jebet's story — I really do — but I also can't ignore what she is doing to the children."

"I know, Nicky. That part makes me very upset as well."

"And that whole thing is really depressing too. Without Jebet saying this, it's like she's using what happened to her as an excuse for being so atrocious to the rest of the world. Like she's entitled to being mean to others, just because of what happened to her. Who gets to do *that*? We've all experienced pain. It doesn't give any of us the right to treat other human beings with anything less than what they deserve."

"I agree."

"It just makes me feel so disappointed in humankind. Like it's a spiralling prophesy of evil . . . if something bad happens to you, you then become evil yourself?"

"Not everyone is like that," Mama Bu said, looking straight at me. "Look around you, and know there is strength closer to you than you realize. Not everyone suffers through pain and hardship only to fall apart afterwards. The truly strong at heart bounce back."

I stared at her, taking in what she was saying.

"Remember Wambua's message? Remember the woman from his story? The one who was raped and became pregnant? Draw from *her* strength, not Jebet's weakness. You need to remember that good people with strong hearts bounce back, no matter what they have gone through. Not everyone collapses when life lets them down. Many rise up in the time of challenge, and they are stronger as a result."

Mama Bu took my hand and squeezed it tight.

"As for Jebet, Nicky, I do not excuse what she has done to the children either. But separate from that, she has still shown good in her own way. Taken people in when they needed it the most."

As if on cue, Johanna came to the porch and collected our empty chai mugs. "Just gonna go wash these up, if you finished?" Johanna smiled, rubbing her growing belly, and returned to the kitchen.

"Johanna. . . ?" I asked Mama Bu.

"Yes, Johanna. As Wambua told us at church that day, Johanna had been abandoned by all of her friends and family when she found out she was pregnant. She had nowhere to go, and no one to take her in. She had no food to nourish herself or her growing baby. And it was Jebet who offered her the shelter she needed. The security she deserved. And, in her own way, love."

I looked down at my tea, realizing what Mama Bu was saying. "Everything about this . . . it's just so very sad," I said. Mama Bu squeezed my hand again.

"It is, indeed, Nicky."

The two of us sat in silence for a long time. We became lost in our own thoughts and the complexity of the situation around us.

After several minutes, I gently broached the subject of staying in Kenya. Despite my overly quick response to Wekesa's sarcastic question, the notion of staying permanently had continually creeped into my mind. "You know, Wekesa asked me who would look after the children if Jebet ends up leaving."

"Yes, we will definitely need to figure that out. There are a few different people who could do it, which is a good thing."

"I was thinking that maybe *I* could do it? What do you think, Mama Bu?" Aside from my family, there was nothing I needed to return to at home. Maggie was never home, off on her own worldwide adventures, and I could go home to visit my parents. My job teaching third-graders seemed mundane compared to the type of teaching I would be doing in Kenya and how rewarding it would be. My mind raced with inspired thoughts of all that I would do in the classroom, and I became increasingly invigorated by the thought of turning the orphanage into a cozy, happy home for the kids I had grown to love.

"Nicky, I do not know about that. You do not want to move here from your home. Your family is there. And Eric too."

"Eric is my past. It would be good for us to have continued separation. And my parents can visit me here. Or I could go home for a vacation every once in a while. Plus, there's always the phone . . . and email . . . and Skype. It's so easy to stay in touch now!"

"Have you spoken with Eric again?"

I shook my head and responded softly, "Eric and I are legally separated. It's best that we not communicate. Our life together ended a long time ago and there's no point trying to pretend it's any other way."

"Are you sure about that, Nicky?"

I nodded.

"We will focus on getting Jebet out of here first. Then we can talk about you staying in Kenya. Golly knows I would love to have you here permanently, but you have got to be certain that it is what you want."

I smiled at my host mother, who gave my knee a big squeeze. "I'd love to be here permanently too, Mama Bu. You and the kids have made this place feel like home to me. I really do — feel at home, that is. And at peace . . . finally. For the first time in a very long while, I feel like I'm where I should be. I don't want to give that up."

"Then maybe you don't have to, Nicky. Maybe you don't have to."

## 26

An hour later, while Jebet was still passed out, Barika came running through the field, calling out, "Bu! Bu! Nicky! Bu! I got so much to tell you girls!"

"We do not want the children to hear you, Barika. Stop yelling so much. Come and sit with us and tell us everything," Mama Bu called back, shushing her with her gestures and telling her to join us on the porch.

By the time Barika came back, we had helped Johanna finish all of the cleaning that needed to be done and the three of us were sitting on the porch, waiting for Jebet to wake up. There was no way Mama Bu or I would leave Johanna and the kids with a hungover monster.

Before even taking her seat, Barika launched into what had happened since she left us. "I got a hold of Lesley right away. She was at work, but I had her cell number so she answered on the second ring. She's great, doing well as she always does, but that's a whole other story. . . ." Barika spoke with her hands flailing.

"Yes, please get to the point, Barika." Mama Bu shook her head.

"I told Lesley all that has been going on 'round here. She is devastated, needless to say. She worked so hard to give Kidaai so much and it all seems to be destroyed now. She asked about the CD player she bought the kids. Is it still here?"

I shook my head, disappointed to hear about the missing CD player. It would have been amazing to share music with the kids.

"I noticed a CD player in Jebet's room when I checked on her this morning," Mama Bu said. "My guess is that she stole it for her room."

"Tsk tsk. And what about the chickens?" Barika asked. "Lesley said she put in a chicken coop so the kids could have eggs."

"She ate them chickens," Johanna responded quietly. "Said the kids don't need no eggs. Then she tore the coop down and used it for firewood."

"Eck — *disgusting*! What an ogre. And I suppose she sold the chicken vaccinations too, yes?" Barika asked.

"I don't know what she did with vaccinations," Johanna replied, shaking her head. Her innocence and gentle nature made me love her even more.

"Here's where it gets good," Barika continued. "I was right about Lesley setting up the rent donor before she left. A lovely English woman named Gloria who lives in Mombasa. Leslie met her one day when Gloria was in Nairobi — I have no idea how they met — and Lesley got to telling Gloria about Kidaai. Gloria was so upset to hear of such poor children with nothing that she agreed to pay for the rent each month so Jebet could fund other things . . . like better food, books, desks and a swing set."

We all looked around. No swing set was in the yard.

"So Lesley gave me Gloria's number — they still keep in touch on occasion. I gave Gloria a ring. Hope you don't mind, Nicky? I had to call three times, but I finally found out that Gloria has been sending Jebet the rent every month for over a *year*! Every *single* month."

Bingo.

Silence took over as Barika paused her rolling update and we all took in the news. I was the first to voice what it meant — and what the others were thinking. "Well, that's it, then. Jebet is a thief."

"Yes, it sounds like she is," Mama Bu answered me. Slowly, she pondered the news. "But we need to be careful in our approach. It is not like where you are from, Nicky. One wrong move on our part and Jebet could be getting away with all of this. If she finds out we know about all of this, and she has lots of money saved up from Gloria, she could easily make the problem go away. And end up staying at Kidaai."

"Gloria's pretty upset to hear about all of this," Barika continued. "She seems like she is a part of the *really* rich folk, so I don't know how much the money part bothered her, but she kept saying that she felt like a fool. That Jebet took advantage of her. She kept saying that she wants to fix this. And that she *will* fix it."

"Fantastic!"

"When I told Gloria all about what has been going on with the children at the orphanage, well, then the real sparks came. She hung up immediately, saying she'd call me back in ten minutes. Sure to her word, she called back almost ten minutes on the nose. She said she's got a social worker friend who works out of Nairobi. Gloria is sending her to help us. She said we can trust her, and that the social worker would never be paid off, but if Jebet tries it, Gloria will just pay more. She wants to be sure that Jebet pays for what she has done and is pushed out of the orphanage."

"So what happens from here?" I asked.

"Paka, the social worker, just called me five minutes ago. She will be calling us back tomorrow — your phone, Nicky. She will meet us in person, but needs the details by tomorrow so she can build a case. We have to be fast, though, because Paka said she is moving to Boston next week, something about visiting her niece."

We had twenty-four hours to build a case against Jebet. Twenty-four hours to collect the proof that Paka needed — or there was nothing she could do to help us.

"Okay, let's get to work. Let's start with the obvious," I suggested. "I have my camera in my backpack. We'll take pictures of the welts on Ita's back and his fat lip too. We can even take pictures of the cuts and gashes on Rhoda and Kevin. We don't have proof that Jebet sold the medicine that would have prevented them from getting sick, but I'm sure it helps show how hurt the children in her charge are getting."

"And we have Wekesa's emails, of course. And Jebet's responses saying that she does not have the rent to give him," Mama Bu added.

"Plus, Gloria said she's got all kinds of emails to Jebet about the rent money, as well as bank slips proving she sent it," Barika chimed in. "And why stop there? Let's go upstairs and take a picture of Jebet passed out on her bed."

"You don't have to, Barika." The deep, raspy voice came from behind us on the porch. We all turned to find Jebet, dishevelled and hung over. "I'm already up."

It was clear that Jebet had been standing behind us long enough to know some of what was going on, but we didn't know exactly what she had heard.

When Jebet crossed her arms and scrunched her face up like an angry black pug, we suspected she knew enough.

Mama Bu spoke first, gently, but confidently, "Jebet, we care about you. We do not want to see you upset. Or hurt. But we also care about the children staying here and we need to protect them. I know it has been so tough on you, but please, think of what it has been like for the children lately. They are all very afraid right now and we need to give them security. We need to make them feel safe."

Silence. I waited for Jebet's response, expecting her to fight back. To contort her voice into a shrill cadence of higher and higher notes as she kicked us out. To flare her nostrils into those perfect saucer shapes that looked like tunnels to her brain. To spit at us. Even hit. Instead, she said nothing. Did nothing.

Mama Bu continued, "What would your *mama* say, Jebet?"

Jebet just looked sad. "I got nowhere to go, Bu." Jebet's voice was quick but honest. "This orphanage is the only place I know now."

"We would find you a place to go, Jebet. You and I have been friends for a very long time and I will help you. This is not about anything but giving some safety and security back to the children. You have been watching over them for a really long time, and it is clear that it has been weighing on your shoulders lately. Sometimes . . . well, sometimes it is time to move on." Mama Bu, with all of her empathetic wisdom, reached out to Jebet with her words. She stood up and placed a hand on her friend's back.

"No! I'm not *leaving*, Bu!" Jebet suddenly screamed. "I've got nowhere to go. I need to stay *here*. And you can't make me leave!"

"Actually, I think we can, Jebet. We want you to step down. To volunteer to leave. But if we have to, we will bring in the authorities to force you out. It has reached that point." Mama Bu paused, briefly. "We found a social worker in Nairobi who will not be paid off. And we have got proof against you — pictures, letters, emails, testimonials from past volunteers. We will take videos if we need to."

Johanna and I stayed silent, watching Mama Bu try to talk Jebet down from the ledge. Shockingly, Barika also stayed quiet.

"I don't know. . . ." Jebet's voice trailed off as she spoke, fear taking over. Jebet had no idea what life would be like outside of the orphanage and it was clear that she was panicked about how she would survive.

"Jebet, listen to me. We have got all the proof we need to make a case against you for stealing the rent money. We know Gloria has been giving you 50,000 shillings a month, and Wekesa has not seen any of it in seven months. Both of them will testify to the fact that you have been stealing. If you make us do this, Jebet, we will. And you know what will happen. They will take you to *jail*. None of us want that, Jebet. Please, work with us. Let us help you."

"You're supposed to be my friend, Bu. . . ."

"I *am* your friend, Jebet. And I always will be. It is why I'm doing this. I want to protect both you and the children."

"Just leave me be! I don't want to talk about this no more, you hear?" Jebet stood up angrily, wobbly from her post-binge shakes, and retreated back to her room. I took it as progress that she hadn't kicked us out.

"What do you think will happen, Mama Bu?" I asked gently after a few moments of silence. All of us were shaken from the clashed alter-cation.

"Jebet knows she has been backed into a corner. She has got no way out. We can work with her, or we can take her down — and she knows that. It is just a matter of time before she admits it." Mama Bu sighed, leaning back in her chair and rubbing her eyes. It had been a long day, and it was only nine o'clock.

"You should all go about your day," Mama Bu continued. "Get going to wherever you need to be, and I will stay here with Jebet. She needs to clear her head, first, and then I will talk to her some more. One on one. I think I can reach her. Make her realize what she needs to do."

I stood, crossing the porch to give Mama Bu a hug, "Thank you for being so wonderful. You are always here for everyone, and we all love you for it."

Johanna rose too and I could tell she was nervous about being in the house with Jebet. I asked her, "Why don't you come help me in the classroom today, Johanna? I could use the help and it will be good for the kids to have both of us there after such an awful start to their day today."

Relief filled Johanna's face and she waddled with me to the classroom. I let her ring the bell.

## 27

At home that night, Mama Bu filled me in on what had happened with Jebet. There had been a lot of tears, cursing and pushing back, but in the end, Mama Bu convinced Jebet that it was in everyone's best interest that she step down as orphanage director.

"Where will she go?" I asked Mama Bu. As much as I disliked Jebet, and hated her for what she had done to the children at Kidaai, I felt sorry for her, given what she had been through.

"That was part of how she finally agreed to go. Barika called Gloria back to let her know what was going on, and Gloria — bless her soul — knew of another family in Mombasa who is looking for someone to live with them and clean their house. I think it is more like a mansion, so Jebet will have her work cut out for her, but at least she will have a place to go and, most important, she will not be around any children."

"The Mombasa family doesn't have any?"

"No, it is just a wealthy couple that lives in the mansion. They have no kids and Gloria told Jebet neither the husband or wife will stand for any antics. Jebet has only one chance with this family, and she knows it, so she better make it work."

"And what about Johanna?" Our pregnant friend had grown increasingly weak as her baby bump had grown and I suspected she needed to be on bed rest until her baby was born. Without the orphanage, she had nowhere to live and no money to pay for food.

"Well, *rafiki*, that is where you come in. Kidaai no longer has an orphanage director, so if you were being serious about thinking you want to stay, well, the role is yours . . . if you want it. Normally the exiting director would be involved in choosing one, but since that is not a good idea in this case, we have more flexibility. I phoned Wekesa about an hour ago and he is fine with you taking over, if you want to stay. It would mean you would move in there permanently, and run the orphanage as you see fit. You could either keep your position as schoolteacher, or find someone new to take over that role."

Silence. My mind raced.

"So, about Johanna . . . if you were the orphanage director, it would be entirely your call about what you wanted to do. If you decide you do not want to take on the role, we will need to find someone new to do it, and that person will ultimately decide if Johanna can stay or not."

More silence. Then a wave of relief, excitement and belonging suddenly washed over me. It just felt right.

"I think I want to do it! I love those kids and know that I could run that orphanage in a way that gives them so much . . . safety, love, opportunity. I really want to make a difference in their lives." My excitement continued to bubble as the realization of me staying in Kenya sank in. "Mama Bu! I think I want to stay! I want to find that feeling of being home again. Feel like I am once again truly a part of something. Be a part of their lives, in a bigger way. Build a home, for both them and me."

"It does not pay much, Nicky."

"Oh, I don't care about that. What do I need to spend money on? I'd just want to love those kids. To give them what has been stripped from them."

"Well, then, it is settled. *Karibu, rafiki!* We are so happy to have you here permanently. Ngong is lucky to have you."

"When will I start?"

"You can move into the orphanage tomorrow. Jebet is packing her things tonight and taking a *matatu* to Mombasa first thing in the morning. I was planning on moving in temporarily until we found a new orphanage director, but if it is going to be you, you might as well start right away!"

"Will the kids be okay with Jebet sleeping there tonight?" I asked, afraid of what Jebet might do given that she was leaving.

"Kiano will be staying there for the night. So he can keep watch over the children and make sure everything is okay. Just to be certain." Mama Bu gave me a squeeze.

"And am I allowed to work here? What about visa issues?"

"I do not know about that, but we can go to Nairobi on Friday and figure it all out. Lucy's friend moved here from Canada to work permanently for a year or so, and she said it was easy to get. I do not think it will be a problem. We will figure it out, Nicky."

"I can't *believe* this. I'm going to need to tell my parents. I'm sure they will be disappointed, but I know they'll also be happy that I'm happy."

"I am sure they will be, Nicky. You deserve happiness. No matter where in the world it finds you."

—

That night, I once again entered the insomniac battlefield, but this time it was excitement keeping me awake. My mind raced with ideas about what I would do in my new role at the orphanage. I wanted to raise money for more bunk beds — the kids were still sleeping three to a bed — and I would pour money into the classroom. With control of the entire orphanage, I could make sure the kids would get the education they needed to regain the start in life they had lost along with their parents.

Johanna would stay at Kidaai, of course, and I would force her to put her feet up and rest for the remainder of her pregnancy. When she had the baby, I would help her at night, with feedings and diaper changes. She could resume her role as house help when she was back on her feet, and I would ensure, somehow, that she would have a small salary for her work.

I considered going back home for a couple of weeks, to organize big fundraisers that would allow me to fix up the kitchen and buy the swing set that should have made an appearance so long ago. I would rebuild the chicken coops and ensure the kids had eggs to eat. And cows! I would get some cows so that the kids could have milk.

Nighttime would be a routine of teeth brushing — which meant I would need to buy each child a toothbrush, given they currently went without — and we would read stories and sing songs before bed. I would leave my bedroom door open at night as I slept, just in case the younger children wet the bed. They would come and get me, gently tugging on my arm and I would rise with them to clean their sheets. They wouldn't be teased in the morning.

If a child got sick, I would hold their hand to make them feel better. I would put cool cloths to their foreheads to beat a fever and make sure the proper drugs and Band-Aids were filled in the medical box for when they needed them.

I turned over in my bed and said a few silent words to Ella, thanking her for all that she had given me, even in the short time we had been together. In the nine months she had been a direct part of me, she had given me an unconditional motherly bond that I knew I would take forward. I would make her proud of the mother I was to become.

I would be the mother the kids of Kidaai needed. The mother I never got the chance to be.

———

As soon as I woke up the next morning, I organized my things and repacked my suitcases, which had never been fully emptied. I didn't want to wait one more minute; I was anxious to get to the orphanage so I could officially begin putting my plans in motion.

Saying goodbye to Kiano, Petar and Mama Bu was tough. I even cried, which was silly since I was just moving ten minutes up the road. But I had spent over two months with them, and it marked the end of my first Kenyan journey. They had been good to me and, above all, had helped me heal.

Kiano left for work, and Petar, school. Mama Bu said she would help me carry my things and get me settled into the orphanage. Jebet was catching a *matatu* to Mombasa at seven o'clock, and wouldn't be there when we arrived.

I couldn't wait to tell Johanna the good news; she could stay and enjoy the remainder of her pregnancy, ensuring the safe delivery of her baby. We could raise the baby together and I would ensure she always had a job, and a safe home, with lots to eat.

Mama Bu and I struggled to wheel my two stuffed suitcases down the red clay road. I carried my swollen duffle bag while she carried my backpack.

When the kids saw us, they came running to greet us. Ita instantly took my duffle bag from me to help, while others helped with the suitcases. We managed to get them up the peeling porch steps and through the front door, when Johanna greeted us, wobbly and swollen.

"Nicky? There someone here for you."

I was confused and wondered if Wekesa had returned to speak with me about the rent details. "Who is it?" I asked, blowing a blonde strand of hair out of my eyes, which had fallen from my ponytail on the walk over.

"I don't know. He in the common room."

More confused than ever, I walked to the common room to greet my visitor. "Hello?" I called out.

Then I saw him.

Eric.

He was perched on the edge of the fraying red couch, looking nervous and out of place. My heart constricted and I struggled to breathe.

"Hi, Nic."

I tried to find words, but could only remain silent. I couldn't make sense of the situation. I was in shock that Eric was actually in front of me.

"Nic, I really need to talk to you. I've tried reaching you over and over, but you won't return my emails or phone calls. I didn't know what else to do, so I got the address to the orphanage from Maggie and caught the first flight I could to Nairobi."

I stared at him. He stared back. Our eyes locked.

"Please, Nic. Just give me ten minutes. I came all this way. . . . I *really* need to talk to you. To tell you something I should have said a long time ago."

Somewhat begrudgingly, and still very confused, I agreed to speak to Eric. "Let's go outside," I suggested, fully aware that Mama Bu, Johanna and the children were still standing behind us. We made our way to the porch, and Eric took a seat, motioning for me to sit beside him.

"Thanks, but I'll stand," I replied, not wanting to get too close to Eric. I was still trying to wrap my mind around the fact that he was even there. Seeing Eric again had shaken me to the core, and having him in front of me, actually *within* my African world, felt as incongruous as it was unsettling.

"Nicky . . . I actually don't even know where to start. I just spent my entire plane ride rehearsing exactly what I wanted to say and, somehow, I can't remember any of it. . . ."

I listened, waiting for him to continue. I had spent too many of my days in a one-sided conversation with Eric, talking at him and begging him to respond, only to find silence. If Eric had come all this way, he could do the talking. He *had* to do the talking.

Eric cleared his throat, then began. "I miss you so much, Nicky. More than words can ever describe . . . even though I'm going to try. Because it's important to me that you know how I feel, and I know now the only way you'll know what I'm really feeling is if I tell you."

"Go on. I'm listening."

"I . . . I have so much to tell you, and I know I should have told you long before now. I just . . . well, I couldn't for some reason. I was totally broken inside and hurting more than I ever thought possible. And to be honest, I didn't know how to fix it. Talking about what happened . . .

even speaking to *you* about it . . . well, it just made it harder. It made it hurt even more, and I wanted to forget everything so I could move on."

He paused, and I waited. I needed him to continue.

"But I couldn't move on. Once you left, I thought I could rid myself of all the memories, like I had tried to do for so many months. But they just wouldn't go. I couldn't sleep. I couldn't eat. I could barely work. I tried everything, but nothing helped. Nothing could make me forget you." He paused, looking down. "Or Ella."

"Because it doesn't work that way, Eric."

"I know that now. Eventually I came to realize that. But it took a long time. Too much time, unfortunately."

I nodded, thinking of all the time that had passed since our separation.

"I joined a bereavement group for dads," Eric continued, sounding almost proud. "Dr. Covert recommended it, actually."

"Oh really? I don't remember her mentioning that."

"She didn't. At least not in front of you." Eric looked down at his hands, linking his fingers together in a way that almost looked like he was praying. "About a month after you left for Africa, I had tried everything else I could think of to make me feel better, so I finally went back to see Dr. Covert for a one-to-one session. In the beginning, I think I subconsciously did it to feel closer to you, because I knew how important your sessions with her were. But then a strange thing happened and I realized that, somewhere along the way, talking through everything with Dr. Covert . . . well, it really helped me. Dr. Covert got me to see things in a way I had never considered. She pushed me to explore everything I was feeling and had been feeling all along. She got me to understand — and, more important, believe — that I needed to feel my emotions, and live through them, so I could move on. So I could find some sense of happiness again."

"And do you? Feel happy now?" I asked.

"I'm not happy yet, but I'm certainly more at ease. And I've learned to cope. How to deal with all of the emotions that hijacked me for so long."

I kept listening.

"Once I was able to sift through what I was feeling, when I started to make sense of it all, or at least some of it, I realized that, no matter what else, I can't live without you. Not for one more minute." Eric glanced up then, and looked straight into my eyes. "I love you, Nicky. More than you'll ever know. And I'm ready to fight for what we had. For what I know we can have again. I know it will take time, but I've got all the time in the world, and want to do nothing more than prove to you how much I love you. To show you how much I believe we belong together."

"And what about when you need to run back to work? What if there's another case that desperately needs your attention?" My voice was lined with sarcasm I wished I could take back the moment the words crossed my lips.

"That won't happen. I quit my job . . . so I could come here and find you."

"You quit? Your job?"

"Yes, I did. Do you remember the McDonnel case?"

I nodded. How could I forget? Eric and a team of about ten other lawyers had been working on it since before we sold our house.

"Well, it goes to trial next week. So, as always, there is a vacation blackout period for all the lawyers who are involved. I pled my case, asking for an exception, because I knew I had to come and find you, but the firm told me I couldn't travel. So I had no choice but to quit."

The words were still not sinking in. "You quit? You really quit your job?"

"I really quit my job. Feels pretty good, actually. No more strings. No more stress." Eric grinned, somehow managing to still tickle my insides with the flutters I hadn't experienced in a very long time. It felt good. Eric continued, "This guy named Jack—he's one of the dads I've become friends with in my bereavement group — well, he really showed me that I needed to do this. That I needed to come here and fight for you. And for us."

I nodded again, taking in all that Eric was saying.

"Jack went through something similar to what we did. Except it was his second child. The baby, Mason, was born at twenty-six weeks and only survived for three days. Jack and his wife, Carol, didn't make it past three months. They separated quickly and were divorced a year and a half later. Unfortunately, Jack realized too late that he and Carol had made a huge mistake getting divorced and, by the time he could tell Carol how he felt, she was already engaged to another man."

I was speechless, still in shock that Eric was sitting in front of me. And somehow he was saying so many of the things I'd longed to hear from him for so long.

"That's why I knew I needed to come now," Eric said. "That I had to quit my job and do whatever else was needed to get you back. And I pray to God that I'm not too late. I love you, Nicky, and I'll do whatever it takes to show you. To prove it to you. I will commit the rest of my life to making you believe this."

Eric searched my eyes and, surprisingly, I fought the urge to run away. To turn on my heel and bolt, just as Eric had done to me. Ironically, after waiting so long for Eric to actually speak with me and tell me how he was feeling, I wanted to flee the conversation. I didn't want to abandon him, just as he had done to me, but I didn't know what to say. And I didn't know what to feel.

Picking up on my hesitation, Eric kept going. "I know I'm very late in telling you all of this, Nicky. I know you needed to have had this conversation a very long time ago. To grieve with me and to deal with everything that had happened. Together."

I nodded, fighting tears.

"You might not believe this, but even back then, I really wanted to talk about everything with you. Believe me, I did. And I tried. On most mornings, I would wake up and promise myself that I was going to sit you down, just so we could talk, and sometimes I would try, but it was like a knife was being sliced through my heart every time we started talking about it."

He looked down, took a deep breath and cleared his throat again. I knew Eric well enough to sense that he was fighting his own tears.

"My God, I miss Ella so much, Nic. I loved her more than I knew was possible. I loved her more than life, and I would have done anything to save her, and somehow we only got to spend an hour with her. How is that fair? How is it right?"

"I don't know, Eric. I ask myself that every day," I responded quietly.

"And what I did to *you*? It's unimaginable. To be honest, I wouldn't blame you if you felt it was unforgiveable too. I know now that I abandoned you at the worst moment of your life, when you needed me the most. And I'm so, so very sorry for that. I wish you could know how much. I hate myself for not being there for you. I love you, Nic. I love you more than anything and I don't know how to go on without you. I'm lost without you and I don't know how to live from day to day without you in my life." Eric's words came spilling out, bubbling up in his throat and, eventually, turning into sobs that yanked at my heart-strings. The tall, silent man who had stood like a stone in front of me for so many months buried his head into his hands and, finally, wept. It was the first time I had seen Eric cry since Ella's death.

I sat down next to him and pulled him into my arms. No matter what had happened, or what would happen in the future, I couldn't bear to watch Eric grieve so intensely and not try to provide some sense of comfort.

Like a baby, Eric curled into me, folding himself into my embrace, and put his cheek next to mine. Our tears mixed, joining together before they fell into our laps, and we sat side by side, linked together in a tight embrace, grieving as one, and mourning the daughter — and the life — we both had lost.

## 28

"Mama Bu?" I called out, walking into the small host home that I had become so comfortable in. I was desperate to speak with her. After Eric and I had spent a long time together on the porch, I left him, saying that I just needed to think.

When I went back into the orphanage to find Mama Bu, Johanna had told me she slipped out the back door to return home to begin her daily chores. Mama Bu knew I would find her when I was ready to talk.

"I am here, Nicky," Mama Bu answered, walking into the living room. She had been scrubbing the kitchen and was wearing a faded orange apron with blue ties around her neck and waist. Her hair was pulled back with her favourite red hair band.

"It's Eric. I just don't know what to think about everything. He came to Africa. To find me. And to tell me that he loves me, and that he wants to get back together."

"I was wondering as much," Mama Bu responded, turning away before she sat down on her favourite couch. I wasn't sure if it was my imagination or not, but it almost seemed as though she was trying to conceal a smile. "And how do you feel about that, chicka?"

"I don't know. Confused, really. I love Eric and, really, I want to be with him too, but I don't know how to do that anymore."

"Did you tell him all of this?"

"I did, and I also told him that I couldn't go back with him because I had made the decision to stay here and be the orphanage director. I told him that I'd given a commitment to you, and to the kids at the orphanage, and that I couldn't go back on my word when the kids needed me the most."

"And what did Eric say?" Mama Bu prompted.

"He said that he would move to Africa. That he would stay here. To help me, and to be with me. He said he would do whatever was needed to make us work."

"I see."

"I don't know though . . . I just don't think that will work. I can't imagine us both here, together."

"First, *rafiki*, I think you must realize what is in your heart. Decide on what you want. Everything else — whether he lives here or you live there — that can be figured out later."

"But how do I do that, Mama Bu? How do I figure that out? How do I know?"

"I cannot tell you what to do or what the answer is. But I will tell you that you already know what it is. Your answer is buried deep within your soul and I am quite certain that you will find it. You will know what is right for you. All you need to do is open your heart to the answer and it will be there. It is waiting for you to realize what it is. To figure out your truth and find your destiny."

"I don't know, Mama Bu."

"I think you should go for a long walk, *rafiki*. Go into Ngong town. Or just walk to whatever spot your path leads you. Go on. Walk, and clear your head, and find your answer. It is there, waiting, I promise you."

I accepted Mama Bu's advice and gave her a hug before I headed out. I walked past Barika's house and, before I knew it, was headed to the market. I wanted to clear my head, yes, but I actually needed busyness. Noise. Chaos.

I walked the hectic aisles, looking past the people around me and, on occasion, accidentally running into them. My mind was far away. A man wearing a hat bumped into me. "*Poleni*," he said. Sorry. I snapped my attention back to all that was around me.

I stopped to hold a ripe red tomato and purchased some bobby beans to contribute to the kids' dinner that night. I bought a banana for my breakfast, but then realized I wasn't hungry. I tossed it in my backpack.

I kept walking through the market. Watched Kenyans shake hands and greet each other good morning. A skinny man with a shaved head called out to a friend buying cinnamon and slapped his back in a friendly salute when he met up with him. His friend responded by putting his arm around the skinny man's neck and pulling him in for a tight hug.

I found a large rock. I sat, not sure what I was waiting for, but also not knowing where else I could go.

After a while, two small children appeared from nowhere and jumped into a leftover puddle from the rain that had fallen a few days before. Once the rain had started, it hadn't stopped, bringing on the wet season and relief to all of Kenya. The children, one of whom seemed to be just younger than two and the other about five, splashed each other with the water, their clothes soon soaked. Within moments, the children surrendered to being wet and sat directly in the middle of the puddle, still splashing each other over and over as their hands hit its surface.

Their laughter rang out loud. I wanted to smile, as so many people would, but the sound actually hurt my ears, reminding me of what I no longer had.

The younger child stood up from the puddle. She took off her pants and threw them aside. Once free, the little girl danced in the puddle, jumping up and down, her diaperless bum soaking up the sunshine.

I wondered where their mother was. How she could leave two young children alone, by themselves, where anything could happen to them?

Sometime later — I can't be totally sure about how long I sat there watching — the mother found her children. She was a young woman, no older than twenty-five. She wagged her finger, lightly scolding them for getting so wet in the puddle. She lifted the toddler into her arms and lightly kissed her on the nose.

It was such a simple maternal gesture and it yet hurt my heart because at that precise moment I realized the toddler was about the same age that Ella would have been.

The mother wrung out the toddler's soaking wet pants and placed them in the sisal handbag she was carrying. She removed a clean cloth and rubbed her children's faces, wiping them free of the mud splatter that had clung to their faces as they had jumped and splashed.

Still holding the youngest on her hip, the mother took her five-year-old child by the hand and the threesome walked away, leaving me, and the now-still puddle, once again alone.

When my legs grew cramped from sitting too long, I rose and walked back through the market. I entered one of the middle rows and almost walked directly into a small woman carrying her baby on her hip in bright red material tied around her waist and in a large knot thrown over one of her shoulders. She had an oversized basket on her head, bursting with breads and vegetables. With the stacked gold bangles around her wrist, and the bright beads she wore everywhere, I recognized her as Maasai.

In our near collision, the woman smiled. "*Samahani*," she said. Excuse me. I returned the smile and kept walking, turning back to look at her baby. He had large eyes that peeked over the red cloth, his hair just starting to come in. In my time in Kenya, I had learned a lot about the Maasai people, and knew the baby's hair would soon be shaved, representing a fresh start that would be made as the baby passed into another one of life's chapters.

"Neeecky? Neeecky!" A familiar voice called to me, yet I couldn't place it. I looked around and saw Moses, energetically waving at me from behind his food stall. I dropped the mango I had been holding at a competitor's stand and crossed the aisle to greet him.

"Where Bu at?" he asked.

"She's at home, tending to her chores. I'm just taking a walk. I needed a bit of a break."

"Well, I glad to see you. I have something for you. I found it after you left that day. It must have fall out of your pocket. I sorry not to give it back more soon. I thought I see you here sooner. Was going to bring it to Bu's, but I work so much. Every day!" Moses walked behind his food stall and pulled something from the portable safe he kept his money in. Holding it up to the sunlight, diamonds danced. Moses had found my cross necklace. He'd had it the entire time.

From out of nowhere, bubbled-up sobs came pouring out of me. Moses didn't know what to do, so he awkwardly handed the necklace over and apologized again for not returning it sooner. I thanked him repeatedly before running as fast as I could back to the orphanage.

## 29

"Eric? Eric! Are you here?" I ran into the orphanage and searched frantically to find him. I had found my answer. I knew what to do.

I flew into the common room and found a handful of kids playing jacks. "Do you know where Johanna is?"

The kids shook their heads. "No, *Mwalimu* Nicky."

I flew into the kitchen, hoping to find Eric having something to eat, or maybe even helping to fix the faucet I knew was broken. He wasn't there.

"Johanna?! *Eric?* Where are you?" As I called their names, I heard my voice becoming more and more desperate.

Silence.

I ran back to the front hall and noticed that my packed suitcases and duffle bags were still at the front door.

I flew outside and into the field, where groups of children were taking part in the circle games that we had spent so many hours playing together.

"Nadia! Have you seen Johanna? Or the man I was talking to on the porch earlier?"

"Johanna is upstairs lying down. I think that man is in the school-room."

I thanked her and ran to the school, flying through its door to find Eric sitting at my desk.

"I hope it's okay that I'm here," Eric looked a bit sheepish, almost apologetic, as though he had intruded on a private part of my life. "Johanna brought me here and told me I could stay as long as I wanted. I didn't really know where else to go."

"No, no . . . it's okay." I took a few steps towards him. I stood beside one of the student's chairs, immediately across from him. He rose to greet me.

"You've done a lot in this classroom," Eric started, complimenting my efforts of the past couple of months. He took a few steps towards me, bridging the gap even more. "Johanna was really excited to show me everything you've done for the kids — the learning stations, the art on the walls, the reading progress charts. It's obvious how much you care, Nic. You should be really proud." His cheeks turned a light shade of pink. "I know I am."

"Thank you," I replied simply. "It's been challenging. But let's talk about that later." I took a few more steps and stood directly in front of him. "For now, I just want to talk about us. About everything you said before." I paused and looked directly into his deep blue eyes.

"I know how painful it was to lose Ella. How much it hurt. And how, even a year and a half later, the ache hasn't gone away, and I don't know if it will *ever* totally go away."

Eric looked down. I took his hand and waited until he looked back up and our eyes were locked.

"And I also know you would never do anything to deliberately hurt me, just as I would never do anything to deliberately hurt you. In our grief, we both did things we shouldn't have. We both acted out because we were trying to deal with our pain in the only way we knew how. The sadness we both felt and the heartache we were both going through, it's the kind that reaches down to the bottom of your soul. And it hit us in different ways, so we responded in different ways . . . and I think that made us treat each other in a way we shouldn't have."

Eric nodded and we both remembered things that had been said, which I knew we desperately wanted to take back.

Squeezing his hand, I continued, "I think, in a lot of ways, we took our pain out on each other. And I'm so very sorry that I did that. I'm sorry for all that has happened and for pushing you to talk when you weren't ready. I was just hurting so much. I didn't know how to cope either . . . but I never wanted to add to your hurt in any way. You are the love of my life and I want to spend the rest of my days showing you that. I want to be with you. I need to be with you because I love you."

Eric dropped my hand, grabbing me around my waist and effortlessly lifting me in a tight embrace. I buried my head in his shoulder. We still fit together like a jigsaw puzzle. Two people, meant to be together. I breathed in the moment and found the home I had been looking for.

"You know, Nic, I had an idea while I was admiring all of your work in here . . ." Eric and I were still sitting in the empty classroom, clinging to each other after so many months apart.

"Oh yeah? What's that?" I looked up, grinning into the familiar eyes that I had missed for so long.

"Well, as you know already, it just so happens that I don't have a job, so I have all the time in the world. I'll stay here with you, Nic, for as long as you want me to. And we'll find the right person, or people, for the orphanage director role."

"I know. And I appreciate that." I had filled Eric in on everything that had happened, and he knew how important it was for us to find the right person to look after the children.

"And if it ends up that we're the right people, then we'll stay. But if you decide you want to go back to Canada . . . well, I think there's still a way we can help."

"How's that?"

"We can start a foundation. Back home. We'll educate people on the need to help and raise money for Africa. We'll donate the proceeds from monies raised directly to helping the kids at Kidaai. We'll make sure the orphanage has the funds it needs to operate efficiently. The kids will have all the food and milk and clothes they need."

I listened, intrigued by the idea.

Eric continued, "And we'll make sure they all get an education. We'll hire an amazing orphanage director and an equally great teacher and buy all of the school supplies they need. We can come back and visit as much as you'd like . . . so we can hand deliver some of the things the kids need." Eric grinned, then continued. "It would be your foundation. And you can run it however you'd like, although I'm hoping the first thing you'll want to do is hire a really great lawyer. I know of one, you know. He's got some great experience working on Bay Street and I know you can get him for a really cheap salary."

I returned the grin, and pulled Eric in for another hug, grateful to have the husband I had known and loved for so long back where he belonged. It was the perfect solution and I knew we could do more to help in Canada, raising money for Kidaai.

"I love that idea." The excitement in my voice bubbled up when I spoke. "But there's only one thing: we can't go until we find the right person to be the orphanage director. I can't leave until that person is in place."

"I know. We'll stay for as long as we need to."

"Then it's a deal." I couldn't stop beaming and pulled him in for a long kiss. "And since it's settled, there's someone I *really* want you to meet. Want to go and find her?"

Eric nodded as he whisked me into his arms. Laughing, he carried me over the threshold of the schoolroom door as we left, together, to find Mama Bu.

———

"We're going to stay until we find the perfect person to be the orphanage director. If it's okay, Eric and I will move in here and take care of the kids until we find the right person for the role," I told Mama Bu. It was later that night and she and I were sitting in the common room of the orphanage, having some tea.

Eric was sleeping off his jet lag upstairs and the kids had all been tucked into bed. Before they all fell soundly asleep, Mama Bu, Eric and I had taken turns reading stories and singing songs to them. Johanna had listened, resting on one of the bunk beds. She said it was for her unborn baby to hear as well, but I think she enjoyed the warmth and happiness that had taken over Kidaai.

"That will be fine, Nicky." Mama Bu winked at me, then grinned. "And you might find the right person sooner than you think. Someone who would do the job that you have intended. She would love the children as her own and make sure they brush their teeth each day and eat the eggs from the new chicken coop. Someone who would commit to the role as wholeheartedly as you would have."

"Oh yeah? Who?"

"Me, Nicky. I was thinking of . . . *me*." Mama Bu smiled over her mug and I instantly returned her grin. I couldn't think of a person who was more perfect than Mama Bu. I was ecstatic at her suggestion.

"What . . . Mama Bu! But what about Kiano? And Petar?" I asked, still smiling.

"Petar's the last of my babies and he will be leaving us soon enough. Our house and property have become a lot to manage, especially with Kiano spending so much time at his sister's place." Mama Bu paused, letting me think through what she was saying.

"So, if Kiano and Lucy agree, and I believe they will, I was thinking both Lucy and we could rent out our homes to other families, and move everyone here. Kiano's working most days anyhow, and I will run the orphanage. I know Lucy really misses teaching — the job she gave up when her kids were born — and this way she could take over the classroom here. Also, she would get to see her kids instead of working as a maid seven days a week and that would mean much to her."

Mama Bu recognized the look of relief that had taken over my face and patted my knee in the motherly way she had done so often since I had arrived in Kenya. "See, chicka, I told you the children would be fine."

I grinned at my host mother and squeezed her hand.

"We will miss you here, Nicky. More than you know. But you need to go, with Eric, back to Canada. You need to return to the place where you belong. To your life. You have found your happiness, Nicky, now go and live in it."

Overwhelmed with emotion, I could say nothing in reply. Instead, I held my mug of chai up to hers and sealed the deal with the clink of Kenyan ceramic.

EPILOGUE

The sun shines on my back and I hunch over sprouted vegetables in the garden I planted months earlier. The tomatoes are glowing red, perfect for picking. Although they still cling to the vine, warm with sunshine, I can already taste their sweetness in my mouth. My thoughts turn to what I will serve alongside them at that night's dinner.

Corn on the cob. Barbecued hamburgers and veggie burgers with toasted buns. Potato salad. Coleslaw. Milk.

The cross necklace I replaced around my neck hangs forward, dancing in the sunlight as I weed the rich earth that surrounds the vegetables of my labour. It tickles my neck, and I feel the weight of its presence.

My legs go numb with lack of blood flow from a position held for too long. I shift. Stretch. Try to lose the feeling of sharp prickles tickling my nerve endings. I stand, stretching further, enjoying the warmth of summer.

I glance at the worn watch on my left wrist; it is shortly after five o'clock. I walk over the freshly cut lawn to the front of the house where I notice new neighbours moving into the house across the street. The woman is directing dressers, chairs and toy boxes, carried by the movers, into the house. Her blonde hair is held back in a ponytail and her brow is creased in stress.

I smile. Wave. Make a mental note to bring them lasagna in the coming days.

She sees my gesture and makes her way towards me. She introduces herself as Beth, telling me they have four kids, all under the age of twelve. Her husband is Bernie.

"Do you have any children?" Beth asks. I pause before answering, wondering what her response might be. It's always different.

"We do. Just one though. He's over there," I point to the giggling group of kids coming from our next door neighbour's lawn, and watch as Bu runs in circles around two of his friends. His dark skin is contrasted against the pale blue sky and, as it so often does, reminds me of days from long ago.

"Which one is yours?"

"Bu, come over here and meet someone!" I call out to him. I raise my gaze and shield my eyes from the sun. Bu runs over and graciously shakes Beth's hand. He is a sweet boy for a seven-year-old. So wise and mature beyond his few short years.

"Boo? That's an interesting name. Is his real name Arthur?"

"Sorry?"

"Boo Radley. His real name was Arthur Radley. In *To Kill a Mockingbird*?"

"Oh, right. Well, no, it's just Bu. Spelled B-U." I grab hold of his shoulders with my right arm, rubbing his head before he runs back to play with his friends. I smile again at Beth and continue, "I'm not sure if you've heard or not, but there's a street party this Saturday. It's our fourth year in a row and they're always a ton of fun. I hope you can make it — it would be a great way for you to meet all of the neighbours. It starts at four o'clock. Hamburgers, hot dogs and veggie burgers are provided. You just need to bring a salad or dessert to share. And there are fireworks when it gets dark."

Beth assures me they will be there and turns to retake her post as official furniture navigator. Within moments, her four children arrive with Bernie, who drives a red minivan into their new driveway and parks alongside Beth's black Suburban. I am happy to see that one of the children getting out of the sliding door is a boy about Bu's age.

I make my way to our front door, realizing Eric will be home in an hour. Before I reach the porch, I hear his Land Rover pull into the driveway. He waves from the driver seat, smiling. I take in the sight of him, his tie pulled loose and the jacket of his suit tossed casually over the back seat of the passenger chair.

"Why are you home so early?" I call out, walking towards him. I let him whisk me into an oversized bear hug. He brushes dirt from my cheek and, for a moment, I am embarrassed that Beth saw me dirt-covered.

"I want to spend some quality time with my family, so I thought

I'd leave the foundation early and come home. After all, you took the day off . . . so I figured I'd follow suit." Eric smiles and pulls me in for a long kiss. Thoughts of Beth leave my mind.

"Well, I'm glad you did. Leave early, that is. It's so nice to have you home."

Eric responds, whispering into my hair. "It's nice to *be* home."

## ACKNOWLEDGEMENTS

First and foremost, my infinite gratitude goes to my beautiful cousin, Rachel Clark. It was through her eyes that I was able to see Kenya; through her touch that I was able to feel its surroundings; and, mostly, through her arms that I was able to hug the delightful children at the Kenyan orphanage where she has repeatedly volunteered. Rachel, it is because of you that I was able to find the words to describe Kenya, both in its hardship and all of its beauty. You continually encouraged me to write this story — from our walk at the cottage when I first told you about the idea for the book (and you immediately pulled out your pictures, journals and videos of Kenya!) to all of the one-line emails you would shoot me back from the small Internet café in Ngong when I had some silly question about what Kenyan dirt felt like. Through this entire process, you remained absolutely committed to sharing every piece of information about Kenya that I needed to bring this book to life, and I will never forget that. I love you, cuz.

Thank you to all of my friends and family who believed in this book and read the manuscript long before there was even a slim possibility of it being published, particularly Wendy Gardham, who was the very first person to raise her hand and ask to read the words that weren't yet a real book. And to the others who shortly followed — Brooke Allen, Ines Colucci and my brother, Ian Clark, who frequently has his nose in some finance or other non-fiction book but would *never* typically pick up women's fiction, let alone remain committed to reading the whole thing in a few days.

My thanks to both Lori Mastronardi and Chantel Simmons, who both read this story not once, but (at least!) twice in order to help turn an unpublished manuscript into a novel. You have both guided me immensely during this process.

To Anthony Iantorno, who immediately forwarded the manuscript on and fought for its chance to be published — and to Erin Creasey who, on the other end of Anthony's pass, immediately embraced it with eyes wide open. I will forever be grateful to both of you for immediately and continually believing in this book.

Thank you to my editor, Jen Hale, who saw something in the story of Nicky's journey from the very first time she read it. She whole-heartedly took on the project with enthusiasm, and it was through her patience, talent and keen instinct that this book became what it is today. And, lucky for me, through our process of many conversations, numerous edits and lots of hard work, I also gained a friend.

To Dr. Kimberly Elford for taking the time to read the manuscript and for sharing her knowledge and expertise within the complex technical world of fertility treatments. And for her encouragement and feedback on the more intimate and emotional side of a couple trying to become pregnant. Her instant and committed willingness to help means more than she probably knows.

And thank you, also, to the others who so graciously gave up their time to make sure the details in this book are accurate: The Honourable Justice Harvey Brownstone, who guided me on separation and divorce law in Ontario; Kulsum Merchant and Franklin Mwango for helping to ensure the Swahili throughout this book is accurate; and Dr. Jane Aldridge for providing glimpses into the medical world that I wouldn't have otherwise known.

To Negin Sairafi, who generously offered her time to take my photo, and who showcased her talent by ensuring I didn't look eight months pregnant in the picture (I hope!). And to Laura DiPede, who has continually offered design suggestions and provided her skilled expertise on so many of the creative materials for this book.

I would also like to thank everyone else at ECW Press who helped turn my original manuscript into what it has become — Crissy Boylan, David Caron, Troy Cunningham, Jack David, Rachel Ironstone, Dave Gee, Jenna Illies, Emily Schultz and Steph VanderMeulen. It has been a true team effort.

As with everything in my life, the most essential influence on this project has been the love and support of my wonderful family, both extended and immediate, and, in particular:

My always kind and loyal mother, who, since I was a small child, told me I would be a writer of some sort — even through my years in business school and a long career in the corporate world. She absorbed every word of my elementary and high school essays with enthusiasm and commitment — and never, ever, stopped telling me that I needed to write.

My exceptionally intelligent and wonderful father, who took every opportunity to teach his children by asking us to count the number of cars on highway transport trucks or insisting on answering the "How *long* until we get there?!" road trip questions with a lesson in fractions. And, most of all, for instilling in me, through both his actions and continual encouragement, that genius is 1% inspiration and 99% perspiration — and that the greatest success happens when opportunity meets preparation.

My brothers, Ian and Steven, who played such a huge role in creating a childhood filled with adventure, constant support and, above all else, laughter. I'm so grateful that our solid 'Clark Kid' foundation has helped to ensure we have become even closer with every day that passes. You are not only brothers to me, but wonderful friends.

My amazing children, Avary, Jacob and Emerson, who, every single day, fill my life with unconditional love, absolute joy and complete perspective. And last, but certainly not least, my eternally supportive husband, Brian, who has taught me so much — and believes in me more than I could ever possibly believe in myself. He never doubted that I would finish this book, even when I did, and inspired me to keep going through his coach-like pep talks that I love so much and, moreover, a constant willingness to ensure I had all of the time I needed to write. Brian, you are my rock.

**artb und**
WHERE ART DOES GOOD

A portion of the proceeds from the sale of this book will be donated to Artbound, a non-profit volunteer initiative that harnesses the power of the arts in support of Free The Children.

Partnering with artists and those passionate about the arts, Artbound raises funds to build schools in developing nations to enrich children with a full education, including art schools and programming. Their programs are designed to empower children through leadership training and the development of skills that will improve their living conditions and generate sustainable income to help break the cycle of poverty.

The Artbound team is comprised of young Canadian leaders from various industries who are dedicated to engaging a global community in volunteer, school building and mentorship. In addition to building schools, Artbound also supports Free The Children's Adopt a Village model that provides clean water, medical care facilities and alternative income programs — all working in unison to allow children to learn and develop in a healthy and safe environment.

In 2011, Artbound travelled to Kenya to assist in the building of the first arts school in the country. As part of the Kisaruni School for Girls, the arts program is a hub for singing, painting, dance, theatre and indigenous art forms.

Still, many more children are left behind, struggling with debilitating poverty and lack of education. Artbound will continue to raise funds to support Free The Children to build new and fully sustainable infrastructures in communities most in need across the globe.

Please visit artbound.ca to learn more.